$\mathcal{B}$

Jared shoved his hands into his pockets.

Standing with her back against the porch railing, her tense shoulders near her ears, she looked fit to be tied. Her beautiful blue eyes searched for him. He stepped closer and cleared his throat.

"He's my horse," she said.

"You can't sell Harley without my say-so."

An exasperated noise escaped her pale lips. "I trusted you."

"Trusting me is the smartest thing you can do, darlin'."

"Don't call me that!"

Her vehement tone caught him off guard. He called lots of woman *darlin'*. Why did she act like it meant something?

Because you mean it when you say it to her.

Dear Reader,

Welcome back to the world of Rocky Mountain Cowboys! I adore writing about these strong, rugged men who shepherd the land and its animals, who fall hard and love forever. In *Falling for a Cowboy*, you'll meet another bold, passionate, fiercely independent Cade: Jared. Everything comes easily to Jared—success, friends and even women—until new feelings for his best friend, Amberley, make him face the biggest challenge of all: winning her heart.

I love a good comeback story. Rooting for the underdog and hoping to succeed against all odds makes a story unforgettable. *Falling for a Cowboy* is a timeless comeback story that was a joy to write. Not only did legally blind Amberley deserve a comeback, but all the characters did, including the children with special needs in her equine therapy program, my hero, and Amberley's horse, Harley. And don't we all love a good horse story full of heart? *Black Beauty*, *National Velvet* and *Misty of Chincoteague* are some of my favorites, and they deeply inspired me.

I hope you enjoy book two in my Rocky Mountain Cowboys series. If this is your first time reading this heartwarming series, I hope you'll check out the prequel, *A Cowboy to Keep*, and book one in the series, *Christmas at Cade Ranch*. Look for book three in the series this April! Visit me at www.karenrock.com to learn more about future books or to let me know what you think about the book and series. I'd love to hear from you!

Happy reading!

Karen Rock

HEARTWARMING

Falling for a Cowboy

Karen Rock

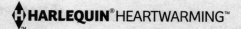

If you purchased this book without a cover you should be aware that this book is stolen property. It was reported as "unsold and destroyed" to the publisher, and neither the author nor the publisher has received any payment for this "stripped book."

Recycling programs
for this product may
not exist in your area.

ISBN-13: 978-1-335-63345-3

Falling for a Cowboy

Copyright © 2018 by Karen Rock

All rights reserved. Except for use in any review, the reproduction or utilization of this work in whole or in part in any form by any electronic, mechanical or other means, now known or hereinafter invented, including xerography, photocopying and recording, or in any information storage or retrieval system, is forbidden without the written permission of the publisher, Harlequin Enterprises Limited, 225 Duncan Mill Road, Don Mills, Ontario M3B 3K9, Canada.

This is a work of fiction. Names, characters, places and incidents are either the product of the author's imagination or are used fictitiously, and any resemblance to actual persons, living or dead, business establishments, events or locales is entirely coincidental.

This edition published by arrangement with Harlequin Books S.A.

For questions and comments about the quality of this book, please contact us at CustomerService@Harlequin.com.

® and TM are trademarks of Harlequin Enterprises Limited or its corporate affiliates. Trademarks indicated with ® are registered in the United States Patent and Trademark Office, the Canadian Intellectual Property Office and in other countries.

Printed in U.S.A.

Karen Rock is an award-winning young adult and adult contemporary author. She holds a master's degree in English and worked as an ELA instructor before becoming a full-time author. Most recently, her Harlequin Heartwarming novels have won the 2015 National Excellence in Romance Fiction Award and the 2015 Booksellers' Best Award. When she's not writing, Karen loves scouring estate sales, cooking and hiking. She lives in the Adirondack Mountain region with her husband, daughter and Cavalier King Charles spaniels. Visit her at karenrock.com.

Books by Karen Rock

Harlequin Heartwarming

Christmas at Cade Ranch
A Cowboy to Keep
Under an Adirondack Sky
His Kind of Cowgirl
Winter Wedding Bells
"The Kiss"
Raising the Stakes
A League of Her Own
Someone Like You
His Hometown Girl
Wish Me Tomorrow

To Dusty, the first horse I ever rode. You bucked me off and broke my wrist, but you also made me fall in love... And a girl never forgets her first love. If you look closely, you'll see yourself on these pages...especially the hugs, the laughs and, most of all, the love.

CHAPTER ONE

"HERE COMES THE CHAMP!" bellowed a rodeo announcer over the Las Vegas Thomas and Mack Center's PA system. "She won her second straight WPRA World Championship title right here last year. Can she do it again? Ladies and gents, this is the amazing Amberley James from Carbondale, Colorado."

Amberley tapped the top of her dad's black Stetson for good luck, lightly kicked her nine-year-old quarter horse, Harley, and galloped out into the arena to raucous applause. Ignoring the buzz of adrenaline inside her, she slowed her breathing and focused on the hunt. She could not—would not—lose. Winning was a state of mind. A way of being. Life. All that she knew and all that she'd ever strive to do.

As her father always told her, if you're not first you're last, and if you're last, you're not much.

Daddy, if you're watching, which I know you are, this one's for you.

She charged forward, leaning low over Harley's neck. The world around her dimmed, muted, then fell away save for her, Harley and the first barrel. Her ears attuned to the sound of her horse's pounding hooves, her body to the muscular rhythm of his enormous strides. A free-runner, the gelding ate up the distance in a breathless few seconds, rocketing beneath her like a locomotive. Then the first yellow barrel flashed up.

Electricity slammed her, straight through the breastbone. Without a moment to lose, she positioned Harley and rose in the saddle. Her leg drew even with the brightly painted side, but then something odd happened to her eyes. Stars burst at the corners of her tunneling vision like fireworks and she felt herself tilt forward. She pushed down on the saddle horn a millisecond later than she should have and dropped.

Air rushed from between Amberley's clenched teeth. In a sport won or lost in hundredths of seconds, she'd just cost herself.

She moved her hand toward Harley's withers, opening him up a little more, squeezed with her inside leg and strove to keep him off the barrel. But that blink-fast delay caused Harley to bend too far. His rear swung, hip disengaged, his hooves kicking up clouds of dirt as he dug in and turned wider than she'd wanted.

Make-or-break time.

Setting her jaw, she pulled her weight forward, brought her rein hand closer, then reached and slid as he accelerated, balancing on the horn and staying out of his mouth to give him his head. She squinted her eyes, straining to keep the blurring world in focus.

Two…three monster strides away from the barrel and then she grabbed the reins with both hands, angling him for the next turn, mentally preparing herself in case he overreacted to the approaching wall, a rare quirk of his that'd landed her in hot water before.

Play it safe or go for it?

Driving Harley hard, they hurtled full out toward the second barrel, making back precious time, she prayed. Her lungs burned and her eyes stung, her face flaming as Harley's silver mane streamed across it. She kept her eyes trained to the side of the barrel that seemed to slide and waver like a mirage.

Keeping her hands still despite the tremors in her gut, she angled her body back to keep Harley from anticipating and turning too soon.

The tension squeezing her chest eased a tiny bit as he responded to her cue. His gait held steady. Still. She could feel him tensing. Better play it safe, especially since the barrel seemed to jump before her eyes. Keeping her hands light on the reins, she gave him extra time she couldn't afford on the back end of the turn in case he blew through it and didn't bend enough. She rotated her entire body as they rounded and squinted in the direction of the last barrel.

Go, Harley.

Go.

She dug her heels into his flanks, asking for whatever Harley had left, and he responded, lunging faster still, closing the distance to the final barrel at lightning speed. Would she be able to judge it with her vision playing tricks? Air stuck in her lungs, and her pulse throbbed painfully in her throat as they committed to the final turn. They had to get around this perfectly. No room for error.

She eased back to her pockets and applied steady pressure, willing him to arc smoothly.

In a flawless pivot, Harley beamed around the barrel like a champ. Then they dashed past and the world rushed back in, a tidal force, the crowd erupting as she swept under the arena and down the gated corridor.

"Fourteen ten," the announcer crowed as she pulled up, then hopped off Harley.

"Not a bad start," she said to him, patting his steaming neck, grateful to have made it through clean given her distorted vision. Her eyesight, corrected with strong contacts, had never been great. Lately, though, she'd begun seeing spots on bright and sunny days. Then parts of her vision started shifting in and out of focus. Exhaustion from her nonstop schedule seemed the most likely culprit, but she'd been through years of touring without anything like this ever happening before.

Harley's silver tail lashed a fly on his rippling black hindquarter. He nickered at her and gave her a sidelong look.

"Not satisfied, champ? Me neither." She threw her arms around his neck for a quick squeeze. His reassuring warmth seeped through her shirt and slowed the gallop of her heart. Her eyesight struggles had been a constant, growing drumbeat these last couple of weeks of the season, a dreadful worry she'd kept to herself.

If word got out, it would set the racing community abuzz. Her sponsors would phone and her endorsements dry up. No sense raising red flags before she had answers. The sooner she returned home, caught up with her rest and got some new contact lenses, a stronger prescription maybe, the better. Hopefully, that'd be the end of it.

And the old, irrational fear she'd once had as a glasses-wearing kindergartener, that she'd go blind, would leave her for good.

The familiar aroma of dust, sweat and leather rose off Harley as she turned and led him back to his stall. Some people associated the smell of apple pie, baked bread, garden flowers with "home," but for Amberley, the smells of the stable—sweet hay, pungent manure, musky animal pelts—embodied her home, and even her church really, where she'd worshipped all her life, most of it alongside her departed daddy.

"We'll do better next round," she promised, guiding Harley past an overturned water bucket. After all, what choice did she have? If she didn't plan on winning, she wouldn't have bothered showing up in the first place.

Hopefully her eyes wouldn't act up again…

Several hours and ten rounds later, Amberley shifted on tired legs beneath a floodlight, trying to look as fresh as she had when she'd begun interviews in the cordoned-off press area. The center of her vision shimmered, and her eyeballs ached with the effort to focus. All around, the humid night pressed close. She held her arms out a little from her sides, her body slick beneath her denim shirt.

Rain had been threatening all day. She wished it'd start and release some of the tension in the black, cloud-covered night. Most of all, she wanted to duck under some covers and get the sleep she needed so badly.

"Congratulations," crowed a big-bellied rodeo blogger named Hank Andrews. Or Anderson. She sometimes struggled to recall names—and lately, faces, too. "Another world championship makes it your third consecutive win."

Powering through her exhaustion, she shot the florid man, and the camera, a friendly smile.

"Thank you very much. I'm just as surprised as anybody. I didn't think I'd be standing here. So. You know. I'm just really excited and thankful."

"No surprise for the rest of us, Amberley," he gushed. Behind a pair of heavy-framed glasses, he had kind hazel eyes. Or were they green? Everything looked a little fuzzy, especially under this artificial light. More evidence of worsening symptoms? Dread rose in her throat. "You've barely lost a round let alone a competition."

She winced and shooed away a bothering fly. "Don't remind me."

When Hank stared at her, confused, she forced a laugh to pretend she joked.

In fact, she recalled every loss in excruciating detail. They served as warnings of the consequences when her vigilance lapsed, like earlier this month when her eyes failed her for the first time. She'd missed a barrel and didn't place high enough to secure a coveted spot on the ERA Premier Tour. All her life, she'd dreamed of traveling with the world's top-seeded rodeo athletes.

"Another great ten rounds. You gave the fans everything they wanted."

Behind Hank, a tall, dark and handsome cowboy ambled out of the shadows. He moved with an effortless athletic grace she'd recognize anywhere, even in this dim light with her eyesight fading fast: Jared Cade, Heisman Trophy winner, Denver Broncos halfback and a member of Carbondale's biggest ranching family. He planted his brown boots wide, hooked his thumbs through his jean's belt loops and shot her an easy grin that gave her a ridiculous beat of warmth—he was her best friend, not a beau or anything…

"I hope so," she replied, feeling her lips twitch up when Jared crossed his eyes at her earnest tone. She couldn't quite focus in on the details of his face given her fatigue, but she knew those features by heart, sight unseen. "I just try to come out here and do my best every night. And, you know, I just got lucky."

Jared rolled his eyes at that. They were both extremely competitive. They'd been friends since they'd met on the rodeo circuit in middle school, trading achievements like some kids traded baseball cards, always keeping score. They shared a hard-work ethic and drive to be the best. Number one. He knew, like she did, that you only spoke about luck, you didn't actually believe in it.

She cleared her throat, shot Jared a stern,

"knock-it-off" look and continued. "I had a good week and Harley worked great and he was real consistent for me. Real solid."

"You've been riding him for..." Hank stopped a moment and whipped out a pad of paper from his back pocket.

Jared held up some fingers.

"Six years," she supplied. A raindrop smacked the tip of her nose.

Jared waved his hand.

"Almost seven," she amended hastily, reminded of when she and Jared had spied the rangy black-and-silver colt going cheap at auction and decided on the spot to train him together. They'd always made a good team, never letting the other quit or coast, never satisfied until they'd pushed each other to achieve top spots in whatever they pursued.

"It was so good to come back here and have another finals with Harley. It's just unbelievable."

Jared brought his fingers up to his temple and fake shot himself in the head, a grin the size of a dinner plate on his face. She could feel the matching one on herself. Good thing this last reporter didn't have video since she must look like a total loon.

"Hey, you nailed it." Hank stared at her a moment, momentarily flummoxed, then continued, "Final round. Did you feel any real pressure? All you had to do was keep him up."

She laughed, despite the rain that'd now kicked in, steady wet mist.

"I don't know about that. You know, I—uh—never even thought about it."

Jared cleared his throat quietly, a scoffing sound, skeptical. True friends like Jared called you out and didn't let you get away with anything...even trying to schmooze a reporter when you just wanted to kick off your boots and eat a pepperoni Hot Pocket.

"It was just kind of the same thing that goes through my head every night. Go fast, be tight, get around the barrels and try to win some money. That was my goal." That earned her two thumbs-up from Jared. Little did he know her other worries—and he wouldn't ever know them since it'd all turn out to be nothing.

She let go of a breath she didn't know she held.

"I don't really have any sort of thought process before I go in other than that." The rain picked up now. Heavy drops pelted them. "I just knew that I needed to focus all day and think about what I needed to do in there. And that's what I did. I focused."

Jared made a circling motion with his index finger. Wrap it up. She gave him a slight head shake. She'd worked hard for this all year and she'd bask in the moment, even if she felt faint, the world growing dimmer. Was it getting even darker out? When she swayed slightly on her feet, she caught Jared's quick, concerned frown and snapped her spine straight.

She couldn't stand being fussed over.

"I didn't hardly talk to anyone today. My mom and my friend were about the only two people I actually spoke to..."

It touched her that Jared had flown out to spend the week with her and help her prepare. They always gave each other pep talks before big games or competitions, sometimes tough, sometimes inspirational, sometimes just to make each other laugh and calm down.

Today, Jared had been full-on comedian, making her giggle whenever her anxieties about the race—and her eyesight—started winding her up. Several times she'd caught herself on the brink of confessing her concerns. Would he think less of her if he learned of her weakness? He didn't know the girl who'd once been called four eyes and been teased so hard she'd spent her lunches hiding in her grade school bathroom.

And he would never know her.

That girl disappeared long ago. Amberley had spent her lonely childhood with her horses until she'd worked her way up into competitive barrel racing and become the winner whom Jared respected. Liked. And winners didn't complain.

They got the job done.

"It just was one of those days when I needed to take it to myself and focus on what I needed to do." Her look clicked against Jared's for a minute. "And it scared me on the first barrel today. I knew that it was going to be tight, and I was thrilled we got around it."

The rain fell heavier, in weighty splats, not that Hank seemed to notice. She shivered in her soggy shirt as he forged ahead with his next question. Would this interview end before she caught pneumonia? If not, her next interview could be from an ICU bed.

"And another world championship for Colorado today. What do they say about you up there in the Rocky Mountains?"

Jared mouthed something obnoxious—it

had to be, given the wicked twinkle in his eyes—and she fought back a giggle. He was the *worst*.

"I don't know what they're going to say." She earned an eye roll for that. "I hope I made them proud. I know I'm proud to be a Rocky Mountain rider. And I have to thank all of my fans today. They've been awesome. I love that they came down and cheered me on. It meant a lot."

That, spoken directly to Jared, wiped the grin off his face and did something funny to his large, wide-spaced eyes, darkened them somehow. For a moment, she glimpsed the heartthrob her girlfriends gushed about, and it unsettled her. Sure, she recognized his attributes. Every female with a pulse appreciated his *lean*, square-jawed, gorgeous face, his towering height, slim hips, muscular torso and endless legs that turned a pair of worn jeans into a work of art. He had the kind of red-blooded American male good looks that made a gal want to salute and thank God for everyday miracles.

She wasn't blind, despite her recent vision hiccup.

But she wasn't stupid either. Fruit flies lived

longer than Jared's romantic relationships, if you could call them that. *Conquests* was more accurate a term. Their friendship worked because she inoculated herself against his ladykiller charms. The only woman to see the frog and not the prince. In fact, she preferred the goofy frog to the prince. Their friendship meant too much and she'd never want him in any other role, especially after losing the only other important man in her life, her dad, to cancer two years ago.

Nope. No way would she ever jeopardize their friendship.

She tore her eyes from Jared and peered at Hank through the steady curtain of water dripping off her hat brim.

"A 13.95 average through ten rounds." Hank whistled. "Pretty neat day. Brings you that average title. How important was that to you?"

"You know, it was real important to me. Every contestant that comes here dreams of winning and that, of course, is one of my goals, and so to achieve it is huge. Though it's surprising, I've worked really hard for this and I just have to thank everyone who's helped me get here."

The rain had turned Jared's long lashes into

dark wet spikes around his golden-brown eyes. He didn't blink, just stared right back at her for a long moment with an unreadable expression she should be able to decipher. She usually knew almost every thought inside his pretty head. "They all helped me get through this week and all through the year. I just can't thank them enough."

Jared mouthed something and pointed to the parking lot where his pickup waited. She didn't have to read his lips to guess he'd said something like, "Let's go."

"Final numbers were one hundred and thirty-five thousand dollars on the week, and that leads you to another world title," pressed Hank.

How many followers did his blog have? Millions? As much as she wanted to please her fans, she needed out of this weather. She felt a sneeze coming on, held it in, then jerked as it exploded in her sinus cavities.

"How does this one stack up?" Hank asked, undeterred.

She took a deep breath and launched into what she hoped would be a good enough answer for him to quote and move on. Please…

"Well. You know. The first one is always

special and so unreal and indescribable. But this one feels so much more hard-earned. And that's what it felt like all this year. Harley got injured right before the season started, so that was a challenge. I didn't think I had a chance to even be thinking of a world title."

Especially with her eyes failing.

A tremor lanced through her.

Jared gave her a firm, "you got this" nod that bolstered her. He'd said those words when she'd worried she and Harley wouldn't be competition ready in time for the season. Every chance he got, he'd come home to work with her and Harley until they got up to speed. She and Jared had always been each other's number one fans.

Would he still stand by her if she had a serious vision problem? She kicked the dumb thought aside. People her age didn't up and go blind for no good reason.

"And I have to give credit to all the girls here because they put on a great barrel race all week and they're tough competition," she concluded and shot Hank a hopeful look.

Got enough?

"World champion barrel racer Amberley

James," Hank intoned into his recorder. "Congratulations on another great year."

She ducked her head and sent a shower of water on her rain-splattered boots. "Thank you."

Please let this be the end. Her heavy lids drooped momentarily, and the ground seemed to tilt a little bit. Or was that her?

"Hank, good to see you," she spied him now standing just a couple of feet away, shaking hands briskly with the lingering blogger.

"Well." Hank's ruddy face turned tomato. "Didn't expect to get a double scoop here."

"Oh, I believe Amberley's done a great job of giving you all the material you need," Jared drawled, polite, friendly and respectful as ever, with just the right amount of firm. "Y'all have a good night, now."

He swept an arm around her waist and led her toward the parking lot.

"Any special reason you came out here? Are you two going to make it official?" Hank called.

Jared halted and peered down at her. She blew out a long breath. Why couldn't men and women just be friends? They'd battled the misimpression they were a couple for years, right down to rumors claiming they dated, held hands, kissed even. She blushed a bit thinking how they'd come close to doing just that right before her father got ill. Luckily, they'd come to their senses and avoided a huge mistake.

"I'd be a lucky man if that were true, but Amberley and I are just longtime friends. If that changes, I'll be sure to give you the exclusive." He tipped his hat and pulled her into the unlit, mostly deserted parking lot.

Under cover of darkness, they ran, hand in hand, splashing through puddles, laughing, soaked and breathless when they arrived at his truck.

"Why'd you do that?" she asked, one heel up and back on the step bar.

He placed his hands on the wet body of his truck, boxing her in, and leaned down. The clean, masculine scent of him, leather, soap and a hint of spice, had her breathing deep.

"To rescue you. Plus, I owe you for bailing me out at the bachelor's auction last week."

A bright laugh bubbled up from within. It felt good after so much worry. "Still not sure if I got my money's worth…"

"Chili dogs and chips?" he scoffed, looking

not the least bit offended. "That took a lot of effort. Planning."

She pressed lightly on his muscular chest. "Yeah. Right."

He trapped her hand against his heart, and for a breathless moment they simply stared at each other.

Tell him about your eyes, urged the angel on one shoulder.

Keep quiet, the devil on her other shoulder whispered.

She cleared her throat and ignored the strange sense of letdown when he released her and stepped aside. "Anyway, I had to even up the score."

"Never," she shot back, forcing a teasing tone, needing to lose this strange awareness tugging her from the friend zone.

He angled his head and raised his thick, perfectly shaped brows. "As in you don't want me rescuing you or pulling ahead in the tally?"

She lifted her chin and ignored the twinge inside about her eyesight. "Neither. Do I look like someone that needs rescuing?"

"Not a chance." He chucked her gently under the chin and considered her. "It might be what I like about you best." Her heart flailed at the deep, serious timbre in his voice. "That and your burned grilled cheese sandwiches."

She laughed, but it didn't break the intimacy swelling between them. "It's an acquired taste."

"Acquired? Maybe. Taste? That's debatable."

The air in her lungs faltered at his tease. Strategic withdrawal time.

She hopped into the truck but left the door open. Today had been a strange day with lots out of focus, especially these all-over-the-map feelings for Jared. Friends didn't look at each like that.

"Get me out of here, you fool."

"Always a fool for you, darlin'." Deep dimples appeared in his flashbulb smile, and for a moment, she almost believed him. He winked, then shut the door.

She leaned her forehead against the window and watched her breath fog the glass. Flirting was as natural and necessary to Jared as breathing.

It didn't mean anything.

And if she ever let herself think so, then she'd be the biggest fool of all.

CHAPTER TWO

"STARGARDT'S DISEASE?"

Amberley strained to bring the wavy lines of her ophthalmologist, Dr. Hamilton, into focus. Shameful tears pricked the back of her eyes. It'd been a long six weeks of appointments and tests since she'd returned home and begun searching for an answer about her failing eyesight, and now this...some strange name that seemed like it had nothing to do with her.

Dr. Hamilton's chair creaked as he leaned forward. "It's a genetic disorder that causes macular degeneration."

Her heart dropped all the way to the floor and splattered.

Was there a cure?

Lately, her central vision had deteriorated at a terrifying rate, hobbling her at home, her spirit and independence vanishing with it.

"Should we have discovered this when she

was born?" her mother asked in what Amberley called her "Interrogation Voice." She'd been a Carbondale county judge for almost ten years and a prosecutor for fifteen before that.

Out of the corner of Amberley's eye, she spied her mother's white face in sharp detail. A line where she hadn't blended her makeup. A mole the size of a pencil eraser. A few strands of gray-brown hair that'd escaped her braid and fell across her cheek.

Strange that while the center of her vision failed, her peripheral vision still worked fine.

"Not necessarily. The condition appears, symptomatically, in childhood with some vision deficit that's correctable with glasses or contacts. However, the loss of sight increases rapidly in the twenties, in some instances progressing to legal blindness."

Her gasp cracked loud in the ophthalmologist's office.

A hand—her mother's—fell on Amberley's knee. Squeezed.

Suddenly it became hard to breath.

"Am I going blind?"

Dr. Hamilton moved his head toward her. That much she could tell, but if he nodded or made a face, she didn't have a clue. He appeared as just a fuzzy blob of tan and brown wearing something white—a lab coat she guessed.

"Complete blindness?" He paused—maybe waiting for her to affirm the question? Her mouth froze along with the rest of her, her heart beating down deep in a block of ice. "That would be rare, but we can't rule it out."

Panic rose. Would her vision be this way from now on? Forever? The world had morphed into a carnival fun house full of twisted, stretched and squashed reflections.

"There isn't a procedure that could help? An implant? Gene therapy?" Her mother's crisp voice turned sharp.

Another knee squeeze.

A drumming sound signaled Dr. Hamilton tapping on his desk. Then a long sigh.

"Gene therapy studies are still too early to be conclusive. Charlotte, I wish I had a better prognosis for Amberley. This is a heck of a thing."

"So—so that's it?" Amberley's voice shook.

"We can arrange for a service dog."

"I don't need a dog," she cried. "I need my eyes back."

My life.

"The Lord doesn't give us more than we can handle—"

Easy for a sighted person to say. Amberley shook off her mother's hand, shot to her feet, stepped forward, then bumped into the desk with her thigh. Hard. Her teeth ground together. She'd become a hermit these last few weeks for this exact reason. At home, she navigated the space well enough, keeping the tormenting sense of helpless, hopeless at bay.

But here—here she couldn't hide from it. In the real world, her vision blossomed into a bigger problem and she shrunk into someone incompetent, dependent, weak, a person she never wanted to be.

"I can handle a fifteen-hundred-pound stallion at fifty miles an hour. But this—I can't deal with this. What am I supposed to do with my life?"

She'd been planning on trying out for the ERA Premier tour team again at their end-of-summer qualifiers. Now she'd never be good enough to ride with them.

Or ride at all...

The life she'd always wanted ended before it'd even started, and she had no contingency plan.

"Honey, let's not think so far ahead."

Dr. Hamilton made a soothing noise. "Your mother's right. Take it day by day."

"And what do I do with those days?"

Unable to pace for fear of smacking into anything else in her obstacle course of a world, she dropped back into her seat. A sense of helplessness washed over her. Crushing. Unfamiliar. Did her life matter anymore? One without riding? Competing? Winning?

If you aren't first, you're last. Her father's words floated inside, stinging.

What am I if I can't compete?

Nothing.

No. Less than nothing.

You may as well not even exist.

She dropped her head in her hands.

"There's plenty you can do," her no-nonsense mother protested. Staunch as her pioneer ancestry.

"Like…"

After a painful beat of silence, her mother cleared her throat. "You could come down and assist my office clerk."

"Doesn't that require reading?"

Metal grated on metal. A drawer opened by the sound of it. Then Dr. Hamilton said,

"There's an equine therapy program for people with disabilities."

"I can't help people with disabilities," Amberley protested. "Not when I'm…"

Silence. Shifting in chairs. A light cough from Dr. Hamilton. A short exhale from her mother.

And then it dawned on her. *She* had the disability. She *was* a disability. And a liability. The realization settled in her chest like pneumonia, cold, dense and painful.

A strange urge to seek out her gelding, Harley, and share the news seized her. He'd always been her rock. Her confidant. Him and…

Jared.

Suddenly she pictured her best friend's wide-open smile and his teasing, amber eyes. What would he think of her if he knew her marginalized status, someone without a purpose or real worth? A loser. Not a winner at all.

She hoped she'd never find out.

Sidelined by an injury last season, he'd return to the Broncos' preseason training in a few weeks. Until then, she'd continue dodging his texts and calls and hole up in her room.

After that…

Her future stretched ahead of her, as narrow, bleak and distorted as her vision.

"So what do I do now?" she asked when the silence in the room stretched to its—her—breaking point.

"I'll give you the number for the equine program and write you a referral to an occupational therapist. They'll help you regain your independence and improve your quality of life."

Her fingers curled around the worn wooden edge of her seat. Her quality of life? That made her sound a hundred years old. Then again, maybe the description fit: someone barely hanging on to a life that was, for all intents and purposes, over.

"No, thanks."

"Excuse me?" Dr. Hamilton's chair scraped and he stood.

"We'll take the number and the referral, Doctor," her mother interjected smoothly, in a brook-no-argument voice which had secured her status as the state's most successful prosecutor turned judge.

Amberley's nose tingled and her eyes ached with the effort to hold back her grief. She needed to get home, crawl into bed and bury herself under the covers.

"Is our time up?" She headed in the direction of the door, unmoored. Her life whirled, out of control, her independence—gone. She couldn't even take off when she wanted—not when she couldn't drive. And she missed her other Harley, a 2010 black Breakout that matched the one Jared bought the same year.

No more hopping on her bike and chasing down sunsets, free, the wind on her face, blowing through her hair, as close to flying as any human could get. No. With her wings clipped, she just wanted to duck under her covers and hide.

Her foot connected with the bottom of a tree stand. It tilted forward and fell on top of her.

"Amberley!"

Her mother and the doctor rushed to help, and she balled her hands at her sides.

Don't cry. Don't cry. Don't cry.

You may not have much, but you still have your pride.

A few minutes later, they were out the door and in her mother's pickup. The warm June air flowed through her cracked-open window as they drove home. She picked out the scent of Smokey's barbecue, sweet and tangy, and pictured the crispy, white-and-red awning and blue-covered picnic tables instead of the passing color smear.

Would she ever see it again?

No.

Another loss, one of the many ahead to grieve. Her future rose black and immutable, her past a cemetery filled with everything she once loved and now lost.

"Listen, sweetheart, I'm going to be with you every step of the way. Don't worry."

"I don't want to be taken care of."

The faint twang of a country song crooned through the radio. "No," her mother said gently. "I suppose you don't. You never did."

Amberley let out a breath. "I love you, Ma. It's just that I need *not* to need you right now."

"Of course."

They rode a while more in silence. Amberley dropped the back of her head to her seat and shut her eyes. When the air turned thick with pine scent, she imagined them crossing out of town and onto the highway that led to their home, a small log cabin with a deep porch that her father had built himself.

What would her dad say to her now?

He'd be so let down.

Sorry, Daddy.

Three more turns and the truck bounced on rough track. When the right side dipped, she imagined the ruts that marked the halfway point up her packed-dirt drive. Then her mother pulled to a stop and Amberley jerked open the door.

"I'm going to bed," she called once she found the porch banister and stepped up the stairs.

"Shoot!" her mother exclaimed behind her.

Amberley stopped and turned—a pointless gesture since she could make out only her mother's tall, thin shape. She pictured the narrow oval of her face, the long brow and upturned nose that'd always given her comfort as a child. Her heart squeezed. She'd never see her mother's face again.

This was real.

Not temporary.

Not fixable.

Forever.

The porch step creaked, and her mother's soft hand fell on Amberley's wrist. "I completely forgot. We have company coming for supper."

"I'll just stay in my room. Tell them I have a headache." A deep ache now clawed her brain.

Her mother guided her up to the porch, then paused by the front door. In the distance, chickens squawked and the American flag atop a flower bed's pole snapped. The warm wind carried the scent of newly blooming wildflowers. "I don't think he'll accept that."

"Why?" she asked through a yawn. Her heavy-lidded eyes closed. Sleep. She just wanted to sleep and not wake up for a long, long time.

Or ever.

"It's Jared."

"JARED!"

Jared Cade waved at a former high school buddy, then swept chalk over the tip of his pool stick. "What's up, Red?"

"Not much." Red clomped over in heavy boots, hitching up drooping work pants, a faint burnt odor preceding him. His short auburn hair stuck up around his smudged face.

"Phew." Lane, one of their Saturday night poker buddies, wrinkled his long nose. "You come straight here from a cookout?"

A couple of the guys guffawed at their long-standing joke with the lone firefighter in their group. Many worked on ranches or in rodeo and gathered at this pool hall most nights.

From corner-mounted speakers, a George Strait tune blared. Pictures of local and state sports teams covered every inch of the wood-paneled walls, jockeying for space. Jared had signed a few of them, he recalled, eyeing a framed eleven-by-sixteen photo behind the cash register. It featured his senior year, record-breaking catch during a state division championship.

One thing he liked best about Carbondale, he'd always be its hero.

"Just finished toasting marshmallows on I-77," Red drawled, referring to the location of a small wildfire that'd broken out over the weekend. He lifted a finger and waved it in a circle, signaling the waitress for a round of drinks. "What can I get you fellas?"

"I've got this," Lane insisted. "Plus, it's my turn to buy." He turned to Jared, eager to please, a fan of Jared's since high school. "Another beer?"

He shook his head, then eyed the striped balls remaining on the pool table. "Heading out to Amberley's in a minute."

Roseanne, the pool hall owner's daughter and part-time waitress, hustled over. She laid her hand on his arm and peered at him beneath lashes so long he guessed they were either fake or she was an alien.

"You goin' to hear Back Country play at The Barnsider next weekend?"

His lips curved into a smile at the flirty look she shot him. She was short and thin and kind of twitchy, filled with the kind of restlessness that set her earrings swinging. A long sweep of cropped platinum hair fell in her face—pale with clean quick features, eyes covered in a haphazard blue.

Roseanne no longer interested him, exactly, seeing as how they'd already been out a couple of times and that'd gone nowhere, but he wouldn't turn his nose up at the attention.

"Could be."

"I might be goin'," she said, coy.

"That a fact?" he answered lightly, shooting for a tone that was friendly but not encouraging.

His brothers, and especially his younger sister, Jewel, teased him mercilessly about his "girl problem," calling him lady-killer or heartbreaker. But the women, they came to him. He never aimed to hurt anybody. Just wanted to keep things light. Fun. No strings roping down this cowboy. If they got their hearts broke, well, he did feel bad about that, but he'd never done it intentionally. That would have required him to put effort into it, which, like most things in life, he didn't since everything came kind of easily to him. Sports, friends, ladies' hearts…

Roseanne finished taking drink orders, snapped her pad closed and turned to him again. "Wouldya like to go with me? If we get too drunk, we could just crash at my place after."

He shot his buddies a quick side eye to stop the guffaws he sensed coming. Roseanne might be misled, but she didn't need to feel bad for it.

"Well, now, I appreciate that offer. I do. But I might have already promised to take Amberley, so…"

"Oh," Roseanne nodded fast. "Of course. You and Amberley, I mean…"

She scurried away, her face aflame. He hung his head a moment. Now he did feel bad. Although he and Amberley were just friends, everyone assumed more. Here he'd gone and added fuel to the fire.

"Thought you two broke up," Red taunted as the guys exchanged knowing, irritating looks.

Jared shrugged, then stooped over the pool table. It bugged him that Amberley had been ignoring his recent calls and texts. The word *friend* didn't describe how much she meant to him. *Family* neared the mark, but then that'd make her a sister. Given how pretty he found her when he forgot to think of her as just his bud—well, thinking of her as a sister was every kind of wrong.

No. Being his best friend made Amberley one of the most important people in his life. Tonight he'd get to the bottom of her freeze-out. Right after he won this pool game.

His fingers tightened around the stick he now angled over the table. He had two shots, he assessed, doing his level best to tune out his exasperating friends and win the game. Fifty dollars rode on it, but more than that, Jared just plain hated losing, especially to a member of his family's longtime feuding neighbors, the Lovelands. His opponent, bull rider Maverick Loveland, a middle child out of five brothers like him, and a smug, tight-lipped, mean son of a gun, not like him at all, had stopped by his table and challenged him twenty minutes ago.

He didn't care about the money. His thirst to win was rooted in decades of fighting with the ranching family that constantly trespassed on their land for nonexistent water access rights, damming up a river that didn't belong to them, and all because they blamed his family for stringing up one of their own over a hundred years ago.

Yet the murdering, kidnapping, jewel-thieving Lovelands started the feud, putting them squarely in the wrong…not that anyone could ever talk any bit of sense into that mulish clan. The Cades and the Lovelands had struck back at each other for so long it'd become a way of life, despite the fleeting truce they'd called last Christmas. For the first time in generations, the Lovelands had attended the Cades' annual neighborhood party, a surprise move that'd ended about as well as could be expected— with nearly all of them sharing a jail cell overnight for brawling.

His deputy sheriff brother, Jack, who'd been visiting from Denver, and local sheriff Travis Loveland had agreed to release the disorderly group in the morning if they hadn't killed each other by then. Somehow, they'd made it through the night without anyone dying. More shocking still, it turned out his brother James's girlfriend, Sofia, had invited Boyd Loveland to the party because he and his ma wanted to start dating.

Jared still struggled to believe that.

And he and his brothers and sister sure as heck wouldn't permit it. They suspected cash-strapped Boyd, threatened with his ranch's foreclosure, sought their mother's money and—of course—those water access rights. Fortunately, Ma came to her senses after the Christmas fiasco and stopped taking calls from Boyd. Still, she swapped too many looks with him at church for his comfort. A plan to rid themselves of Boyd for good was in the works.

For now, he'd content himself with Maverick.

He eyed his shot choices again, evaluating the easier target. He hated losing and avoided it at all costs.

"Heard Amberley dumped him stone cold," Lane guffawed.

The eight ball jerked forward and smacked into the lone solid ball left on the table. Loud laughter followed on the heels of a brief stunned silence when it sunk into a pocket.

Maverick Loveland clapped him on the shoulder. "Thanks, dude. Though if you wanted to give me fifty bucks, you could have just handed it over. Saved me some time." He plucked the cash off the table and ambled away, as sarcastic and conceited as every other rotten Loveland.

Jared swore under his breath, stung.

"Sorry, Jared!" Lane jittered around him, shoving his hands in his pockets, then yanking them out again. "That's on me. If I hadn't distracted you, you would have won it for sure."

The rest of the crew nodded quickly, and Jared relaxed a tad. Lane was right. He hadn't lost. He'd been sidetracked by thoughts of Amberley.

Why was she avoiding him these past few weeks?

He fitted his stick back in the holder. "Loveland got lucky."

"Yeah, he did," Red vowed. He lifted the mug Roseanne offered him and sipped.

"Exactly," murmured another friend.

"Heck, yeah," said a third.

The tight group, former high school football teammates who'd won the state division championships together, shared plenty of glory days. He'd missed them when the NFL drafted him out of college. After last year's injury, an ACL tear that sidelined him from his starting Broncos position, they'd rallied around him, supportive of their hometown hero.

Life was simpler in Carbondale, where he wasn't some nobody with nothing much to offer. What good was being in the middle of the pack? When his agent called recently with the Broncos' offer: a one-year contract, at a lower salary—basically a benchwarmer position— he'd turned it down.

He'd rather be here, where people knew him, appreciated him, where he could fulfill his vow to his dying father.

"Later." With a wave, he headed outside, hopped on his motorcycle, donned his helmet and roared out onto the two-lane route that cut through Mount Sopris's eastern side. He let out the throttle and ripped through the dark night. Around the edges of his light beams, a dense forest crowded each side of the road. Each breath dragged in the spring-fresh scents of fresh earth, pine and growing things mixed with gasoline fuel. Waves of heat rippled up from the engine, and the wind rushed past.

Life was lived for moments like this, he thought, effortlessly guiding his Breakout around a fallen branch from this morning's storm. Astride his Harley, listening to the rumble from his straight pipes, seated in his low-slung seat, he felt in control of the elements regardless of their severity because only the ride mattered. Sure, not returning to professional football bugged him, but he'd made that call, not the team. An important distinction. One that preserved his status as a winner. Not a failure.

He slowed at a flashing red, then stopped, peered side to side, and peeled off the line with a deep burrrrrooomboomboomboom. At the top of a steep incline, his Breakout went slightly airborne, and for a quick second he imagined himself flying. Nothing above or below him. Just moving through space, wind, and its feeling of force on his face and body.

Dad would have enjoyed this ride, he thought, glancing up at the full moon crowning over a distant peak. Growing up, his father called Jared a star. He'd attended every football game, cheered the loudest and told Jared nothing made him happier than seeing Jared win, especially during his final months of life when he'd battled liver cancer.

Jared's wins on the football field distracted his family and gave them moments to cheer in a dark time. His pa insisted Jared was the glue that held the family together. Before passing away, his father told Jared his siblings would need someone to look up to after he'd gone. He made Jared promise to be that hero.

Since things came easily to Jared, he'd had no trouble fulfilling his pledge until his injury. When he'd tried, and failed, to make a full comeback, however, he realized he'd never fulfill his designated role as family hero if he remained a bench warmer. He opted, instead, to return home. At least here he remained a small-town hero, his reputation intact. Much better than enduring seasons as a second-stringer with little chance of making it back under the big lights.

Or worse, getting cut.

Still. Returning to the ranch hadn't fulfilled him either, no matter how much the community treated him like the "big man" in their small town. A champion. Maybe because such treatment left him feeling like a fraud. He needed something to take his mind off wondering what he'd do with his life now that he couldn't play ball. He sped faster. Amberley was just the distraction he needed.

A few minutes later, he pulled up beside Amberley's cabin, cut the engine and lowered the kickstand. Something immediately seemed off about the place. Light streamed from every window, and the front door hung open.

"Hello?" he called, swinging his leg over the bike seat. His boots clattered on the porch steps. "Amberley?"

He swept off his hat, ducked inside the cabin and peeked at the kitchen. No signs of cooking. No evidence of anyone anywhere. Huh.

Striding across the small space, he stopped at the start of a short hall that led to the back bedrooms. "Amberley?" He listened. Nothing.

"Charlotte?"

Concern brewed along with his confusion. He'd spied Charlotte's white pickup outside. They were here. Just not in the house.

He paced back outside and tramped down the stairs, his heart picking up speed when he spotted Charlotte walking his way, her hands cupped around her mouth.

"Amberley!" she called.

He caught up to her and his breath whistled fast, pulse thrumming. "Something wrong? Where's Amberley?"

"I don't know!" Moonlight reflected on her damp cheeks. "She ran off when we got back from the doctors. I tried following but I twisted my ankle. Now there's no sign of her."

He peered at the shed where Amberley stored her bike.

"She go for a ride?"

"No. She can't because—" Charlotte stopped and clamped a hand over her mouth. So many expressions collided on her face, and he couldn't read any of them. She didn't seem to breathe.

Neither did he. Worry punched him in the gut. Hard.

"Because why? Charlotte, what's going on? I don't see…"

"She can't either."

"What?"

"She's going blind. We just learned about it today and—"

"Blind," he cut in, repeating a word that suddenly made no sense. Not when it came to Amberley.

A rising wind lifted the hem of Charlotte's

long skirt and ruffled her sleeves. She twisted at the waist, eyes darting every which way.

"It's a genetic disorder that starts with blurring of her central vision. She's been having trouble with her eyes for a while but she didn't tell anyone. Didn't want to worry us."

A short burst of air escaped him. "That's Amberley." As tough as they came and not one for sympathy. He'd never met a stronger woman. Or a more stubborn one. He had to get to her. Darn it. She needed him. Whatever the issue, they'd work it out together like they always did.

"She was upset when she found out I'd invited you to dinner." Charlotte's voice kept taking on air, getting higher and higher, thinner and thinner. "Jared, what if she's hurt? Trapped out there?"

A long low howl rose in the dark night, and the hairs on the back of his neck rose. Wolves. And they weren't the only animals a person had to worry about in the Rocky Mountain wilderness.

He slammed his hat back on, mind racing, thinking as Amberley would. He knew her as well as he knew himself. Maybe even better. Where would she go?

The answer smacked him full in the face.

Of course.

Dirt sprayed from beneath his boots as he sprinted down a familiar trail.

"I'll find her, Charlotte!" he called over his shoulder. "I'll bring her home safe and sound. Promise."

CHAPTER THREE

AMBERLEY STUMBLED ALONG a rutted path, her gasps of breath harsh in her ears. Her boots sunk into puddles forming atop the hard-baked soil. Soaked, her plaid shirt clung to her like a frigid second skin. It'd begun drizzling only ten minutes ago. Then, in that unpredictable way of Rocky Mountain weather, the sky turned on the world with what appeared to be crack-white flashes of lightning. Thunderous booms shook the electric air and thick sheets of rain pelted the earth, shaking her from the inside out.

Worst of all.

She was lost.

Clamping her chattering teeth, she trudged on, one foot in front of the other. Where was she? She'd run off a half hour ago, she estimated, and should have reached her destination: a small, abandoned one-room schoolhouse that had once served the local ranching families a hundred years ago. Its shape should have caught her attention by now. The dirt path that ran from her cabin led straight there, yet somewhere along the way she'd gotten turned around. Now she didn't recognize which path she followed since staring straight at anything was like looking through a smudged, cracked, warped windshield. Reining in her mounting panic, she used her side vision to guestimate her location.

The waterfall of sky blurred the dim landmarks worse than her slipping eyesight. Skyscrapers of pitch-green trees, pines she supposed based on the smell and shape, loomed to her right. To her left, the land turned to beige shale and seemed to slope down. In fact, it seemed to disappear—

Her foot encountered air and she teetered for a gut-cramping moment on the edge of a drop-off. Her arms pinwheeled. A flash-thought forked in her mind. Would it matter so much if she tumbled right off this mountain? What difference would it make?

A wild shriek flew from her, voicing her anguish, her fear, her hopelessness, her rage, her despair.

Then a strong arm snaked around her waist

and yanked her back. Hard. She and her rescuer smacked to the boggy earth with a sploosh. The man grunted, the air knocked out of him, and she blinked up at the shifting, whirling sky, winded herself.

An instant later, she scrambled away and rocked back on her heels. A tall, lanky man leveraged himself up on his elbows, then shot to his feet in a smooth, agile move she'd recognize anywhere.

Jared.

He opened his mouth to say something, but just then a deafening flash-bang splintered the fizzing air. The sky lit up and lightning burned through a nearby tree, amputating a crane-sized branch. It crashed with deadly force inches from their feet. Burnt wood and sulfuric fumes rose.

The sky growled, low and ferocious, readying for another salvo. Goose bumps broke out across her skin.

Jared gestured. "Come with me!"

Amberley nodded. No time to argue. He laced his fingers in hers and together they slid and stumbled through the howling tempest. The streaming air launched debris at them, hard bits of wood whizzing fast enough to strike with maximum impact. When a trail marker sign winged at them, she didn't spot it fast enough to duck and it bashed straight into her forehead, sending her to her knees. She clutched her stinging face, and her fingers came away a sticky, blurred red.

She felt dazed. She shook her head to clear it, but the move only shot a bolt of pain through her. Without a word, Jared scooped her up in his arms, held her tight to his broad chest, and jogged down the trail until the outline of the old schoolhouse appeared. She grasped her thrumming head, afraid it'd either fall off her shoulders or explode if she didn't.

Without pausing, Jared kicked open the door, shoved it closed behind them, strode inside the dark interior, then lowered to a tottering wooden chair at the front of the room. All at once, the world muted itself. The now-muffled rain snare-drummed softly on the roof. The fangless wind batted against the rattling windowpanes. The dank, musty space closed in. Their ragged breaths mingled. Beneath her ear, Jared's heart galloped and the hands smoothing up and down her back shook.

She'd never sensed Jared flustered a day in

his life, and for some reason this scared her as much as anything.

"Shhhhhhhhhhh," he murmured, low in her ear. "I've got you, darlin'."

She stiffened.

"You're safe," he crooned in a rumbling, husky voice.

Enough. She didn't want to be safe. Least of all because of someone else rescuing her or seeing her at her weakest. Even worse, that person was Jared.

She wriggled free of his arms and faltered back a couple of steps. Her hands groped the emptiness behind her, a new habit, to feel for what she couldn't see. Frustration and helplessness brewed in her belly, toxic and nauseating. When her fingers encountered the soft edge of an old desk, she leaned on it, testing her weight partially, before trusting herself to sit atop it.

"Let me." Jared brushed back the hair sticking to the gash on her forehead. Something dripped from her temple. Warmer than water.

She'd never fainted in her life. Yet suddenly, a light-headedness stole over her, and she grasped the edges of the desk with both hands.

"Stop." She jerked away and nearly cried out from the pain. A red drop splattered on the dusty floor.

Jared pivoted with her. "Hold still." He flipped off her hat, grasped her chin in one strong hand and studied her. A deep longing to see his amber eyes seized her. Yet if they held pity, she'd rather not know. "This is going to need stitches."

She started to shrug and realized that even the slightest movement made her head whirl and her stomach revolt. "A flesh wound," she said, trying to joke, a reference to one of their favorite Monty Python movies, but her voice cracked like a thirteen-year-old boy's.

"Not funny, Amberley," Jared growled. "You could have gotten yourself killed out there."

He pulled something from his back pocket, wrapped it around her head and tied it in the back. It smelled like him, she thought, breathing in the crisp cotton, clean soapy smell. His lucky bandanna, she guessed.

"So what if I had?"

He knelt in front of her and gathered her hands in his. Though she tried to stop them, tears of pain welled. She didn't cry easily. In fact, she could count the number of moments on one hand. The time her glasses got knocked off and she'd had to crawl around on the playground looking for them while other kids laughed. And once when she'd dislocated a shoulder during a barrel racing accident. Then the day they'd buried Daddy.

"Well, if you'd gotten yourself killed, then I would have lost my mind," he said, his voice thick with emotion, almost a croak.

Her frog prince. Back.

Only she didn't want him anymore.

She didn't want anyone.

Not even herself.

At least not who she was now.

She screwed her eyes shut. Jared brushed at her damp lashes with his thumbs, the gesture so tender it ached. "Your mother told me about your eyes."

A painful lump formed in her throat.

"Amberley, talk to me."

She stood. Halting steps carried her to the window. Although she couldn't see much in the writhing darkness, she imagined the tumult and wished it'd sweep her away, too.

"I want to go home."

Jared joined her. When his fingers laced

with hers, she jerked her hand away. "Charlotte told me you've been having trouble for a while now. Is that why you've been avoiding me?"

She shrugged.

"Why didn't you tell me?"

"I didn't want to."

Because I couldn't bear for you to think less of me.

To pity me.

"Why? I'm always here for you."

"I can manage on my own," she fired back.

"But you don't have to."

"Yes, I do."

"We're a team."

Only when they were both equal. But those days were over. "Not anymore."

"Just tell me what I can do, Amberley."

"This isn't about you, Jared," she snapped.

"The heck it ain't." She flinched at his suddenly angry tone. In all their years, they'd never fought. Not seriously. Sure. They'd had their share of good-natured arguments from time to time. Squabbles. Bets. Competitions. Rivalries. But this? It was foreign and felt every kind of wrong.

Still. She'd rather he be angry than sorry for

her. Angry meant you mattered. Pity? That rendered you inconsequential.

"We'll get through this."

"Get *through* this?" She pressed her burning forehead against the cold glass. "I'm going blind, Jared. I'm never getting *through* this."

He cupped her shoulders and turned her slowly. "There's got to be a cure," he insisted. "Surgery. A donor list. Didn't I hear once—something about cadavers..."

"Stop." She put her hands over her ears. "Just stop. Everything comes easy to you. Heck. You've never had to work for just about anything in your life, so I get your not understanding this. But I." She poked a finger in his chest. "Am. Not. Getting. Better."

"So you won't even try?"

"I just want to be left alone."

"What's that mean? Holing up in your room? Hiding out from the world? Ignoring your friends?" He cleared his throat. "Me?"

"It's not hiding. It's being realistic. Facing facts."

"About what?"

"That I can't do anything anymore."

"You can do plenty."

"Not barrel race."

She angled her head and viewed him from the corner of her eye, using her working, peripheral vision. Those perfect brows of his slanted over his straight nose, and white rimmed his golden-brown eyes all around. He appeared every bit as uncomfortable and confused as she felt.

And she couldn't bear it.

He surrounded himself with capable, successful people. Winners. She couldn't blame him for not understanding how to handle someone disabled like her. *Disabled*. She already hated the word. It meant not able. Who wanted to be known as that—even if it was true?

"You can't see at all?"

"Not dead on. Everything's a blur of color in the center of my vision. From the sides, I can focus some."

"You can't see my face?"

Her insides shriveled at the pained note that entered his voice. "Not all of it. Not at once. And soon." Her voice fractured. "Soon I might not be able to see even that."

He brought her hands to his warm, smooth cheeks. When he swished her fingers over his down-turned lips, she yanked free.

"Let me help you," Jared insisted.

"Do what? I can't compete anymore. Can't ride. Can't drive. Heck. I can't even walk alone on my own. I don't want to depend on anybody for anything. I don't want to be reminded of—"

"Reminded of—" he prompted.

"Of how helpless I am."

"No one's saying you are."

"But they'll be thinking it. You're thinking it."

The beat of silence spoke volumes and hurt way more than she'd imagined it could. They'd never lied to one another, and she didn't expect anything less than brutal honesty from her best friend now. Outside, the battering rain eased, then trickled. The thunder and lightning moved off to torment another mountain.

She glimpsed Jared's chest rise, then fall with a long exhale. "You're no quitter, Amberley. That isn't the gal I—" he stumbled, fumbled for a word. "I care about."

She flushed. What'd he been about to say? Oh. No matter. None of it did anymore. Jared liked being around her because she challenged him. Once it sunk in that those days had ended, he'd come around only out of pity.

She didn't believe for a second he'd abandon her. His decency and loyalty meant he never turned his back on his friends. But she wanted to be his equal, not his charity case. Better she cut things off while she still had her pride. Jared ran with a fast crowd and she'd only slow him down.

"Then stop caring about me," she forced herself to say, "because that girl's gone."

"Not happening."

She paused, thinking fast. She needed to get rid of him once and for all. For both their sakes. "So as my friend you'll do anything for me?"

He nodded quickly. "Now you're seeing sense."

"Promise?"

"Promise."

"Anything?"

"Name it," he vowed.

"Alright. Then bring me home and don't ever come around again."

"Amberley…" he protested, his voice full of air like she'd sucker punched him.

She shook her head. Firm. "You promised."

"AMBERLEY, PHONE!"

At her mother's call, Amberley roused herself ever so slightly from the 24/7 stupor she'd fallen into these past few weeks. "Tell them I'm sleeping!" she called without opening her eyes. She turned and burrowed deeper under her covers, ignoring the slight bump up in her heart rate.

So far, Jared had kept his word and not called since that night on Mount Sopris, but a part of her, a lowdown, cowardly, traitorous part, still hoped, every time she heard the phone ring, that he hadn't respected her decision...

Hadn't given up on her.

She missed him. Missed her friend. Missed that smile. Not that she'd ever see it again anyways.

Oh. Stop bellyaching. It was for the best. If she cared about him, she'd let him go. She sighed and flopped over on her back, arms flung wide, her best thinking position.

What was the saying? "If you can't fix it, you just have to stand it."

She glanced over at the bedside table cluttered with cans of pop, bags of chips and dishes left over from eating meals in bed the last few weeks.

Or wallow in it...

Inertia. Another good word for her current state. Suspended animation. That summed it up, too. Maybe she should request to be cryogenically frozen. Least then she'd do something for science.

"Amberley!" shrilled her mother again.

She shoved herself upright, and her covers dropped to her lap in a messy heap. "Can you take a message?" From the corner of her eye, she spied the digital clock with the oversize display her mother had brought home recently. It read 1:20 p.m.

Outside her open window, the sky was a blue so brilliant even her eyes picked it up, the air was still washed clean from recent rain, and birds warbled from the two rustling maples that stood sentinel at the end of their drive. It was the kind of weather that usually woke her feeling elated, glad to be alive, wishing she could belt out some musical number like "Oklahoma" or the "Sound of Music."

Not that she could sing a lick, but on days like this she'd always felt anything was possible. Even singing on key. Like maybe she could ride to the end of the earth and back before it'd even had a chance to circle the sun.

"It's about Harley!"

Harley? She tossed off her covers and stumbled down the narrow hall to the kitchen, hands brushing the walls to keep her bearings. Her wrinkled sleep shirt swung around her knees.

She mouthed "Thanks" to her mother and brought the phone to her ear. "Hello?"

"Sorry to bother you, Amberley, what with, ah, all you're going through and all."

Harley's stable owner, Benny Jordan, an asthmatic former champion roper turned rodeo clown who'd retired to this area fifteen years ago, breathed noisily into the phone.

"Is Harley okay?" Her fingers gripped the handle hard, and she dropped into the seat her mother pulled out. Inside her chest, her heart skittered every which way. Although it'd been weeks since she'd seen Harley, not a day passed where she didn't wonder how he was doing and if the stable was taking good care of him. Prior to her accident, they'd spent most of every day together. Now, the thought of seeing him again only reopened the wound of all that she'd lost.

When her mother pointed at the phone, then her ear, Amberley nodded, fumbled around for the speaker button, then pressed it.

"Well, now. That's the thing. See. He's not eating like he should." More wheezing, then, "Been skittish when folks come near. This morning, I sent in Joan to muck out his stall."

Joan? A former rodeo pro herself, she'd become the local horse whisperer and founded the equine therapy program they ran out of Harley's stables. She had much more important things to do than clean stalls.

"Did something happen?"

A kettle whistled, and her mother's chair scraped back as she rose to grab it.

"Well. Now she's going to be fine."

"Benny. What happened to Joan?" Her pulse picked up tempo and her fingers drummed along with it on the wooden tabletop. Across the way, she glimpsed her mother's form twist to face her. Something hung from each hand. Mugs, Amberley guessed.

"The doctor says it'll heal in about six weeks."

Alarm bells shrilled in her ears. "What happened?"

"Harley busted out her kneecap. Kicked her full on."

Every bit of air in her lungs rushed right out of her. "I'm so sorry."

The sound of poured liquid reached her ears followed by the rip of paper as she imagined her mother opening tea bags.

"Not your fault."

But it was. She saw that suddenly. "I should have been down to care for Harley."

"Understandable that you haven't." She heard a couple of quick inhaler puffs from his end. Then, "Sorry to bring you the bad news, but I'm afraid we're not going to be able to house Harley anymore."

She hung her pounding head. "Is that final?" Jordan Stables provided the only home Harley had ever known. If he couldn't manage there, who knew where he'd end up?

The painful thought of being separated from him branded itself on her heart, burning straight through.

And it's not like you've done anything to help, whispered that angel on her right shoulder.

What's the point? whispered the devil. *Not like you can ride him again. Care for him.*

But she and Harley had a bond that went deep. Besides handling him morning and evening, she'd talked to him a lot. While grooming him, or letting him eat "better" grass on the stable's front yard, she'd filled him in on rodeo winners, cried over barrel racing icon Scamper's passing, sympathized with his "picked last in gym" herd status, and generally kept up a running conversation. She believed she could rattle on about the rising price of corn feed and Harley would think all was right with the world.

And after her father's cancer diagnosis, Harley had been there. She'd cried lots of tears into that silver mane of his. Had hung on to him when it'd felt as though her whole world was falling apart. He kept her from crumbling, too. She never could have gotten through that terrible time without him…or Jared…

Abandoning Harley was inexcusable.

A spoon clanged against ceramic. Her unflustered, steely-souled mother stirring the tea.

Daddy's last words came back to her. "I know you're going to be okay. You are strong."

And she'd believed it, until now.

"When do you need Harley gone by?"

"Joan's in quite a state, as you can imagine. She's got students booked for her program, and now she's laid up. Plus, we won't be able to get anyone to care for Harley. So—"

"I'll come down," she cut him off.

A hand appeared in her line of vision, and the mug her mother set down banged against the table. Puffs of pungent steam swept off the surface and curled beneath her nose.

"Not sure if that'd make a difference."

"If I keep up his stall, can he stay? Least until I figure out next steps?"

She could see general shapes when she was close-up and in small spaces, like a stall. Heck, she'd cleaned the stable's stalls so many times, she could do it blind. It'd hurt to be nothing better than a stall mucker, but she'd do anything to help the horse that'd done so much for her.

Benny made a noise like a shrug. "Well. That'd solve some of the issues."

"Some?"

"He's not socializing well with the other horses in pasture. Acting out."

"Needs exercise," her mother murmured beside her.

"That Charlotte?" Benny hollered.

"Howdy, Ben!" her mother called. "Just thinking there isn't anything wrong with Harley some regular riding wouldn't sort out."

"That a fact."

Amberley's body tightened, her muscles

clenched. She'd been resisting her mother's plea to sell Harley. Now it seemed she faced a rock-and-a-hard-place decision. Sell Harley, or find a way to interact with him that wouldn't leave her feeling worse than ever.

She'd avoided anything that reminded her of the old days. Had asked her mother to remove all her trophies. Stopped listening to rodeo on the radio. Cut Harley and Jared right out of her life. Now she understood how much her decisions affected others. Jared called her selfish, and he had the right of it when it came to Harley.

A steel band tightened around her chest at the thought of letting Harley go. Yet Harley's needs mattered most. First step, visit Jordan Stables, settle him down, get him comfortable and put out feelers for buyers.

Champion barrel racers like Harley sold quickly. He might even make the ERA Premier touring team she'd dreamed about, and he deserved that spotlight. The glory. He'd trained hard for it, right alongside her.

She recalled something she'd read on a poster once: "If you love something, let it go, even when you know it's never coming back."

Or something like that.

It applied to her and Jared, too.

"Just give me fifteen minutes and I'll be down."

"Mighty appreciated," Benny said, then hung up.

A little while later, her mother pulled to a stop in front of Jordan Stables. The familiar scents of manure, hay and horse assailed Amberley as she eased out of the car and stood with a hand on the warm car hood. Memories, sharp and sweet, rushed through her, stinging her eyes and heart. Once this had been her sanctuary. Now she felt like a stranger. Worse. Like she didn't belong.

"Howdy, ladies." Benny's unmistakable twang rang out.

She turned in the direction of his voice and recognized the barrel shape of him, the rolling gate of his bowed legs. He wore the same ten-gallon hat. That much she could make out. As for the rest, her memory about the grizzled man filled in the blanks.

"How's Joan?" Amberley jumped, then swatted at a biting horsefly. In the distance, a group of riders lined up atop horses in one of the corrals.

"Resting for now, otherwise I'd take you to her."

"Please give her this and our apologies." Charlotte handed over a couple of banana walnut loaves she'd baked this morning. The sweet, nutty smell passed beneath Amberley's nose as the foil-wrapped rectangles exchanged hands.

Now that Amberley thought about it, her mother cooked a lot lately and she'd taken time off from work to care for her. Was her career suffering? Did she resent being tied to the house alongside Amberley? Regret flashed inside. She didn't want to be a burden to anyone. She'd been taught better than that.

Amberley's life might be done, but that didn't mean the same was true for her mama. Or Jared. Or Harley.

She had to find a way to cut ties with all of them. Otherwise she would bring them all down.

"That's mighty kind. Thank ya," wheezed Benny.

"Wish we could do more," her mother demurred.

Speaking of which...

"Mind if I go and check on Harley?"

"Still got him in the third stall." A sweep of movement, Benny's arm, she guessed, pointed her in the right direction.

"Thank you." She took a tentative step toward the long, ramshackle building that housed most of the stable's horses. Overhead, birds twittered among the rustling branches of the mighty oaks that covered much of the property. A horse's neigh spurred on two more, and a shifting movement from the mounts in the corral caught her eye. Her foot encountered something sticking up from the ground, a root maybe, and she stumbled forward, only to feel her mother's hand at her elbow, steadying her.

"Got you, honey."

Amberley swallowed down the loss of all that she couldn't see and focused on Harley. Several paces farther and her fingers brushed the rough edge of the half door to his stall. Inside, a large black shape lifted its head and twisted its neck to eyeball her.

"Hey, Harley," she cooed, and he lowered his head and blew. His stamping hooves shifted through the straw bed. "Sorry I haven't been around."

Lifting the hard metal latch, she eased open the door and made to slide inside.

"Honey. That may not be safe," her mother cautioned.

"It's *Harley*."

In an instant, she threw her arms around his warm neck and buried her face in his tangled silver mane. When had he last been brushed? The rise of dust from his pelt itched her nose, and she sneezed.

"I'm sorry, baby," she crooned, and Harley dropped his head to her shoulder at last, nickering, shaking slightly in his withers. "Should never ever have abandoned you."

Another rumble emerged from the back of his throat. His soft lips brushed against her jawbone and his warm breath rushed by her ear.

"I was scared. Still am. But I'm going to do right by you now," she vowed, feeling around for a brush. Harley needed her and she needed him. That was plain.

An hour later, she and her mother led Harley by a corral on their way to the pasture. The rise and fall of excited children's voices indicated a lesson in progress.

"You need to wear your helmet," she heard an adult exclaim.

"Watch her back brace," someone else warned.

"No! I don't want to!" she heard a girl scream. "Please don't make me. Please!"

Harley slowed and his ears twitched. She clucked to keep him moving, but he seemed more interested in the commotion. Was this the therapy program her doctor had mentioned? If so, good thing she hadn't joined it. Why force people with disabilities to confront everything they couldn't do? It was demoralizing.

"Is that Amberley James?" she heard someone squeal. She froze.

"Yes, it is!"

"Amberley!"

A rush of movement, color and shapes, closed in on the fence. Harley sidestepped but otherwise stayed calm.

She'd gotten recognized plenty in her old life. But now, she just wanted to be forgotten. Since she had stayed away from the news, she hadn't yet heard how the rodeo community responded to her vision loss. Her mother and her agent resolved her former contract obligations. That much she knew, but little else.

Still, she couldn't deny that a bead of warmth

expanded inside at the children's excitement to see her.

"Howdy," she called in their general direction.

"Ride? Ride? Ride?" demanded a little boy. A blur of motion at his sides suggested he flapped his hands.

"Can you teach me to be a barrel racer?" asked a child who didn't appear to have any hair given the bare flesh tone surrounding her head.

Cancer?

Her heart squeezed.

"Oh. No. I—uh—I don't ride much anymore."

"See!" cried the child she'd heard earlier. "Amberley's blind like me and she won't ride, so I don't have to either. I want to go home!"

"Well. Ah…" She stalled, unable to agree with that sentiment. Riding helped her during the years her thick glasses made her feel different from other kids. Working with horses gave her a taste of success and achievement. She didn't want this little one to leave defeated because of her.

"It sure would mean a lot to the kids if you'd join us today," said a voice she recognized.

Joan's daughter, Belle, home from college. "Not to mention we're a bit understaffed at the moment."

Amberley winced, thinking of injured Joan and Harley's role in it. She owed it to the Jordans to help. At least for today.

"I might take Harley around once," Amberley said slowly, hardly believing the words as she spoke them. "If you will, too. What's your name?"

The little girl bowed a head of what looked like blond curls. "Fran."

"Alright, Fran. If I walk Harley around, do you think you might try for me?"

"Okay."

A moment later, she guided Harley into the corral, surprised at his lack of hesitation. He stepped forward, sure-footed and eager. In fact, she'd never sensed him this excited, not even before a barrel race.

Was he showing off for the kids?

"Here you go." With an oomph, Benny hefted Harley's saddle over her horse's back. She didn't need her eyesight for this, she mused, while her fingers flew nimbly, fastening and cinching out of habit. A budding light of confidence flickered inside.

With a boost from Benny, she swung her leg around Harley, and her lips twitched up in an unstoppable smile. Settling back in the saddle felt good. Like coming home.

"Fran? Kids? You ready?"

"Yes!" they chorused.

"I'll lead you around," her mother called from below, but Amberley shook her head. She could manage this small-sized corral, and she'd discern the fence in time to avoid it.

Most important, at least for today, she wanted to imagine that she could ride Harley on her own. She owed it to her horse, to injured, shorthanded Joan, and to her mother, who needed to stop fussing and get her life back.

Maybe, in this insular little world, Amberley could pretend she had a purpose after all.

CHAPTER FOUR

SWEAT TRICKLED DOWN Jared's jaw as he rode his eleven-year-old quarter horse, Chance, behind a herd of ambling longhorns. Petey, a stray who'd become one of the ranch's top work dogs, loped along. Overhead, a vast blue sky arched above craggy mountaintops. The musky smells of livestock and leather mingled with the sweet pine of the tree breaks in the clear, dry air.

Nothing invigorated him like riding in high open spaces, he thought, chest expanding in a deep breath. Well, nothing except winning under the big lights and watching Amberley's eyes light up in a smile.

He tamped down thoughts of his best friend. Amberley wanted nothing to do with him. Last week, she swore she didn't need his help, and her rejection stung, leaving a rawness inside that hurt anytime his mind turned her way.

How was she?

Had her vision worsened?

Picturing her holed up in her house, giving up, bothered him to no end. It killed him to think of his gutsy, fearless pal that way. She'd never been a quitter and had succeeded in everything she'd done. Not a day passed without him staring down at his phone, willing himself not to call.

To leave her be.

He was a man of his word.

With a slight tug of the reins, he guided his sleek gray stallion around a depression in the field and clamped his teeth. But it made no lick of sense for her to walk away from their friendship. She meant a heck of a lot to him, and he'd thought that went for her, too.

Guess he'd been wrong.

Or she was just being stubborn.

His money was on his second guess, but how to know for certain?

Don't interfere with something that ain't botherin' you none, his pa always said.

But it did. Maybe too much.

Enough.

He swayed slightly in the saddle and forced his mind on the day's tasks. His gaze traveled over the brown-and-white-spotted cattle, checking for stragglers. Black-and-white herding dogs prowled on the edge of the low-ing, bleating group, working seamlessly with him and his siblings as they drove the cows and their offspring toward the day's pasture on the western edge of Laurel Canyon.

As a grass-fed, organic beef operation that guaranteed humane treatment of its animals, Cade Ranch avoided artificial fertilizers and pesticides. Instead, they moved their cows daily on a two-week rotation system that allowed the land time to recover between graz-ing periods. The labor-intensive work entailed traveling on horseback instead of ATVs to keep the cattle relaxed and used to their pres-ence. The natural, chemical-free environment, begun by his father shortly before his passing eleven years ago, was good for the herd and for the business. They commanded top dollar on the beef market.

He sure wished his personal life was that successful.

Life had gone his way before his ACL in-jury and now this roadblock with Amberley. He'd made grudging peace with giving up pro-fessional football, his lifelong dream. But how long before he'd let his longtime friend go?

His nonstop thoughts of her suggested no time soon.

When a couple of longhorns halted and dipped their heads to a grassy spot, he squeezed Chance's side, trotting closer. He pursed his lips, but Petey rushed forward before he whistled, anticipating human directives in his uncanny way. Jared yanked off his hat and waved it in front of his flushed face as Petey's lunges got the cows hoofing again. The heated air barely stirred the hair plastered to his forehead.

He had a date tonight with a new gal. A pretty little thing. Sweet and friendly and easygoing. Uncomplicated—just the way he preferred. And she liked daisies, he recalled. She'd told him so when he'd complimented her flower hair clip at last night's county fair. As for her name, he struggled to recall it since they'd spoken only briefly at her busy 4-H fair booth.

Laureen.

He shook his head, shooed away a nagging fly and settled his hat back on, pulling the brim low against the sun.

Loranne.

No. Still not right.

Laurie-Anne.

Aw. Shoot. He'd have to ask his little sister, Jewel, who loved giving him grief about his pathetic (her words) dating life. But seeing as the only male in Jewel's life was her black stallion, Bear, Jared didn't put much stock in her opinion. He'd never had any trouble with women except keeping their names straight from time to time, and now Amberley freezing him out.

But Amberley wasn't just a woman. Well. Not the dating kind. Sure, when he'd first spotted her at a local junior rodeo, he'd wanted to ask her out. He'd never seen a prettier girl. Astride a mount that looked too big for her dainty frame, thick, honey-blond hair swinging beneath a black cowboy hat, eyes so blue a boy could drown in them, he'd frozen in his boots, sure he'd glimpsed an angel. Her white teeth flashed when her rosy lips parted in a smile at the fawning crowd of young men. Then her gaze tangled with his and she'd rolled her eyes, ever so slightly, a comical gesture, a private communication, that began a connection that'd strengthened through the years.

Until now.

His personal life wasn't much without her

in it. As for his professional life—he stifled a yawn—it wasn't exactly fulfilling these days either. Chance's head bobbed up and down as he wove in between the cattle with Petey sticking close, checking individual cows for signs of fatigue or distress.

Once he'd imagined his destiny the way his father described it: cheers, trophies and records, a hero's life, not this sedate ranch work punctuated by local wins at rodeo or pool competitions. He needed more, something to divert his attention longer than another evening with the latest gal to catch his eye. What that was, though…well…he couldn't put his finger on it. He'd gone so long seeing his life, his future, through his father's eyes, he couldn't envision it on his own.

If you're not makin' dust you're eatin' it.

Ever since returning to sleepy Carbondale for good, he'd battled a constant choking sensation. Seemed his old life wasn't as easy to swallow anymore.

The returning shadows cast by a cluster of ponderosa pines suggested they'd passed lunch without a break, a fact confirmed by his rumbling stomach. They'd been laboring since dawn, ahead of the heat that now made his plaid shirt cling to his sore muscles and his thighs chafe beneath leather-chaps-covered jeans. Even his toes, crammed inside dirt-splattered boots, slid against each other.

He could sure use a drink right about now.

A whistle cracked through the air. He craned his head and spotted his brother James riding up with a three-month-old straggler secured across the front of his saddle. James pointed at a young heifer that'd wandered from the herd, shaking its head. Peering closer, Jared spied its leaking eye. He reached for the rope coiled at his side.

Pink eye.

They'd need to doctor it on the range before the infectious condition spread. He freed his rope and circled it as he closed in on the wayward steer.

Suddenly the calf spooked and bolted for a tree line fifty odd yards away. If it broke through there, it might tumble into the ravine on the other side and break its neck.

"Yee-haw!" hollered a familiar, blood-thirsty voice. He caught sight of his little sister, Jewel, streaking by atop Bear, her lariat lassoing above her Stetson.

He kicked Chance and galloped after her,

clods of dirt spewing behind them as they thundered after the panicked cow. They didn't need to exchange a word or a look to execute this familiar roping routine.

Giving Chance his head, his trained heel horse flashed past the young cow before pivoting to block its escape into the trees. Rope snaked through the air, and the lariat's noose dropped neatly over the heifer's head, checking its flight.

Jewel rode closer, the line held fast in her fist, her slim, freckled face set, dark eyes flashing beneath the wide brim of her hat.

He whistled under his breath. Jewel was greased lightning with a lariat. He'd expect nothing less of his talented little sis, who could, despite her size, outride, outshoot and outdo any of the Cade boys. She was headstrong and full of grit, and it had never occurred to his brothers to give her breaks for being "a girl." To be honest, they were all a little bit afraid of her and her shoulder jab that kept them in line.

Most of the time.

The heifer wheeled, straining against the rope, while James continued circling his cord, waiting for the balking animal to settle enough for him to snare its hindquarters. Trying to shake Jewel's rope, it swung its head, then spread its front legs, bracing and pulling. Getting nowhere, it raced back to the herd, then jerked to a halt at the end of the tether.

Jared advanced a couple of paces, then stopped, patient, steady, holding himself and Chance still, save for his circling rope. The blowing yearling dropped its head. A tense minute went by while Petey expertly hemmed in the animal, wearing it down without stressing it. Then, without warning, it reared up and kicked out its back legs.

Bingo.

Jared tossed his loop neatly around the calf's hindquarters and lowered the lariat's bottom edge to the ground, keeping it loose and flexible. His breath lodged in his throat as he waited, willing it not to slide off before he could cinch it around the animal's girth. Petey charged the yearling so that it stepped back, straight through the noose.

"Got it!" whooped Jewel.

In a flash, he pulled, tightening the loop around the runaway's belly. Jewel secured her line to her saddle and hopped off Bear, the jerking, straining yearling trapped between their ropes. In the grass, Petey sat on his haunches, his mismatched eyes intent, over-size ears pricked forward as he assessed the unfolding situation, eager as always to help the humans who'd once rescued him.

Jewel crept forward, a tie-down rope clamped between her teeth. Her horse, trained like all the ranch's mounts, backed up a cou-ple of steps to keep the line taut and the calf from thrashing. One kick could bust a kneecap or knock loose teeth, not to mention the risk of the animal injuring itself. Grabbing hold of the heifer's head, Jewel expertly worked Jared's rope over its hips and down with her other hand.

He wheeled Chance so that the loop slid to their quarry's ankles. Then he jerked the rope, knocking it off its feet. It flopped into the soft, deep grass.

"Hold!" Jewel hollered. He circled Chance back and watched his sweating, straining sis-ter tie up the heifer's front legs, trussing the winded animal in a blur of movement. Then she hopped back on Bear and they walked their horses toward one another, slackening the ropes to give the straining calf more breathing room. It lifted its head, struggled to get back on its feet, then sank down again.

James trotted up, unbuckled his saddlebag and passed them eyewash. His dark eyebrows met over his nose. "Anyone seen Justin?"

A yowl rang out, answering that question. Their reckless younger brother, Jesse's twin, raced by after a breakaway calf. Jared's heart stopped at its proximity to the tree line and ravine. Riding that fast, Justin might not stop in time to avoid a fatal plunge.

At the last possible moment, Justin launched himself from the saddle and tackled the animal, wrestling it to the ground in a tangle of limbs, hooves and feet. A cloud of dust and grass rose. In two wraps and a hooey, he bound three of the heifer's legs while his pinto circled back.

James swore a blue streak. "Someday he'll kill himself." He kicked his mount and joined their daredevil sibling.

"That's the plan," Jewel muttered, dropping to her knees beside their four-legged patient.

Jared joined her and ripped off the eyewash cannula's wrapping. "He hasn't been the same since Jesse."

Jewel held the calf's head as he flushed its

red-rimmed eye. "It's as if he's daring death to take him like it did Jesse."

"Justin loves playing the odds." Using a sterile cloth, he carefully wiped the discharge from around the heifer's eye.

"Playing a fool more like," Jewel huffed. "Next time we hog-tie *him*."

Their shared chuckle died off quickly. Justin wasn't the only Cade affected by Jesse's murder these past two and a half years. Jack, their oldest brother, had left home, became a bounty hunter and returned only once he'd captured Jesse's killers. James, second oldest and ranch manager, had turned their operation into a fortress, determined to keep out the kinds of outsiders who'd taken their brother. Of course, all that changed once Sofia Gallardo, Jesse's ex and mother of Jesse's five-year-old son, Javi, showed up at the door and stole James's heart.

As for Jewel, his fun-loving sister had thrown herself into her ranch jobs, working every minute of every day, as if she'd just as soon avoid life altogether. And Ma. Well. She'd mostly kept to her room until Sofia and Javi came along.

"Looks good," Jewel confirmed once he'd finished. She began disentangling the calf.

"Nice work, yourself." He stowed the eyewash and secured the rope she passed him. "For a girl," he couldn't resist adding.

His shoulder exploded in pain. "Ow!" When he whirled, Jewel grinned at him smugly and lowered her fist.

"You had that coming."

"Probably," he agreed good-naturedly, rubbing his arm.

The calf wobbled to its feet, sniffed the air, then bolted for the herd. Jared swung back into his saddle and trotted after the rest of the longhorns. His mind returned to his mother.

It'd been a long time since he'd seen her smile as bright as the night she'd welcomed Boyd Loveland to their calamitous Christmas party... He shook away the memory. Jesse's son, Javi, along with his siblings, would help Ma overcome her grief the right way. Letting scheming Boyd into her life would only break her barely mended heart again.

As for himself, he wasn't sure how Jesse's death had changed him, though he knew he didn't want to let his little brother, who'd idolized him, down. It pained him to imagine what Jesse, or his father, would think if they'd seen Jared warming the bench game after game.

Good thing he'd quit before breaking his vow and letting them down.

Better to be a big fish in a small pond than a minnow in the sea. In Carbondale, people still looked up to him. Saw him as somebody important. Not some loser wasting his time hoping for a chance that might never come.

And that mattered most, right?

He shook off the unease that coiled sour and thick in his stomach and shifted his focus back to the herd.

This was his life now. He was man enough to accept it.

A couple of hours later, he hunched over a ham and cheese sandwich in the ranch's main house kitchen. Lifting a glass, he downed half of the cool, sweet milk.

"How'd Justin get that black eye?" asked his mother as she passed a bowl of her sweet bread-and-butter pickles.

He met her large hazel eyes behind wireless frames. Save for the silver bob that swung around her pretty face, her age would be hard to determine. No wonder Boyd Loveland thought he'd found a prime widow to scam when he'd courted her this winter. His mother would be a catch for any man, just not a low-life Loveland.

"Wrestling a heifer."

Air escaped coral-lined lips that perfectly matched a similarly colored blouse tucked into a denim skirt. Coral earrings swung. Some mothers liked sewing. Some cooking. His ma obsessed about matching, right down to her toe polish. It was a way of life, she claimed.

"Can I wrestle a cow?" piped up Javi, his five-year-old nephew. He jumped in his seat, and his eyes, so dark they looked black, twinkled beneath a mop of brown hair.

"No. And feet on the floor, honey," Javi's mother, Sofia, a lithe brunette with golden-hued skin, murmured from the stove. Something exotic smelling sizzled as she stirred it in a wok. Looked like she was continuing her "Mysteries of the East" cooking marathon this week. Ever since she'd arrived at the ranch, she'd shaken up James's carefully arranged rules intended to preserve their way of life and keep change at bay.

And he'd never seen his brother happier.

"Why must he scare me so?" sighed Ma.

"He's working through things."

She brought a steaming cup of tea to her

lips and met his gaze over its rim. "How about you?"

He stopped chewing and swallowed. "Me? I'm fine."

"Mmm-hmm," she mumbled as she sipped her drink, sounding unconvinced. Then, "Javi, carrot sticks are for eating, not sword fights."

"But I have to kill the Joker." Javi poked the jelly container one more time, then bit off a piece of his carrot.

"*I* chose not to go back to football," Jared insisted, thinking of the latest call from his agent, who'd urged him to reconsider. A carrot snapped between his fingers.

"And you're happy about that?"

"I'm here aren't I?" Out of the corner of his eye, he glimpsed Sofia and his mother swap a glance.

"That didn't exactly answer my question," Ma chided gently.

He frowned, not liking where this conversation was headed.

"They don't want me as a starter."

His mother passed a slice of apple to Javi. "That still doesn't mean you can't be part of the team."

"I didn't want to be just part of the team."

"Yeah!" Javi piped up. "Uncle Jared's number one."

He felt his skin heat a little at the familiar hero worship. Jesse had used those exact words growing up.

His mother nodded slowly. "Right. Number one or nothing."

He shrugged and headed for the fridge, nervous energy shoving him onto his feet and moving. She didn't know about the private conversation between him and Pa before he passed, or the promise his father asked him to keep between them. "We got any mustard?"

"Bought some yesterday. Ran into Charlotte James at the store, too."

He straightened so fast that he banged his head on the fridge door.

"Are you okay, Uncle Jared?" Javi giggled.

"This thing?" He knocked on his head and winked at the cheeky child. "A sledgehammer couldn't dent it."

Javi snorted a milk bubble from his nose.

"Was Amberley with her?" he asked, heading back to the table.

"No."

His chest tightened as he pictured her stuck in her room, hiding out from the world. The chair scraped across the wood-planked floor when he pulled it out and dropped back into it.

"She was at Jordan Stables. Charlotte says she's participating in their new equine therapy program."

He stopped squirting mustard on his sandwich, set the bottle on the table and pressed his bread back on top.

Amberley…taking steps to get better…the heaviness in his chest eased a bit.

"Shame they'll have to close it," Sofia said, then sighed. She held a seasoning jar in each hand, her head swiveling between them. Then she shrugged and began shaking both heavily over the stir-fry.

He swallowed his bite. "What?"

"Joan got injured and her daughter's heading back to college next week," Ma said. "What with Benny's asthma getting worse, they might shut down."

His heart lurched as he thought of Amberley, taking her first steps back into the real world only to have another door slammed in her face.

"Heard Maverick Loveland might lend a hand since his PBR tour's out for the season, but it still won't be enough," Sofia added over her shoulder.

He rolled his eyes. Of course, a Loveland volunteered. The cash-strapped clan contributed to the community every chance they got in the only way they could, with time and labor. No denying it was admirable. Noble even. He'd give them that much.

He pictured Maverick helping Amberley on and off her horse, holding her waist, her hand, as the two of them talked, laughed and cared for horses together.

His bleached knuckles tightened around his glass.

"I can help, too," he blurted.

His mother's eyebrows rose.

Javi leaned forward, eyes shining. "I want to help! Can I help?"

The kid, homeless for much of his childhood, had gained an insatiable need to help others from his hardships.

"It's for grown-ups, honey," Sofia answered without turning. "Plus, you're already training Milly."

Jack had rescued Milly, a troubled roan, from the dude ranch where he'd captured Jesse's killers and met his fiancée, Dani.

"You want Milly to pull Jack and Dani's wedding carriage, right? Well, we've only got three more weeks to make sure she's 100 percent ready."

"Okay." Javi dropped a slice of cheese to Clint, their obese tabby, who stretched in his usual position beneath the table.

"Honey, remember what the veterinarian said," Sofia said. "No more treats for Clint."

"He's just fluffy," James pronounced with a chuckle as he entered the room and doffed his hat. He mussed Javi's hair, then wrapped his arms around Sofia from behind and pressed a kiss to her cheek. They exchanged a private smile that made something bang inside Jared, a lonely hollow sound.

"There'd be no glory in the work," his mother said, a wistful smile playing on her lips as she, too, watched the affectionate couple. "No medals or awards. No fame. No win-or-lose challenges."

He shrugged.

Just Amberley.

The name whispered in his head. He could keep an eye on her there and ensure her well-being. She'd told him not to come around, but she hadn't warned him away from equine therapy, from private property she had no claim to. Going there wouldn't break his promise exactly.

Looking at the situation closer, he saw that it was his civic duty to help others. If it was good enough for a Loveland, it was darn sure good enough for a Cade.

He'd been frustrated and at odds with himself lately. Working with Amberley would give him someone to focus on besides himself. Plus, she needed him, even if her stubborn nature kept her from admitting it.

He scooped up the rest of his sandwich, jammed on his hat and grabbed the keys to his truck.

He was going to help her.

And this time he wouldn't take no for an answer.

CHAPTER FIVE

HARLEY HEAD-BUTTED Amberley's shoulder, and she whirled in his direction. The humid afternoon air inside his stall stuck her shirt to her back. She shoved back the limp hair strands that'd come loose from the haphazard braid she'd managed this morning and let out a quick breath. All around rose the sweet, soothing smell of freshly spread hay.

"I'm hurrying," she groused, glowering at her horse's black shape. It was only her second day back at Spirit Ranch, yet he hustled her like he did in competition seasons, eager to get to the ring, not cutting her any slack. A blur of silver, his tail, flicked dismissively.

"Sheesh. This isn't exactly easy."

A high-pitched whinny erupted and she caught a flash of white as his lips must have peeled back, signaling just how little he cared about excuses.

And he shouldn't. He deserved better than

a visually impaired former barrel racer. Last night she'd wrestled with posting an ad for him and couldn't bring herself to list it. Delaying was just cruel. A champion like Harley couldn't be happy stuck in a small stable like this, his activity restricted, his glory cut off at the knees.

"Everything alright in there?" called a deep male voice.

Maverick Loveland. A PBR bull rider who must be home for the off-season. She remembered him from high school when he'd introduced himself earlier, but couldn't recall his face since they'd rarely crossed paths on the rodeo circuit. The way he'd blotted out the slanting sun and cast her in shadow suggested he was very tall and very built.

"Just dandy!" she squeaked, then cleared her throat. "I mean fine. We'll be out in a sec."

"Sounds good. Class starts in five."

She listened as the sound of his clomping boots faded, then ran a trembling hand over Harley's cinch. "Now, don't you worry. You're going to do just fine out there. I won't let you down."

Warm air blasted by her cheek as Harley gave an exasperated blow.

"Okay. Fine. Maybe I'm the one who's worried." She gulped over the ball that'd lodged high in her throat since her mother dropped her off. "A lot."

Without her full sight, she no longer trusted the world, or herself. She felt like she'd been drop-kicked onto another planet where none of the old rules applied. She couldn't navigate a world that left her helpless and weak. In fact, she wanted nothing to do with it.

Why had she promised to come back today? She wished herself back in bed, covers pulled over her head, blocking everything out.

"Amberley? Is Amberley here?" piped up a child's voice. The shape of a buff-colored pony and a small form astride it paused outside the open, upper half of the stall door.

"Here," she called.

"I told you she'd come, Fran," crooned an adult woman.

Fran. The blind girl Amberley met yesterday.

"Amberley's no quitter."

She forced a smile to hide her misery. This youngster needed nothing but encouragement. "Nope."

Liar.

"Hurry, Amberley," Fran called, and a moment later the silence suggested she'd ridden away.

Amberley's head hung and her fingers tightened on Harley's bridle. She wanted to quit this whole moment, but she'd given her word. Besides, riding Harley around the small rink yesterday had helped her remember, just for a moment, the rider she'd once been. It'd given her a break from the shadows growing inside, from the whispers that taunted her.

Loser. Useless. Nothing.

She'd thought she had left those voices behind when she'd become a rodeo champion. Now they howled within, louder and inescapable.

She couldn't run or hide from her vision loss.

And she wouldn't accept it either.

Doing so meant accepting what she'd lost— whom she'd lost—herself.

"There's nothing better for the inside of a man than the outside of a horse," her mother said over breakfast, quoting one of their favorite cowboys, Will Rogers.

Yet the reminder only increased Amberley's gloom. Now she'd never be one of her Western heroes, a fearless rough rider. Her disability trampled her confidence and spirit into dust.

She must have made a noise because suddenly Harley's warm neck wrapped around her. No horse loved giving hugs more than Harley.

I got you, he seemed to be saying. *I've got your back.*

"I know," she whispered, breathing in the clean, lavender smell of his freshly washed mane, loving her horse so much. If only she could keep him, though she'd never commit such a selfish act. "But I want to have your back, too."

In the distance, a motorcycle engine roared, growing louder and louder before falling silent. Yearning seized her for a ride on her other Harley. She should post an ad to sell it, too.

"Come on, boy," she urged, then groped for the latch. Just as she pressed it down, the door swung open.

"Hey, Amberley."

"Jared?"

Incongruously, her hand flew to her untidy hair. Who knew how it'd turned out or even how she looked? She'd never worried much about that before, especially around Jared.

Now that she had to go out in public with no reference at all, except her mother's clearly biased opinion, she worried that her buttons weren't done up right or that her shirt didn't match her pants. Then again, everything went with jeans and cowboy boots, so she supposed she looked halfway decent.

And why was she suddenly obsessing about her looks around Jared?

"Miss me?" He must have grabbed Harley's lead and tugged because her horse stepped quickly out of the stall, nearly leaving her stranded. "Keep your hand on his side until we get to the gate."

She pressed her palm to Harley's moving hindquarters and staggered forward, confused and hurt. "What are you doing here? You promised—"

"—to leave you be?" he cut her off and slowed the pace when she stumbled on a bumpy bit of terrain. "Right. Well. I'm here in a professional capacity. Not as a friend."

"Yeah. Right," she scoffed. He didn't fool her one bit. "What's this *professional capacity*?"

"I work here."

"What?" Anger and humiliation warred

within, shame winning out. She didn't want him seeing her in the ring like this, so incapable, so needy. "How? Shouldn't you be training with the Broncos this summer? Getting ready for the season?"

"I might not be going back."

"You're quitting?"

"Not exactly..."

"What's that mean?"

"Look. I don't want to talk about it."

Stubborn cowboy. "And here you are telling me not to quit!"

"Jared called from the road when he heard we're shorthanded," said Benny, wheezing slightly as he joined them "—on account of—" He stopped and cleared his throat.

"How's Joan?" Jared inquired, solicitous.

Amberley's cheeks heated. By neglecting Harley, she'd gotten Joan hurt and shorthanded Spirit Ranch. And was Jared really quitting the Broncos? If so, he must be mulling over a better offer from another team. It was the only possibility that made sense.

"Doctor says her knee will be good as new in a few weeks. Till then, we sure appreciate Jared volunteering to help."

She could feel Jared's eyes on her and forced

a neutral expression while nodding in the direction of Benny's voice. It'd be selfish to demand that Jared leave, so she'd stay silent.

Never miss a good opportunity to shut up.

Plus, she didn't plan on attending the program regularly, if at all. From now on, she'd care for Harley earlier in the day, before the program began, and avoid Jared altogether. In fact, that'd work out better since she'd finish in time for her mother to pick her up before she headed into morning court.

Would her tactic deter her old friend?

She snuck a sidelong glance at Jared and struggled to focus on his handsome profile. The firm set of his dimpled chin and full lips wavered, then held. She noted his "ready to rumble" expression, the same look he wore before jogging onto a football field.

A sigh escaped her.

Deep down, she appreciated his loyalty and determination to help. They never quit on each other, but things changed. She wasn't the same person. Why couldn't he see that?

He hated losing, and that's all she represented now...a losing proposition. In time, he'd grow impatient and give up on her, his rejection hurting her more than anything. What's more, she couldn't bear failure either, especially when she didn't live up to Jared's notoriously high expectations.

Like her father's.

Harley halted and she rushed forward a couple of steps, groping for the button to activate the gate, wanting to prove herself. Her hand collided with Jared's calloused flesh. She jerked back as if stung, her heart beating every which way.

With a metallic squeal, the gate swung open and she walked beside Harley into the ring.

"Amberley!" squealed several children. Their small shapes squirmed atop motionless mounts. A few of the other horses answered Harley's exuberant neigh. His muscles quivered beneath her fingers the way they did before a race. Strange to see him so excited over this sedate interaction.

"Hey, everybody!" she called, then slid one foot into the stirrup before starting to swing herself into the saddle.

Suddenly the toe of her boot slipped, the ground rushed up to meet her and her teeth bit down on her tongue.

Surprise and shame burst within her like fireworks. The chattering children fell silent.

Strong hands gripped her elbows and pulled her to her feet. Her quick, hard breaths drew in Jared's scent: boot leather, cologne spice and clean, male skin.

"Are you okay, Amberley?" called one of the children. Her voice rose several notes in concern.

"Just fine," she answered, ignoring the pain that flared up her hips. On the scale of riding mishaps, this barely registered, but the blow to her ego shot off the charts.

"Are you hurt?" Jared asked, his voice low and urgent in her ear.

Since when had either of them ever worried over minor accidents? No one fussed about injuries unless a bone was showing or you'd lost feeling...and even then you should cowboy up and walk it off, they'd always said.

They were tough as nails, bulletproof.

No more.

"No." She kept a smile pinned on for the little ones watching and willed back the humiliating sting in her eyes. "Stop fussing and let go."

Instead, Jared settled his large hands on her waist and hoisted her into the saddle. Her face heated again at his high-handed treatment. He'd just ignored her wishes. Is that what happened to the disabled? Did the world stop treating you like you had a right to your own opinions, to make your own judgments?

Did your body, your life become others' to control?

She couldn't stand that.

Wouldn't tolerate it.

"Welcome, everyone," she heard Maverick say. She suspected Benny had put him in charge because of his ring experience as a professional bull rider.

"Howdy, all," interjected outgoing Jared. "Who's ready for some fun?"

Several of the kids hollered back, many recognizing him from football.

"Can I get your autograph?" one of the mothers standing by her child's horse asked. "For my husband."

Yeah. Right.

"Sure thing, ma'am," Jared drawled, always in his element around adoring women.

"Let's begin with stretches," Maverick continued smoothly, ignoring Jared's interruption in that firm, no-nonsense way that Lovelands had.

They were men of few words but deep convictions, her mother always said. Descended from an army cavalryman and his Cherokee bride, their unique good looks—black hair, tawny skin and deep blue eyes—made them the most sought-after bachelors in the county, next to the Cade cowboys. The air of mystery surrounding the private crew only furthered the female population's obsession with them.

However, out of loyalty to Jared and his family's generations-long feud with the group, she'd steered clear of them. Whenever she'd glimpsed Maverick at rodeo competitions, she'd kept her distance.

"Arms overhead," Maverick urged.

She raised her hands to the sky and peeked down at the top of Jared's brown Stetson. He'd tipped it back, she guessed, since she could now make out the tan streak of his forehead. The shine of black—his boots, she supposed—were now planted far apart, as if he braced.

Did he worry about her? She didn't need him guarding her, drawing more attention to her deficiencies.

"Arms out to the side." At Maverick's directive, she reached with her fingertips and locked her knees around Harley, getting a sense of her balance without visual cues.

"How are you doing?" Jared asked.

"Trying to concentrate."

"Can I help?"

"Really?" she huffed, earning one of his deep, warm chuckles.

"Now breathe," Maverick instructed. "Deep breath in through the nose, then all the way out through your mouth. In. Out. In. Out."

She inhaled the laurel-scented air, and her lashes drifted to her cheeks. "Now picture your favorite place." Without the blurred world visible, her imagination took flight.

She pictured a spot atop Mount Sopris that overlooked Laurel Canyon. Purple flowers waved in the deep valley below, yellow-and-white butterflies fluttering above them in a colorful cloud. Patches of verdant green broke up the flower patches and rolled down to the edge of the sparkling Crystal River.

Jared, beside her on a checkered picnic blanket, swam into focus. His chiseled features knocked the breath out of her. The touch of gold that radiated in his amber-brown eyes glowed at her... She'd forgotten how handsome he was, or maybe she'd just never let herself look as closely as she did now—when it wasn't real, when she simply lost herself in a dream.

Was he her happy place?

"Alright everyone, let's go once around the ring now."

Jared tugged Harley without warning and she swayed forward, off balance. Her hands landed on the pommel, the only place she could grab since Jared had the reins in his overprotective grip. Hooves plodded in the soft, packed dirt. The chattering children's voices rose and swelled.

"Speak gently to keep your mount," cautioned Maverick from somewhere close. "Otherwise, let your hands and legs do the talking."

She made out his mammoth shape beside the gate as she lurched by atop Harley, uncoordinated and ungainly.

"Looking good up there, Amberley," Maverick called.

"Quiet, dude," Jared retorted. "Only hands and legs doing the talking…"

"Jared!" she exclaimed, taken aback at the edge in his voice. It took a lot to rile the easygoing cowboy.

She'd never had a front seat to the Cade-Loveland feud before. After over a hundred years of it, did they even know why they hated each other? Of course, Maverick and Jared had competed on the junior rodeo circuit, their rivalry to outdo one another legendary. Something about this tension, though, seemed fresher. More personal, somehow.

"Just a friendly reminder to avoid unnecessary chitchat," Jared protested. "Just like he said."

"Much appreciated, Jared," Maverick called, not sounding the least grateful.

"Anytime, *bud*."

Maverick's guffaw followed them around the ring.

"Friendly, huh?" Jared didn't fool her one bit.

A horse nickered behind them, and the child riding it made a low humming sound.

"I'd like my reins, now."

"That's not safe." Jared's face flashed up at her, and she pictured his left eyebrow rising in that skeptical way of his.

Her fingers tightened on the horn. For the first time, he didn't trust her judgment, and it hurt. "I did it yesterday."

"Maybe you were lucky yesterday."

She leaned over Harley's neck and whispered, "Don't make me beg," near Jared's ear.

In an instant, the reins slid across the tops of her hands. She curled her fingers around them, and the familiar, comforting sensation snapped her spine straighter. She lifted her chin.

"Don't go crazy," Jared warned, an undercurrent of worry weighing down his attempt at a lighthearted tone.

A knot filled her aching throat. "Oh. You know me," she croaked. "Always up for a little excitement."

"Amberley," Jared began.

"Don't," she whispered, dangerously close to humiliating tears.

"Don't what?"

"Don't *care*."

They plodded along in silence for a few paces before he said, "Well, now. That's impossible to do."

"Then fake it," she insisted, wishing him gone and, contrarily, glad to have him close— just not in a way that left her feeling smaller and no longer his equal. "Don't treat me differently."

"I'm not," he insisted.

But he was. He just couldn't see it.

"Pull up now," ordered Maverick.

Before she could react, Harley stopped. Something moved near the bridle. Jared's hands. Her gut clenched. While she'd held the reins, he'd guided Harley—giving her the equivalent of a pony ride.

So now he was treating her like a child.

"Think of this rail as all of the challenges you're facing," Maverick said. "You're going to lead your horse over those challenges. You're going to conquer them. Got it?"

A chorus of "Yes" rose from the kids.

"Bet Amberley and Harley can jump over it!" one of them hollered.

"I want to see that!" another yelled.

"Please, Amberley!" the group pleaded.

"Sorry, kids," she heard Jared say before she could speak. "But—"

"I'll do it!" The rail had to be on the lowest setting, six inches above the ground, if Maverick thought the kids could simply lead the horses over it. No challenge at all. She could do it blindfolded.

Or legally blind.

Her jaw set, she wheeled Harley away and brought him into a trot that carried her swiftly to the blurred shape of the gate. She couldn't quite judge the height, or her proximity, just yet. Unease fluttered in her belly. How many paces to it? Time to jump?

Relying on instinct, she squeezed Harley's sides at the right moment, but he balked. She flew over his head and landed flat on her back. At the children's cries, she struggled to sit up, but the fall had knocked the wind out of her. Calloused hands cupped her face.

"Amberley!" Jared's baritone sounded urgent and anxious. "Say something."

"Something," she croaked.

"Still got her humor," she heard Maverick drawl from a distance. A deep sound rolled from him, not so much an outright laugh... more of a quiet admission of amusement. "Need a hand up?"

"I've got her," Jared insisted, possessive.

"*I've* got it." She heaved herself into a sitting position, furious with herself, with Jared's hovering, with everything.

Angry tears pricked the backs of her eyes. She had to leave before she embarrassed herself more. "Where's Harley?"

"Here!" Maverick brought her horse close.

"Is Amberley alright?" one of the kids whimpered.

"I want to go home," another sobbed.

Harley dipped his head, sniffing her.

"It's okay, boy," she whispered, then gripped his bridle and pushed to her feet. The world tilted and spun, and she locked her knees to keep them from buckling. She would not scare the little ones. "I'm just fine. Got a little ahead of myself is all. Y'all go ahead with the fun and I'll see you soon."

With that, she led Harley to the gate, one hand trailing along the ring's fence top for guidance.

After pushing the automatic opener, she marched out into the empty space, squinted for the stable's brown, rectangular shape, and more or less followed Harley, who headed directly for his stall out of habit.

She needed to do this on her own.

If someone rescued her, that person owned her. Not because she'd owe them—she could always find a way to repay a favor. They owned her because she'd stop being the lead in her story anymore. She'd become the poor struggling loser/helpless damsel who was saved from danger/dishonor/humiliation by the brilliant, brave, compassionate hero, and he got to decide which, because she wouldn't be the one running this story, not anymore.

Once inside, she collapsed into the soft hay and buried her face in her hands.

"Cowgirl up," she whispered to herself.

But her shoulders shook and hot tears splashed down her cheeks. She. Could. Not. Take. This.

"Amberley?"

Strong hands fell on her shoulders. She squeezed her eyes shut and shook her head, unable to speak without her voice betraying her.

The hay rustled as Jared kneeled before her. His thumbs brushed the damp from her cheeks, the gesture achingly tender. "Tell me what I can do." His voice was deep. Gentle. The same tone she'd heard him use a hundred times when soothing frightened foals.

"Please." The single word emerged in a sob. "Leave."

He pulled her into his arms instead, and his steady heartbeat drummed against hers, the warmth of his lithe, muscular body seeping through his shirt. "Anything but that."

She lifted her tear-streaked face, trying to

meet his eye, to convey everything she felt, the despair, the anguish, every black emotion welling up inside her. She couldn't bear any of it. A choking sound escaped her.

His hands smoothed down her back. "Shh-hhhhhhhh," he breathed in her ear. A shiver tore through her. "I've got you, darlin'." He squeezed her waist. "I've got you."

Her fingers landed on his rounded shoulders and dented the firm flesh. His body was warm and hard…solid in a way nothing in her life was right now. She buried her head in the cords of his neck. "Please," she whimpered, not even sure what she begged for anymore, a flood of sensations at his proximity jumbling her emotions.

His hands rose to cup the back of her head, and then he angled her face up to his. The unexpected move struck the air from her lungs. Was he about to—

His mouth grazed hers, the barest of touches, and then, when she didn't move away, he kissed her properly, with increasing pressure, the brush of his lips electrifying, scattering her thoughts. He tasted like caramel apples and smelled like leather and sandalwood. Was this real?

With a low moan, her mouth parted under the cowboy's onslaught and her body reacted at once: a prickling at her legs, a thumping heart. Her bones lost their snap, and she melted against him. Their short breaths mingled in the stall. Fast and hard. His arms wove around her and held her close. When her head tipped back, her hat fell off and her braid whisked over the curve of his tensing bicep.

A deep groan ripped out of him, a sound she'd never heard from him before. Passionate. Masculine. Primal. Frissons of delicious awareness skittered over her flesh. Then he kissed her more urgently and she responded in kind. Light-headed, she held on tight, the world in a tailspin. Their tongues tangled in a dance that made her pulse race and her skin burn.

"Amberley." He breathed her name like an invocation, barely breaking their kiss.

"Hmm?" She threaded her fingers in the crisp strands of his hair, unable to open her eyes.

His lips slid across her jaw, nibbling the sensitive flesh of her earlobe before they glided lower along her jaw. "You're beautiful, babe."

Babe?

He called all of his girls babe. Especially when he couldn't remember their names.

Tension locked up every inch of her. She propped an eye open. Then the other. Despite her lack of vision, she could suddenly see this disastrous moment clearly. In minutes, he'd gone from treating her like a child to seducing her like one of his flings.

And she was neither.

She leaned away, inserting space between them without untangling their arms. "Jared!"

Sparks continued exploding along the skin his mouth explored. She pushed against his hard chest. "Stop."

He lifted his head slowly and gazed down at her. For the first time, she felt glad she couldn't read his expression. His hold loosened and she wiggled back until her spine bumped against the stall's wooden slats. Her chest expanded, drawing in a shaky breath.

"Why did you do that?" she demanded.

"I wanted to—to—" He faltered, suddenly uncertain, his usual brash confidence gone. "Comfort you," he finished quickly.

"Comfort me?" she echoed, not sure if she'd heard him right.

"You were crying and I felt..."

"Sorry for me?" She pushed to her feet on trembling limbs, her entire body aflame. Her spine pulled tight as a rope. "You kissed me out of pity?"

He stood, too, and his hands waved. "No."

"What, then? So, you don't feel sorry for me?"

"I do, it's just—"

"Just what?" she demanded.

"You kissed me back."

She pressed her lips together, forcing herself to ignore the remembered feel of his mouth gliding over hers. Her blood throbbed in her veins. "That was a mistake."

"You didn't like it?"

"That doesn't matter."

He closed the distance between them. One finger skated down the side of her cheek. "Doesn't it?"

"Get out." She pointed toward the sunlight glinting over Harley's head. "Now."

"But I—"

"Now!"

"Everything alright in here?"

She ducked her head at Maverick's voice and turned, wiping her eyes on her sleeve. "Jared was just leaving," she said without turning.

"That right?" Maverick drawled, a hint of menace entering his voice. "Glad to show him the way, then."

"No need." The ache in his voice made her heart clench as tight as a fist. "Bye, Amberley."

She didn't release her breath until she heard the stall door click closed behind him.

"You sure you're alright?" asked Maverick, his deep voice now full of concern.

"I'll be fine."

When the world fell silent again, she buried her face in Harley's soft mane, not fine at all.

How could she have kissed her best friend?

CHAPTER SIX

"HEY. ARE YOU listening to me?"

Jared nodded quickly at the attractive woman sitting across from him. They occupied a narrow wooden booth in a honky-tonk on the outskirts of Carbondale. The dive reeked of spilled beer, burnt popcorn and stale body odor from the herd of cowboys who'd stampeded in for tonight's ninety-nine-cent wing special and the latest Diamondbacks game. Wall-mounted speakers blasted a thumping Tim McGraw tune he recognized. "A Real Good Man." A crowd of line dancers dipped, clapped and twirled on the scuffed wooden dance floor.

His stomach twisted. He'd been anything but a good man to Amberley today. And nowhere near a good friend.

"Jared!" Long, glitter-tipped nails drummed on the tabletop.

"Yep. Sorry." His eyes drifted over the petite blonde whose electric blue eye shadow matched her camisole top and the floral clip in her hair. She'd sure gone to a lot of trouble for their first date, and she deserved a better time than he was showing her. He'd been looking forward to tonight, right up until the unforgettable kiss with Amberley that'd left him staggering and off balance all day.

Why had he done such a fool thing?

And why couldn't he stop thinking about it?

She'd felt right in his arms, her mouth beneath his sweet and incredibly tender.

"Yes, *what*?" his date demanded.

Now, what was her name...? He'd been in a fog since leaving Spirit Ranch and forgot to double-check with Jewel.

"Sorry, Lori. I—"

Penciled brows met over her short, flat nose. "It's Layah."

"Well, that's a real pretty name. Just like you," he said sincerely, ducking his head and smiling at her from beneath the brim of his hat. His friends called it his lady-killer smile, though Jewel told him serial killer was more like it.

A preen replaced Layah's pout. "Why, thank

you. You see, my grandma's name is Leigh and my pa is a big Star Wars fan so—"

The woman's voice drifted as his mind replayed earlier events. Seeing Amberley struggle in the ring today nearly broke his heart and then, when he'd found her crying—*crying*, when, he'd never so much as heard her sniffle in all their years as friends—the effect devastated him. For the first time in his life, he'd felt helpless. He needed to dry her tears, heal her wounds, stop her pain. He'd swept her into his arms before he thought twice about it. In an instant, she'd become someone else, a stranger, a warm, beautiful vulnerable stranger that his heart responded to in an altogether different way.

He relived the feel of her in his arms nonstop. The unguarded expression on her face had done something crazy to his heart, like nearly stopping it altogether.

"So when my ma went into labor during *Return of the Jedi*, well my pa said they couldn't just leave—"

Jared nodded and smiled along to Layah's harmless prattle, trying hard, but failing to focus. Amberley's accusation echoed in his head.

"You felt sorry for me!"

No denying, he had pitied her, the last thing in the world a gal like Amberley ever wanted or deserved. He'd be lying to himself, though, if he blamed sympathy for his passionate response.

No woman ever affected him that way, and it blew his mind that Amberley, his best friend, had done him in. The way she'd responded had made him lose his head and nearly his control. Electric. Passionate. Unbridled. It'd been like holding on to a rocket ship that'd lit out for the moon.

And he hadn't wanted to let go.

"The contractions started coming fast when the Emperor—" Layah paused to sip the last of her beer "—when the Emperor shot Luke with those laser fingers. Never could figure out why he could do that since Jedi used light sabers."

Jared caught their waitress's eye and crooked a finger, signaling for another round. "He was a Sith."

Layah's navy-coated lashes blinked at him. "A what?"

"He was a Sith Lord."

"Huh." Layah lifted the edge of her empty

bottle's label with a fingernail and shrugged. "Anyways, the usher told my parents—"

Jared grabbed his bottle and gulped the rich local brew, his eyes peeled on Layah's fast-moving mouth, his thoughts adrift despite his best efforts.

Could he have feelings—romantic ones—for his longtime friend? Impossible. Amberley was a pal. A rough-and-tumble gal far different from the girlie-girls he dated, like Layah. In fact, strange as it sounded, he'd never thought of Amberley being a woman much, given she gave as good as she got whenever they'd competed, raced motorcycles, camped, fished and ridden the range.

Yet that kiss had ripped off his blinders. Would he ever see Amberley the same way again? Could he forget the responsive woman who'd driven him senseless and transfixed his heart?

She'd been right to send him packing. Crossing the line didn't come close to describing the wrong he'd done to her...done to both of them. The kiss tested their friendship's bond, but would not break it, he vowed. From here on out, he'd keep his distance, romantically.

He wouldn't stop helping Amberley, however. He'd find another way was all. She'd looked good up on Harley, and come hell or high water he'd get her back in the saddle and out into the world. Life was a dimmer place without her in it.

He needed to apologize for starters. Then he'd present her with a new plan of action, a grand gesture that'd convince her to give him—and herself—another chance.

"So, they stuck me in the popcorn maker to keep me warm until the ambulance arrived," Layah finished with a flourish. She beamed a bright smile at their returning waitress and accepted her new beer.

"The popcorn maker?" he echoed after their server whisked away their empties.

"Mmm-hmm," Layah murmured, the bottle to her mouth.

He stared at her for a minute, and then she lowered her drink and burst out laughing. "I got you!"

"Was any of that story true?"

Her left eyebrow twitched. "My dad is a Star Wars fan."

"I'm sorry." He reached across the table and took her hand in his. Her fingernails scratched against his palm. "Guess I'm not at my best tonight."

The tip of her tongue appeared between her teeth as she regarded him. "Even halfway for you is still awesome."

"Now you're being too easy on me."

"Probably." She giggled. "But you're worth it."

And that was the problem, he thought, staring into Layah's twinkling, iridescent coated eyes. Things came too easily for him. Somehow that didn't set so well anymore after watching Amberley and the kids at the program battle their challenges. Despite their hardships, they fought on. That seemed more heroic than his life, no matter his achievements.

If he didn't work hard for his blessings, did he deserve them as much as they did?

Amberley was correct to call him out for quitting football when he wouldn't let her give up. And she didn't even know the full story. If she did, she'd call him a flat-out hypocrite.

And she'd be right.

"I've got to get up early tomorrow for my hospital shift, so…"

"Occupational therapist, right?" He threw

some cash on the table, stood and walked around the table to pull out her chair.

"You remembered." She slid her purse strap up her arm.

"Miracles happen."

A smile played on her lips. "Yes, they do."

"Can I make it up to you another time, darlin'?"

"Depends."

"On...?"

"If whoever you were really thinking about tonight will still be on your mind."

His eyes dropped at her direct stare. "I'll make sure of it." No more dwelling on Amberley as anything other than a friend, he vowed silently. Or on that kiss.

"I'll hold you to that." She trailed a finger up his bicep, then squeezed. "My," she breathed. "How many footballs you think you've caught with these?"

"Not enough," he said as they headed to the exit. His agent had left another "last chance" message about trying out as a free agent again.

As they passed the line dancers, a familiar silver-haired woman caught his eye.

"Ma?"

She didn't hear him over the thumping

music and continued stomping forward and back next to, of all people, Boyd Loveland. A few of her church friends fanned out on each side. Did they meet by chance or plan?

Their beaming smiles suggested this was no coincidence. Why keep this from the family? Sure, they'd all landed in jail the last time she'd tried dating Boyd, but she owed them the truth.

Just last week the Lovelands sold off their antique tractors at a local auction to raise cash. Everyone knew Boyd would do about anything to scrape together the money to save his ranch…and it seemed courting Ma still topped that list.

Not on Jared's watch.

His boots carried him to the edge of the dance floor. He crossed his arms and waited for his mother to notice him. The hem of her skirt floated around her knees as she twirled, and her smile flashed beneath the twinkling lights strung from the overhead beams.

When was the last time he'd seen her so happy and relaxed? he thought with a twinge.

"Is that your ma and pa?" asked Layah, pointing to the laughing couple.

"My father died eleven years ago."

The song ended and Boyd brought Ma's hand to his mouth. Their eyes locked.

"Ma!" he called.

Her head whipped around and her face fell. She hurried over, Boyd hot on her heels. Behind her, the DJ and his crew began dismantling their sound equipment.

"I—I didn't expect to see you here," she said, breathless.

"You look pretty tonight," he said. She smoothed down her skirt and returned his uneasy smile. "What are you doing with *him*?" He angled his head at Boyd.

"Howdy." Boyd stuck out a hand and Jared shook it reluctantly.

He wouldn't be rude and make a scene like he and his siblings had at last year's Christmas party. It'd devastated his ma. Afterward, she'd retreated into the sad silence that had surrounded her after Jesse's death. Tonight, she resembled her old self, though—the vibrant mother he missed.

"I came for the line dancing." Boyd faced Jared full on, eyes steady, jaw firm. "And for Joy."

Ma twisted the turquoise pendant that matched her skirt and dyed snakeskin boots.

"May and Jessica drove me. We met Boyd here."

"You planned on seeing each other?" Jared asked, careful to pitch his voice low. If his siblings knew about this, they'd blow a fuse.

"I'm Layah Jennings, by the way." Jared's date smiled politely at his ma and Boyd.

"Layah, this here's my ma, Joy *Cade*." He stressed the last name, his intent gaze never leaving Boyd's unflinching face. He'd give the old cowboy one thing. Like all Lovelands, he was tough as boot leather and didn't give an inch.

"Bye, Joy. Bye, Boyd," called May and Jessica on their way out the door.

"Don't you need them for a ride?"

Boyd swept an arm around Joy's shoulder and they swapped a long, indecipherable look. At Joy's nod, Boyd said, "I'll see her to her door."

"So you two are…"

"Friends," Boyd finished, resolute. "And I'm honored that Joy will allow me that much. She's an incredible woman."

Yes, she was. No one knew that better than her kids. He didn't need Boyd telling him so.

"Cades and Lovelands aren't friends," Jared

said through clamped teeth. Boyd might claim a platonic relationship, but Jared had believed the same about himself and Amberley…right up until they'd kissed.

Boyd released his mother and stepped closer. His expression softened. "Son, may I give you a bit of advice?"

"I'm not your son." Jared shoved his balled hands in his pockets. Once he filled his siblings in on Boyd's reappearance, they'd figure out how to get rid of this Loveland once and for all.

"Well, now." Boyd rocked back on his heels, looking more thoughtful than offended. "True enough. But age has a way of teaching you a thing or two, and here's one I've learned. Best get your own life in order before ordering others around."

His mother enveloped Jared into a vanilla-scented hug. "Sorry, honey," she whispered in his ear. "We'll talk at home."

He squeezed her back. He wouldn't blame his lonely mother for wanting attention. Boyd was just the wrong guy to lavish her with it. "Sounds good."

Layah squeezed his arm once his mother

and Boyd disappeared through the exit. "You alright?"

"Fine," he assured her.

But he wasn't fine, he mused, as he held the door for his date and walked her to his pickup. Much as he hated admitting it, Boyd had a point. His life wasn't in order.

And he'd spent a lot of time recently ordering others around, starting with Amberley. He'd selfishly used her to distract him from dealing with his dismal future.

Seeing Amberley struggle in the saddle today made him question how he'd handled his career setback. A zero chance of achieving glory didn't mean Amberley should give up.

Did that apply to him, too?

He'd thought quitting while ahead meant staying a winner. A hero like he and his father wanted.

Now he wasn't so sure.

After a chaste peck on the cheek, he dropped Layah home and headed to Cade Ranch. A new moon hung high in the bright sky and his headlights bounced off long stretches of rail fences that ran along the deserted rural route. Out here, in the pitch-dark, it felt as though he floated through space, aimless and drifting, without direction or purpose.

But that wasn't living, was it?

Not a hero's life after all.

He'd contact his agent tomorrow and give him the go-ahead to float his name as a free agent. In the meantime, he'd begin working out on the ranch. Maybe he'd prove those sports doctors wrong and get back into top athletic condition again.

It'd be hard work with no guarantee of success, but he demanded that from Amberley. Much as he hated admitting it, Boyd's point resonated. Jared had to put his own life in order and lead by example, become another kind of hero, if he had any chance of getting through to his friend.

And despite the kiss, that's all they could—should—ever be, especially when they needed each other now more than ever.

His tires churned up the gravel-lined drive to his front door, and he cut the engine. Petey bounded his way, tail beating harder than a helicopter blade.

He hopped out of the cab, slammed the door, then ruffled the mutt's soft, floppy ears. "Hey, boy," he crooned.

A rough tongue licked every inch of his face. He'd never owned a pet as affectionate and devoted as Petey. Despite being smaller than the other cattle dogs, and a stray, he never quit, working hard to prove himself to the humans he adored.

Then a thought struck him.

Petey.

He could train Petey for Amberley. No dog on the ranch took direction better. His siblings often joked Petey could read their minds. He'd be an excellent service dog and the tool Amberley needed to regain her independence.

Better yet, Petey personified the big gesture he needed to convince Amberley to give him, and their friendship, one more chance.

And this time, failure was not an option.

"AND HOW OLD is he?" asked a caller responding to the online ad Amberley placed last night. Beyond Harley's stall, a rooster crowed and the blurred morning completed its shift from gray to pink to golden. The clear, crisp air brushed cool fingers against her skin.

Amberley groped for the shelf at the back of Harley's stall and stowed a pair of clippers, blinking gritty eyes. She'd gotten up at 4:00 a.m.

to care for her horse and avoid Jared. Not that she had been able to sidestep her nonstop thoughts of their kiss.

"He's eleven years old. I bought him from Sunnyside farms. His grand-sire was Scamper."

Harley stretched his neck and pressed hard against Amberley's hand, shamelessly begging for a scratch and nearly knocking the phone from her hand.

"Behave," she whispered. Harley nickered and stamped his hooves. "Fine." She shifted the phone to the other hand and ran her fingernails lightly behind his ears the way he liked.

Would his new owner know how to give Harley affection? Would they cut the apples in quarters the way he preferred? And that overdramatic yawn of his. Harley opened his mouth really wide and threw his head way up and off to the side. If his halter was adjusted too tight for him to open his mouth all the way, he'd get testy, do a little half rear and give a squeal of anger.

A sigh escaped her. She needed to write a long instruction list for Harley's new owners, though it didn't guarantee they'd follow it.

Would he be happy without her?

She sure wouldn't be without him.

Harley lifted his head, his signal for his favorite thing: a hug. Her chest tightened as she wrapped her arms around his neck and he laid his head on her shoulder. The familiar musk and warmth of him enveloped her. Letting him go would break her in two, but Harley's needs came first.

After a couple more questions and answers, the caller promised to contact her again after he'd talked it over with his wife and daughter, an aspiring competitive racer.

She pocketed her phone and pictured Harley, his tongue between his teeth, his lips curled back, when he acted silly. The caller had sounded a little stern. What if they didn't appreciate Harley's goofy side or got scared when he shifted around for a butt scratch, thinking he might kick them...especially when he raised his back left leg like he often did?

Keep him here, whispered the devil on one shoulder. *That way you won't have to worry.*

Think about Harley. The exciting life he deserves, trilled the angel on the other side. *Do the right thing, Amberley.*

"I will," she exclaimed. "Stop nagging."

"Amberley?"

She cringed at Jared's deep voice. Her heart beat a fast staccato.

"Morning, Jared."

"Mornin'. Didn't expect to see you here till later. Hey, Harley-boy. Got this for you."

Harley advanced to the front of the stall, and she heard him crunch on something that smelled sweet.

Apple.

How kind of Jared. He'd always been sweet like that. Thoughtful.

And the way he'd made her melt in his arms...

Amberley shoved her hands in her pockets. "Oh. Yeah. About that. I don't think I'm going to class today."

The wood beams of the doorway groaned a bit where Jared must have leaned on them. At over six feet, he blocked out the strengthening sunlight.

"Just today?" he asked.

"Anymore," she amended, head lowered. Was he thinking about their kiss? Had he relived it, over and over and over, as she had? Her pitiful lack of experience didn't match up to his Don Juan reputation. Her only serious relationships involved horses.

"Is that because of yesterday?"

Her feet shuffled and a flush started up her neck and crept into her cheeks. "No." She groaned. "Yes."

"I'm sorry, Amberley. I should never have kissed you. You're my best friend, and I crossed the line."

Strangely, his apology only made her feel worse. Didn't she want him to regret it as much as she did?

But you don't regret it, do you? whispered the devil on one shoulder. *You liked kissing him.*

Accept his apology, twittered the angel on her other shoulder. *Then you can both move on and forget it ever happened.*

"No, you shouldn't have."

His hard-tipped fingers reached across the stall half door and laced in hers. "I'm also sorry I let you think I kissed you only because I wanted to comfort you."

Her pulse stuttered. "What other reason was there?"

"Because I wanted to." His voice deepened and grew rough. After a beat of awkward silence, he cleared his throat. "You're beautiful, Amberley."

She jerked her hands away and dropped her gaze. "I'm not one of your girls."

A short, humorless laugh escaped him. "No. You're my best friend and I won't jeopardize that again. In fact, I have a surprise for you if you'll come meet him."

"Meet him?" She lifted the latch and stepped gingerly outside. Immediately a warm, wet nose butted into her hand. An insistent tongue rasped against her palm.

A dog.

She went to her knees and a shaggy, medium-sized dog pounced on her lap, dropping heavy paws on her thighs. "Oh, aren't you a cutie."

"His name's Petey."

"Hi, Petey." She ruffled his long ears, feeling the large notch in one that suggested Petey hadn't had a very easy life.

"And he's yours."

She blinked up at Jared, trying to read his face but catching only flashes of teeth in what might be an uncertain smile.

"I can't take care of a dog." Petey sniffed behind her ear, then began vigorously licking her jaw.

"Not yet, but you will after I train him."

"Train him?"

"He's going to be your guide dog."

"Jared, I don't…"

"Petey, fetch me a soda."

With a bound, the dog flung himself from her lap and disappeared. "Did you just send him to the store?" she joked.

"Not quite."

Scattering pebbles heralded Petey's return a moment later.

"Give." She heard Jared say, then, "Good boy." Petey woofed.

A second later, something cool and metallic pressed into her palm. She ran her fingers over the tab, marveling. "How did you… How did he?"

"He got it from the cooler—a trick he learned in one night."

"You taught him?"

"Yep. He's a stray who showed up on the ranch a couple months ago. Only took him a week to catch on to cattle herding and become one of our best. He's the smartest dog I've ever known and yours if you'll have him."

She buried her nose in Petey's soft fur. "You don't have to spend all that time. The doctor said he could find someone—"

"Please let me do this for you."

She released a breath. "Okay. Thank you. And I accept your apology."

Jared cared for her more than anyone besides her mother. He'd seen her at her weakest, her worst, and yet here he stood, still by her side, not giving up on her, as pushy as ever, and she loved that about him.

She really did.

"An apology isn't the only reason I stopped by."

Petey stuck close as she pushed to her feet, stick in hand and tossed it. With a joyous bark, he raced after it. "What do you want?"

"Your help. Your tumble yesterday taught the kids something valuable."

"It did?"

"Yeah. That even champions get thrown and make mistakes. What counts is the getting back up."

She chewed that thought over, then nodded. "True." When Petey dropped the stick on her boots, she grabbed it and winged it away again.

"I was wondering if you might come back to class as an assistant," Jared continued. "It's clear you don't need help with horses."

As if to emphasize the point, Harley leaned

through the stall door and pressed his clenched teeth into her shoulder with his lips slightly parted, another quirk of his when he wanted attention.

"Was this your idea or Maverick's? Yesterday you wouldn't let go of Harley's bridle."

Jared's head seemed to tip back. "I'm sorry about that, too," he said to the sky. His face lowered and she felt, rather than saw, his eyes on her. "I was just being—"

"A jerk?"

He chuckled. "I was going to say protective, but I suppose both are true. Anyways, the idea's mine and Maverick agrees."

"You talked to him?" she asked, surprised. "Alone?"

Petey's panting breath sounded as he returned at a gallop.

"Down," Jared instructed, and she glimpsed the dog's furry outline drop instantly to the grass. "You know I'd do anything for you, darlin'. Even if that means conversing with a Loveland."

A short laugh escaped her, then she sobered. "But how can I really help without my...my... vision? Won't I be a burden?"

"You?" scoffed Jared. "Not a chance."

Pride spread like warm honey in her veins at his admiring tone. "Just seeing you out there is motivating to the kids, but more than that, you can teach them how to handle the horses, groom them, clean their stalls…"

She turned and eased back into Harley's stall. "I'm still aces at that, at least."

Jared joined in her ironic laugh, and suddenly it felt like old times, the rhythms of their friendship returning.

"You'll do a lot of good. Maverick and I also need help planning and running new activities like taking the horses through obstacle courses with barrels and such. I'd appreciate your expertise."

She cocked her head, considering. As an assistant, she'd regain some of the pride she'd lost yesterday, but how to handle being around Jared, and her unwelcome new feelings for him?

"We'll take it day by day," Jared said, sensing her silent reservations. "And anytime you want to quit, you just say so."

"I don't like quitting." The words flew from her lips, from the gut-level spot where her grit used to be. It felt good to find it again.

"I was counting on that." She could hear the

smile in Jared's voice. "Class starts in thirty minutes."

"See you then, *friend.*"

His hand cupped the side of her cheek, and the fluttering in her stomach made the gesture feel anything but "friendly."

"Later. Come on, Petey." He whistled.

After Jared left, she rested her head on Harley's back and closed her eyes. What had she just committed herself to? She'd be working with Jared in the program and with a service-dog-in-training.

Since the kiss, an even more bittersweet memory haunted her: the feel of Jared's arms wrapped around her, the strength, the firmness of them, the way they'd made her feel safe and strong again and something more... something that'd made her heart pound harder than ever before around him.

Was she developing romantic feelings for him? If so, the timing couldn't be worse. Even on her best day, she didn't remotely resemble feminine types he usually dated. Crazy her to keep thinking of him that way.

A shiver tore through her. *Get a grip, girl.* Even if Jared could get serious, he'd have more power in a relationship with her because of her blindness.

Better to keep her distance and work on regaining her confidence all on her own.

And forget that kiss ever happened.

CHAPTER SEVEN

"WHAT'S MMA?" AMBERLEY eyed the blurred, boxy shape of a white vehicle as it bounced up the rutted drive, then stopped in the parking area outside the corral. Someone—she couldn't make out gender—hustled to the back of the vehicle. The grating, mechanical whine of a wheelchair lift sounded.

"Methylmalonic acidemia—a genetic disorder. Metabolism problems," Benny supplied. Like Amberley and Jared, he huddled out of the afternoon's intense sun in the stable's shadow. "Emily had a stroke a couple years back because of it."

"She's so young," Amberley murmured, straining to focus on the small shape an adult bundled into the wheelchair. The trauma of learning about her genetic disorder at twenty-six paled in comparison with the challenges that Emily must face daily.

Amberley set her jaw. She'd ensure that

Emily, while on Spirit Ranch, would forget her troubles and just be a kid for a while, like any other.

"Ten years old, I'm thinking." Two rasps of Benny's inhaler reached Amberley's ears. He lowered his voice. "Jan, her mother, says Emily started dialysis this week, which is why she can't make the regular group. Really appreciate you two staying longer to give her a solo lesson."

"Of course," she and Jared said at the same time.

A warm hand settled on Amberley's shoulder, and she glanced up at the fuzzy brown of Jared's large eyes. She sensed his thoughts. They still made a great team, even when the goal wasn't about winning.

"Howdy!" hollered a female voice that belonged to whoever pushed the occupied wheelchair to the corral's gate.

Amberley hustled to the opener and hit the automatic button without hesitation. Working in the ring this week boosted her confidence. She'd even begun doing more at home and had cooked dinner last night.

Despite the overdone eggs and burnt toast, her mother declared it the best meal she'd had, then burst into tears. Seeing her no-nonsense parent break down hit Amberley hard. Reclaiming her independence meant giving her mother peace of mind and her life back. She'd vowed then and there to work as hard as she could so no one would sacrifice on her behalf again.

A motorized engine hum announced the gate opening, and Amberley stepped back. Her boots automatically tested the ground for uneven terrain before she trusted her full weight on them. Harley dropped his head over her shoulder, eager to welcome another child.

All week, he'd showered the kids with affection, seeking them out, grabbing hugs wherever he could…the shameless scamp…but still, he wanted to help as much as she did. It touched her that he still found a way to thrive outside the spotlight of barrel racing.

Too bad his sale fell through. She'd reacted to the news with relief, followed by guilt for feeling relieved. Harley deserved more than walking around a ring all day. He needed to go as far as his hooves could carry him, right onto the ERA Premier team she'd once dreamed of making. Hopefully this morning's email response to her ad would pan out.

Harley lowered himself to his knees, then laid his head on Emily's shoulder. "He's so soft!" she squealed.

"Careful, big guy," Amberley warned, feeling for Harley's bridle, then slipping her fingers through it.

"He likes me!" Emily flung her arms around Harley's gleaming black neck. A flow of silver— the luxurious mane Amberley painstakingly brushed this morning—signaled he'd tossed his head in agreement.

"I love you, Harley," Amberley heard Emily whisper close to where she imagined her horse's ear to be.

Amberley's chest grew tight. Watching the children find acceptance, happiness and success moved her deeply. Spirit Ranch let them forget their limitations as it did her. It gave them all a place to belong, a spot where they felt capable and appreciated. For a while, they could forget about their disabilities and simply live.

"Who wouldn't like you, Emily?" Jared declared in that warm, easy way he had of making everyone feel welcome, wanted and included. Working together this week reminded her why they'd become friends in the first place, though it hadn't helped her forget about their kiss...

"For one thing, you've got cool wheels," Jared continued, holding up a finger Amberley guessed. "Two, you're wearing Broncos'-colored brace bands. Three, Harley likes you and—" Jared dropped his voice to a conspiratorial whisper "—he hardly likes anybody, but don't tell him I said so."

Harley snorted while Amberley struggled to hold back an eye roll. Jared the hambone. He loved exaggerating and making outrageous remarks he claimed as truth.

Emily clapped her hands. Zen Harley didn't seem to flinch, as far as she could tell, save for a quick, fly-slapping tail flick.

"You're sure it's okay if I leave for my hair appointment?" asked Jan.

Amberley's heart went out to the woman. Like her mom, she guessed Jan struggled to take time for herself, something she and all parents of high-needs children deserved.

"Emily will be fine with us. Right, darlin'?"

A shivering awareness tripped over her skin at Jared's husky drawl. Was that darlin' meant for her or Emily? Or Jan? Not that it should matter, especially since he used that endearment with all women…even their seventy-year-old female lay minister for goodness' sakes. Yet after their kiss, she heard it differently, and it flustered her.

Would they ever get back to their easy friendship?

"Am I going to ride him?" Emily's voice rose.

Jared's head angled to the side. "Well. That depends."

Amberley squinted at him, wishing she could read his expression, though she recognized the mischievous note that'd entered his voice.

"On what?" Emily quavered.

Oh, no. Jared's teasing might be shaking the little girl's confidence.

She opened her mouth to interject.

"Can you keep a secret?" he asked.

What?

Intrigued, she leaned closer. Jared told the best tall tales.

"What is it?" Emily demanded.

"First I have to know if you can keep a secret. Only a couple people are in on this. Me, Amberley and Benny, so we're taking a big risk telling you."

Emily nodded, her reservations apparently settled. Jared's playful nature, a hindrance when it came to serious relationships, worked perfectly with children.

He'd make a good father, whispered the angel on one shoulder.

And a terrible husband, huffed the devil on the other.

Amberley shook her head clear of the voices. Jared was not husband material—least of all for someone like her. If he ever married, he'd wed a model like other NFL stars did. A gorgeous peacock. Not a dusty sparrow with a broken wing like her.

"You see, Harley isn't just some regular horse," she heard Jared declare when she tuned back into the conversation. Her mouth quirked. "He's a Pegasus who lost his wings."

Amberley clamped her lips to muffle her gasp. Where on earth did Jared come up with these things?

"How?" Emily breathed, all in by the sound of it.

"One day they stopped working and fell off," Amberley said, guessing where Jared was going with this and wanting to play along. "The doctor diagnosed a genetic condition."

"Like me." The swoosh of flesh color moving across Harley's black neck indicated Emily stroked him. "Sorry, Harley. That's sad."

"Well. You'd think so," Jared said. "But Harley here didn't let that hold him back. Even though he can't do what the other Pegasuses can do, he never quits and he always tries. He tries real hard."

"Like me?" Emily's voice rose in question.

"Exactly," Amberley and Jared affirmed in tandem.

Amberley heard someone blow their nose. Emily's mother?

"When he walks around the ring, he can still pretend he's flying," Amberley embellished.

Jared's hand flashed up and she guessed he gave her one of his "thumbs-ups." Pleasure, sweet and golden as warmed honey, poured through her veins. He saw her as a partner again, not someone to pity.

"I can pretend with Harley," Emily declared.

Amberley smiled. Never had she appreciated Jared's ability to motivate others more than she did now, a gift that lifted this little girl from her wheelchair so that she could fly.

"Then it sounds like you're the right rider

for Harley after all." Jared helped Emily out of the wheelchair while Amberley led Harley around to the special stairs the kids used to get into the saddle. Thanks to hours of practice, she'd finally mastered leveraging herself onto her horse without them.

Not that it'd stopped Jared's hovering.

"Aren't you going to say bye to your ma?" Jared asked. Based on their routine, Amberley gleaned that he now held Emily's hands, balancing her as she wobbled forward.

"Bye, Ma!"

Amberley smiled at Emily's offhand, dismissive tone. Thrilled at the prospect of riding a "Pegasus," she didn't need, or want her mom here, and that was a good thing.

Jan wavered at the gate.

"We've got your cell phone number, so we'll call if anything comes up." Amberley aimed a reassuring smile in Jan's direction. Was the protective mother worried about leaving her daughter with a legally blind volunteer? "Better hurry or you'll miss your appointment."

"Right. Love you, Emily!" Jan called, still lingering, clearly struggling.

"Can I be alone now?" A note of impatience entered Emily's voice.

Jan laughed. "See you in an hour, honey."

A moment later the van's engine turned, loud in the still, humid air, then grew quieter as it sped back down the lane.

Amberley guided Emily up the stairs. She fit her small foot into the stirrup, impressed with the brave girl. Having a disability made you appreciate independence. No matter your limitation, the drive to push forward, to reach a goal, big or small, took grit. Children with physical restrictions shouldn't be labeled "disabled." *Challenged* fit better as a descriptor since they battled to overcome limitations every day. That made them special. Fighters. Survivors. A testimony to the strength and will of the human spirit.

They worked harder than the athletes with whom she'd competed, and for less glory, too. These children's accomplishments might not seem big to some. If you judged sheer effort, however, there was no comparison. Working with them filled her with pride.

Was she proud of herself, too?

Her father's face flashed in her mind's eye.

"You're a winner," he'd vowed. "Never forget it."

And she couldn't. Especially now that she'd never be one again.

Sorry, Daddy.

Still, working with these kids gave her a new perspective about her own limitations. More than one way to succeed or accomplish a goal existed. With Harley's help, she'd guided the children through activities that helped build their strength and self-esteem. What's more, they were eager to talk to her about her blindness. Perhaps her "handicap" was, in some ways, an asset as it inspired kids, like Emily, to keep trying.

Jared swung Emily's other leg over the saddle and secured it while Amberley handed up the color-coded reins. She moved to Harley's head and looped her fingers through his bridle. He opened his mouth wide, jerked his head up and back and yawned, not the least bit flustered by the bouncing child on his back.

"Nice molars," she teased, then pressed a quick kiss to his soft nose.

"All set?" Jared called from his position by Emily's side. The high-backed saddle helped keep her upright, but they still needed to ensure she maintained her balance as she worked on strengthening her core and the leg muscles that had lost functionality after her stroke.

"You bet," Amberley responded with their old catchphrase, the one they'd used when they'd just been pals, not friends who kissed…

Stop.

"If it's alright with you," Benny said, sounding winded, "I'll check on Joan. She's due for some meds, and I need to get out of all this pollen."

Amberley opened her mouth to object, then shut it. Since the kiss, she'd avoided being alone with Jared. Surrounded by crowds of kids and assisting adults, it'd been easier to keep up her "just friends" act, despite the awkward, self-conscious feelings that dogged her.

"Not sure, Benny. This filly looks like she's up to no good and ready to get into all kinds of mischief."

Emily giggled at Jared's warning. "No, I'm not."

"I was talking about Miss Amberley James, actually," Jared clarified, a current of humor running through his somber tone. "Never take your eye off her. I know I don't."

She blushed at his words' double meaning and forced herself to laugh along with a departing Benny. She'd sensed Jared's gaze on her a lot lately. Yet without her vision, she felt more in the dark than ever. Had his naturally flirty nature crossed into the same no-man's-land her seesawing emotions now occupied?

Better not to speculate, she told herself firmly, and focus on the work. Oh. And act normal…whatever that meant anymore.

She ducked her head, pulled some brightly colored beanbags from her pocket and passed them up to Emily. "Ready to play beanbag toss?"

"Yes!"

"When we lead you past a barrel, you toss in the matching color bag. Got it?"

"Got it," Emily shouted. "Yellow first."

Amberley squinted at the barrels. From this distance, she could just make out the color strip Maverick painted on them after they'd come up with the game.

"Cluck to tell Harley to walk." Jared imitated the sound. "Then pull the green rein to steer him over there. And whatever you do, watch out for Amberley."

"What's Amberley going to do?" giggled Emily.

Harley's head bobbed up and down as they ambled to the yellow barrel.

"She likes to steal things."

Amberley's mouth dropped open. "No, I don't," she protested.

"Pull lightly with both reins to make Harley stop," Jared advised, ignoring her.

Harley, ever the highly trained athlete, immediately planted his hooves in the dirt.

"Now throw it in."

Something yellow whizzed by Amberley's head.

"Did I make it?"

She squinted into the barrel, then scanned the ground, cursing her faulty vision. "I don't see it." She fought back the familiar rise of helplessness.

"Did Amberley steal it?" Emily accused.

"Nah." Jared came around the front of Harley's head to join in the search. Within seconds he swooped down and grabbed the bag beside Amberley's feet.

She bit the inside of her cheek to hide her frustration and disappointment. With a little more time, would she have found it?

Jared's finger pressed lightly under her chin, and he tipped her face up to his. "The only thing you have to worry about is her stealing your heart. She's a pro."

And with that, he returned to Emily's side, leaving Amberley gaping, her mind in a whirl.

Jared's flirtatious nature was messing with her head and preventing her from regaining her "just friends" footing. Should she say something? If she did, things might get even more awkward.

A half hour later, they finished the games designed to help Emily's coordination and strength.

"How do I fly?" she asked as they led her and Harley around the ring.

"Close your eyes and stretch your arms out to the sides." Jared moved, imitating the pose, Amberley guessed.

"I'll fall off."

"I won't let you."

The firmness of Jared's voice had the desired effect. "Okay, I'm ready."

"Now say, 'Harley, fly!'" Jared boomed, theatrical and dramatic enough to make the crazy thought seem possible.

"But he can't really, right?"

"Sure he can. You can do anything in your imagination."

Emily giggled. "I like that."

"So where do you want to fly to?" Amberley asked.

"Can we fly to the sun?"

"You'll get burned," Jared warned.

"Not on a Pegasus," Amberley insisted, enjoying this game with her oldest dearest friend. "Remember. They have fire protection."

"Good one." The blinding white of Jared's teeth flashed at her. "Okay, then. To the sun."

She clucked and led Harley slowly around the corral.

"Keep those eyes closed, Emily. No peeking," Jared directed.

"I won't."

"Okay. Here we go." Excitement bubbled inside Amberley. "Tell Harley to fly."

"Fly, Harley!" Emily shouted.

Amberley made a smooching sound that kicked up Harley's gait so he high-stepped it around the ring.

"We're crossing over the treetops now," Jared said, his voice so full of wonder he nearly convinced Amberley this was really happening. She didn't need to close her eyes since she could barely see. Instead, she let her mind wander where Jared's words took her.

"Wow," he exclaimed, all boyish excitement. "It looks like a green sea down there. The leaves are rustling, moving together like waves. Can you hear them?"

"I can hear them!"

"Now we're soaring over the mountains. There's a family of billy goats grazing right on the very tip-top."

"Even the babies?" Emily breathed.

"Yep. One of them just bahhhhhhed at you."

"Baaaahhhhhh!" Emily blared back.

They completed one go-round, and Amberley signaled Harley to pick up the pace. His old barrel racing quirk of balking at fences came in handy now. In the past, she'd compelled him to run at barriers before turning at the last minute. Now, he could give them the wide berth he preferred.

"Ladies and gentlemen," Jared said in a comical imitation of a pilot's voice, "we're cruising at an altitude of ten thousand feet and blasting through the clouds."

"What's it look like?" Emily asked, eager.

"White. Everywhere," Jared answered. "Like spun sugar. If you stick out your tongue maybe you can taste it."

"I can!"

"Good!" Jared crowed. "You're using your imagination. The sun's just ahead. It's getting warmer. Can you feel it?"

A trickle of sweat wound down Amberley's cheek at the exertion. She'd lost her stamina if this activity tired her.

"It's hot!"

"But not too hot. Remember, Harley can protect you," Amberley assured her.

"But he's not a real Pegasus."

They neared the dismount stairs and Amberley pulled Harley to a stop.

"Just because he lost his wings doesn't mean he's not a Pegasus anymore." Jared helped Emily off the saddle and down the stairs.

Emily threw her arms around Harley's neck. "You're a real Pegasus, Harley. You are."

Harley's head bobbed in a flash of black and silver, and Amberley smiled through the tears that sprang to her eyes.

Jared was right. Wings didn't make a Pegasus. Working limbs, perfect eyesight…they didn't make a human either. What we imagined and strived to be counted. Real strength rooted itself inside, where it mattered most.

Except when it came to winning. No amount of imagination could transport her into its circle again, or earn her one of her father's rare smiles, the kind she'd fought to receive all her life.

Now she'd couldn't even picture it.

"Emily!"

Amberley backed Harley from the gate to make way for the rushing parent.

"Mama, you look pretty!" gushed Emily.

"Did you have fun?"

"Yes! Harley flew me to the sun."

"Well, now. That's extra special. Thanks, Jared and Amberley. It's awful nice of you to do this for us."

"Nice?" scoffed Jared. "Harley would have had a fit if he couldn't have seen Emily. He didn't give us a choice...not that we would have said no."

Emily giggled. "Can he come here so I can give him another hug?"

Harley pulled on his bit. "Just try to stop him," Amberley exclaimed, nearly dragged over to Emily's wheelchair.

"Want to stop by my ranch later?" Jared asked after the mother and child departed. "Petey's got something he's dying to show you."

"Petey, huh?" Her lips quirked up in the corners. "In that case…"

A few hours later, she rocked beside Jared on his porch swing. Crickets thrummed in the brush, and fireflies lit up the deepening twilight. Cade Ranch's trademark tea roses must still twine around the railing and pillars, she mused, breathing in their intoxicating, floral scent. The swing's chained hook creaked as they pushed forward and back. When the firm curve of Jared's muscular bicep brushed against her shoulder, she shivered despite the balmy June air.

"Cold?" His deep baritone seemed to vibrate through her.

"No," she said, then clenched her teeth to hide their chatter.

"Want something to drink?" He must have gestured because their hands brushed. An electric spark shot up her wrist.

"No."

"Do you want me to take you home? Petey can do his demonstration another time."

She shook her head, annoyed at herself for acting like one of Jared's besotted girls. Since the kiss, she'd become hyperaware of him. Hearing him work with the children

in his confident, caring and humorous way
kept her in turmoil over her confusing new
feelings. She "saw" him differently than the
success-driven athlete who'd had one single
focus: himself. Even though she no longer had
a visual, what she imagined filled her with
longing to touch the smile she pictured on his
handsome face...to kiss it, too.

They'd given in to a moment of weakness,
but this week's camaraderie proved their
friendship was special. She needed to control
her burgeoning feelings or risk losing one of
the most important relationships in her life.

"Can't we let Petey go yet?"

She peered at the furry black-and-white blur
sitting motionless on the porch's edge.

"Nope. We've been practicing. He's got to
learn to wait for you when you run errands
and such."

"I'm not planning on running any."

"Who's going to do your shopping? Bring
you to the post office? Take you to church?"

She opened her mouth to say "my mother,"
then snapped it shut. No. She wouldn't rely
on her mom or anyone else. Jared was right.
She needed Petey. Could the rambunctious dog

sustain his perch much longer? It'd been nearly five minutes.

"Stadiums allow service dogs, right? I could attend a Broncos game again, like old times, or whichever team you're signing with."

"No."

The perch twisted on its chain as Jared shoved off it and paced the porch.

No? Shame twisted through her. Maybe he didn't want a disabled girl cheering him on. He probably had a harem of pretty women to do the job. "I see."

Suddenly his long strides halted before her. "It's not what you're thinking."

"What am I thinking?"

"That I don't want you there."

In the silence, a small whimper escaped Petey. She wanted to cry with him.

"Look. This isn't easy for me to say, and I should have told you the whole truth before."

"You don't need to spell it out." She grasped the swing's arm, stood and sidestepped him. "Petey, come!"

With a joyous bark, the dog launched himself across the porch and leaped at her knees.

"Yes, I do, Amberley. Down, Petey."

The pup flopped back to the floor at Jared's stern command. An exasperated woof escaped him.

"Up, Petey." Toenails scratched on wood as he scrambled back to his feet, then seemed to settle. Something thumped steadily. His tail, she guessed. "Look. I get it."

A strong hand caught her elbow. "I didn't quit the Broncos exactly. And I'm not signing with another team. They just don't want me back as a starter. No one does."

Surprise walloped her behind her knees, making them wobble. "As in never, or just until your ACL is healed?"

A long breath blew past her ear. "Let's sit."

At her nod, he led her back to the swing. Petey threw himself across her feet once they'd settled into the deep cushions.

"Could you still play for them, even if you don't start?"

"I'd be a second-stringer at best."

She let that sink in a moment. Returning to the Broncos as a second-stringer would be unacceptable to him. He always strove to be the best, number one, just like her.

"But you could work your way back up…"

A raspy tongue glided over her bare ankle.

She reached down, groped for Petey and scratched behind his ragged ears.

"It's possible. But our sports doctor said there's not much chance I'll improve beyond this."

Understanding welled. They'd bonded over their thirst to win, and now she felt an even deeper kinship with Jared.

They'd lost their dreams. But maybe not each other.

Would having him back in her life full-time, just as a friend, be enough?

"What'll you do now?" she asked once Petey scampered off the porch, barking madly after a squirrel, she supposed.

"I was going to ranch full-time. But then I started thinking about you and the kids in the program. Seeing how hard everyone tries made me decide not to give up. Maybe I can't play professional ball, but I could still start on a local semipro team. I shouldn't give up what I love doing just because I can't be at the top."

She considered that a moment, then nodded. "Good."

He clasped her hands and squeezed. "And neither should you."

She blinked up into his blurred face. "What?"

"I've got an idea about getting you back into barrel racing."

She jerked her hands away. "That kind of pie-in-the-sky nonsense only works on little kids like Emily."

"Hear me out."

Anger washed hot inside her. "Stop telling me what I must and mustn't do."

"But…"

"You're acting just like my father."

"You say that like it's a bad thing. Your father was a great man."

"He was…but he was also a taskmaster. He pushed me hard and I let him, I wanted to make him proud—something I never did unless I won."

"Not true. He talked you up all over town."

"Talked up my wins, I'll wager."

Jared's silence was affirmation.

"Anytime I placed second or worse, my dad wouldn't talk to me for days, he'd be so upset. Now, whenever I think about trying and failing, I remember those silences, how much they hurt, how it felt not to be perfect, number one."

"He rejected you."

"No. He was trying to teach me a lesson and make me the best I could be."

"But he's not around to judge you anymore. You can judge yourself."

"It's impossible anyway." She shooed away a buzzing mosquito. She'd only just gotten used to her limitations. She wouldn't let Jared get her hopes up. The fall, when reality returned, might finish her off completely. "I heard from a buyer today. I have an offer on Harley."

"You can't accept it."

"Because you say so?" she demanded, done with Jared's high-handed control.

"Yes. Since I own half of Harley."

CHAPTER EIGHT

JARED SHOVED HIS hands in his pockets to keep from reaching for Amberley. Standing with her back against the porch railing, her tense shoulders near her ears, she looked fit to be tied. Beneath that, he glimpsed fear. Fear of failure. The result of a well-meaning parent unintentionally doing a bit of harm. Hearing about her experiences with her father only strengthened Jared's resolve to get Amberley back in the rink. She alone would decide if she was worthy, and he'd make darn sure she did. Somewhere in the distance, thunder rumbled, and humid air pressed all around, dark and heavy.

"Your stake in Harley's just a technicality." Her beautiful blue eyes searched for him. He stepped closer and cleared his throat so she could locate him. "He's my horse."

"You can't sell him without my say-so."

Her blond brows lowered and met over the

straight bridge of her nose. "I should have bought out your share."

"Glad you didn't."

An exasperated noise escaped her pale lips. "I trusted you."

"Trusting me is the smartest thing you can do, darlin'."

"Don't call me that!"

Her vehement tone caught him off guard. He called lots of woman darlin'. Why did she act like it meant something?

Because you mean it when you say it to her, a voice said inside him.

Since their kiss, he couldn't keep his eyes off Amberley. Her beauty was undeniable, but his attraction went deeper than physical. He'd always admired her fearlessness. Now, he saw real courage, conviction and strength in her work at Spirit Ranch. Her patient, supportive approach with the awestruck children inspired them, and him, to try harder.

Not one for complaining, she faced her vision loss head-on, determined to keep her independence. That took true grit. The real measure of a man—or a woman—wasn't counted in wins, but in how many times you got up after you'd been knocked down.

Amberley's no-quit attitude made her a real champion. A hero like he'd promised his father to be. She'd transformed from his win-or-bust, competition-hungry kindred spirit. Adversity had stripped her of her sight, and he'd never seen her, and her big heart, clearer.

Did he have any right to it?

He slid his fingers through the silky strands of her blond hair. "What should I call you?"

Her eyes widened and her mouth trembled. "Stop."

Her fresh, citrusy scent made him breathe deep. "Stop what?"

"Stop flirting with me!"

She brushed him aside and moved forward a couple paces. Petey leaped between her and a rocking chair, herding her the way he did the cattle, halting her momentum before she stumbled into it.

"I'm not flirting with you," he objected.

Liar.

He flirted with all women, and, until now, it'd seemed harmless. But with stakes high, his friendship with Amberley on the line, he shouldn't be sending mixed signals.

He had no business messing with her emotions. He dated casually, and Amberley was anything but casual to him. If he jeopardized their friendship, he'd lose her.

Yet deep down, he sensed friendship wasn't enough anymore.

"Sell me your stake in Harley," she insisted. Her eyes flashed his way.

He ran a hand over his face. "No."

"He'll be miserable stuck at Spirit Ranch," she cried. When she gestured, her hand smacked the chair spindles, and she winced. His protective urge reared up. It took every ounce of willpower not to pull her clear of the chair and shield her from this hurt and every other pain that might ever come her way.

He forced his mind back to Harley and his antics with the children. "Looks happy enough to me."

"But it's not good enough."

"For him or for you?"

Her lashes dropped to her red-stained cheeks. "He deserves a shot at being a champion."

"So do you," he said, meaning it. The world needed real heroes like Amberley. It killed him that she didn't see herself the way he did.

She opened her eyes and scrunched them, skeptical. "And how are you aiming to make that happen? Harley being a Pegasus is more likely."

"I'll guide you through a course with a walkie-talkie."

"How?"

"We'll fix one to Harley's saddle. I'll call out when you're coming on a barrel and need to turn."

A short laugh burst from her. "That easy, huh?"

"No. But it's a start," he insisted, defensive. He'd always been a risk-all, fear-nothing, have-no-regrets kind of guy. Amberley had been that way once, too. He needed to remind her and plant her back in the winner's circle where she belonged, no matter what it took. The odds might be against them, but he'd bet on Amberley every time.

"It's too dangerous."

"I won't let anything happen to you." His voice broke as a picture of Amberley, crumbled on the ground, flashed in his mind's eye. Barrel racers hit speeds of fifty miles an hour. A shiver ran behind his ribs. He could be sending her to the hospital or worse.

His back teeth clenched. That. Would. Not. Happen. He'd keep her safe. "Promise."

Bright headlights passed over the porch as a sedan approached. The purring engine slowed and a car door slammed.

"Hey there, Jared! Looks like a storm's comin' on."

"Hey, Mrs. James."

Amberley groped her way to the railing, then trailed her hand along its top until she reached the stairs.

"Amberley, wait."

She whirled, and the anguish on her face shot an arrow straight through his chest. "I'm sorry, Jared, but I can't."

"Can't or won't?"

"What's the difference?" Her hands stretched his way. He leaned forward so she could reach him, and her fingers landed on his arm. "If you really care about me, sell out Harley's share."

"I care," he vowed. Precious girl. He loved her more than anyone else in the world.

"But you won't sell."

"I won't, *because* I care."

For several seconds, only the burbling car engine disturbed the silence. Then, when the quiet stretched to its breaking point, she shook her head, stepped off the steps, grasped her mother's hands and disappeared into the car.

He stared down the dark, empty drive, feeling as if somebody pumped a numbing agent into his arteries.

His brother Justin clapped his shoulder. "Real men don't make war on women."

Jared nodded slowly. "I'm trying to convince her I'm not the enemy."

"She'll come around. You always get the girl."

Funny how that'd never really mattered to him before now. He hooked his thumbs in his belt loops and stared at the heat lightning cracking the mountaintops. "Maybe not this time."

Jewel joined them, her fingers fiddling with a sparkling band wrapped around one of her braids.

"You look pretty," Jared observed.

"She took a two-hour bath." Justin lifted a dark brow. "And those are new jeans."

"Cowgirls don't take baths, they dust off," scoffed their older brother, James. The screen door creaked as he closed it behind him. "What's the occasion?"

Jewel's shrug appeared a mite too casual. "Just going to the pool hall."

Jared's eyes narrowed. "Isn't Heath Loveland's band playing there tonight?"

Jewel toed a circle in the birdseed that'd spilled from the porch feeder. "Could be."

He and his brothers exchanged a long look. Teasing Jewel about a supposed crush on Heath had been one of their favorite ways to torment their little sister. Tough as nails, little got her goat except this ongoing joke.

Could it be true?

He shook off the crazy thought. Cades and Lovelands didn't mix. Speaking of which...

"Saw Ma and Boyd line dancing last night."

Justin swore a blue streak and Jewel stomped a boot. Strangely, James remained suspiciously quiet. "Did you know about that?" he asked his older brother.

James eyed each of them steadily. "Sofia mentioned Ma might see him there."

"And you didn't put a stop to it?" Jewel demanded, a fair-enough question for their controlling brother.

"Nope. Promised Sofia I wouldn't interfere."

"Were they dancing together?" Jewel asked.

"Yep. And Boyd called me *son*," Jared said.

Justin kicked the railing. "Low-down, son of a—"

"Better watch your mouth, sunshine," James growled, angling his head up at Javi's open bedroom window.

"Something's got to be done, and if you ain't gonna then it's on us," Jewel declared, slowly, as if puzzling out a problem.

James spread his hands. "Like I told Sofia, I'm not interfering."

"Want some company at the pool hall?" Jared doffed his hat and ran a hand through his damp, matted hair.

Jewel peered, back forth, between Justin and him. "Maybe. Why?"

"We need a word with Heath Loveland." Justin laced his fingers together and cracked his knuckles.

Jewel's eyes widened. "You're not threatening him!"

"Why? You want to do it?" Jared asked easily. "Ladies first after all."

"N-no," Jewel stammered. "Heath's harmless. He's not like the other ones."

Justin hooted. "Jewel's got it bad for Heath." He trucked down the stairs to avoid her left hook, hopped on his chopper and grabbed his helmet. "Last one there's a Loveland."

Jared scrambled after him, "Unless you want that being your last name, better hurry, Jewel."

A couple of hours later, Jared, Jewel and Justin crowded around a high-topped table with Maverick, Heath and Daryl Loveland. The place reeked of whiskey and sweat, but that could just as likely be the Lovelands.

"Everyone agreed on the plan?" asked Maverick.

All nodded.

Jared forced himself to shake Maverick's hand. "It's a deal. You hold up your end of the bargain, we'll keep ours, and our parents won't want anything to do with each other when we're done."

"Pa should have had more sense in the first place," Daryl muttered under his breath.

"What'd you say?" Justin bristled, spoiling for a fight.

Daryl leaned forward, chin jutting. "I *said*—"

Jared slapped a hand on the table, and the glasses jumped. "Enough. We got plenty to do keeping our parents apart without fighting each other. We're on the same side—for now."

"Guess hell has frozen over," Justin grumbled.

"They could wind up hitched if we don't stop them," Jewel mumbled around a mouthful of peanuts.

"That'd make us brother and sister," Heath observed, his eyes on Jewel.

A collective groan rose from the group, all except Jewel, whose bad swallow ended in a coughing fit.

"Everyone set on the details? You Lovelands sure are good at forgetting things." Justin's black eyes glinted. Beneath the table, Jared spied his hands clenching and unclenching atop his legs.

"Like?" growled Daryl.

"The whereabouts of the fifty-carat sapphire your great-great-great-great-granddaddy stole from us," Jewel huffed, red-faced but recovered. "That's a start."

"How about the water rights yours stole from us?" Heath interjected, one side of his mouth curling up.

Roseanne, their waitress, stopped by the table, interrupting the standoff.

"Can I get you fellas anything else?"

"And lady." Heath nodded over at Jewel, who turned a violent shade of purple.

"No, thanks, darlin'." Jared pulled out his wallet and handed her enough cash to settle the tab along with a generous tip.

"I've got this." Maverick waved a fistful of green.

Roseanne wavered until Jared ducked his head and shot her a slow, lazy smile from beneath the brim of his hat.

Her crazy-long lashes batted as she beamed back, nodded, then scooted away.

"Thanks, darlin'," he called after her, eying a seething Maverick.

"How about some pool?" Maverick challenged once the rest of the crew grabbed their keys and headed for the door. "Wouldn't mind taking some more money off you tonight."

"You got lucky last time," Jared replied automatically, scanning the tables for his friends. Lane and Red waved him over.

"I could have beaten you blindfolded," Maverick taunted.

Jared stopped in his tracks, an idea occurring that might solve Amberley's trust issue after all.

"Meet me here tomorrow night." He jerked his chin up at Maverick, his statement more a command than a request. "I'll do you one better."

"IF I BEAT Maverick Loveland at pool, I win your half ownership in Harley?"

Jared tucked Amberley's hand into the crook of his arm as he led her across the pool hall's parking lot the following night. He'd worn cologne, she thought, inhaling the familiar spicy scent, her pulse jumping.

"And if you lose," Jared drawled, "Harley stays on Spirit Ranch."

Their boots splashed through puddles created from last night's rainstorm. The humidity had broken, leaving the air clean, crisp and smelling of freshly turned earth. A smudge of white glowed down from the dark, sparkling sky. Somewhere in the distance, a car door slammed and laughter floated from what sounded like a large group arriving at the local dive.

Little chills ran up her spine. She hadn't been out in public, other than the doctor's office and the ranch, since her diagnosis. No doubt there'd be plenty of whispers and pity-filled stares in her direction. What would they be thinking? Saying?

Poor Amberley, she could hear them cluck. *Can't do a thing for herself anymore.*

She used to be something once...now she ain't nothing much...

She shook her head to stop the voices, especially the last one that'd sounded too much like her father.

As if reading her thoughts, Jared squeezed her hand. He leaned down and murmured "You look beautiful" into her ear.

A rush of air escaped her. "No flirting."

Was she being hypocritical? Considering she'd driven her mother crazy donning tons of outfits, asking for detailed descriptions, she'd wanted to look good for Jared. Plain and simple.

"Just making a factual observation, ma'am." He must have tipped his hat since the brown of it lowered over his brow momentarily.

She rolled her eyes. "Ma'am, huh?"

"You said you didn't like *darlin'*."

"I like it better than being called the same thing as my grandma."

"Then darlin' it is," he drawled, sounding completely unrepentant.

Despite her nerves, her lips curved. "You're incorrigible."

"I prefer tenacious. Less old cuss, more cowboy."

"Real cowboys don't call themselves cowboys."

Jared laughed and pulled her closer. His solid warmth lit a golden glow that radiated through her chest, filling the space behind her ribs. She'd avoided him around the ranch for most of the day, but when he'd approached her with this outrageous chance to win back his stake in Harley, she'd agreed to meet him.

Anything for Harley, she thought, even taking a crazy bet she had little chance of winning. It'd be humiliating to lose in front of people who'd once looked up to her, respected her, but she had to try.

They must have reached the door because Jared paused and suddenly a rectangle of light, and a boot-stomping honky-tonk tune, spilled into the night.

"After you."

"Can we go in together?"

She didn't want to wobble inside looking lost and blind, a fallen champion.

Jared swept an arm around her and firmly

led her into the pool hall. His sure grip kept
her from stumbling as he steered her though
the maze of crowded tables she only barely
glimpsed.

"Amberley!" someone cried to her right, and
Jared halted. "It's me. Brianne. From school.
You look so—so—"

Amberley gritted her teeth. Brianne, a notorious gossip, lived, ate and breathed drama.

"Beautiful?" Jared supplied. He leaned
down and brushed a lingering kiss on Amberley's cheek.

She felt her heartbeat everywhere, right
down to her fingertips.

"So y'all are together, now?" Brianne
gasped. Amberley could practically hear the
woman's brain teletyping the message she'd
eagerly broadcast to the community.

She opened her mouth to refute Brianne's
claim, but Jared jumped in first.

"We'll just leave y'all guessing on that for
now."

He swept Amberley away and she held in a
chuckle at his deft handling of the town's one-
woman rumor mill.

Gratitude for her friend rose. Jared just
made the story of her appearance about a pos-

sible romance instead of her pathetic fall from grace. Like always, he had her back.

Until this roadblock with selling Harley...

She had to win Jared's stake. Her dim vision flickered over the area where the pool tables were. They blurred and jumped, rectangular shapes stretching into green and brown smears of color. Despair wrapped around her heart and squeezed.

If she couldn't bring the table into focus, how would she play on one and beat Maverick Loveland? Notoriously skilled at just about everything, Maverick was one of the few people to give Jared a run for his money.

They stopped and Amberley slid her fingers on the sleek edge of a pool table.

"Hey, Amberley," she heard Maverick say. "Nice seeing you."

"You won't say that after she beats you," Jared said beside her.

"Thought I was playing *you*," Maverick replied, his voice cool and unruffled like all Lovelands, such a stark contrast to the passionate, rowdy Cades.

Jared nudged what felt like a pool stick and a cube of chalk into her hand.

"Nope. You said you could beat me blindfolded. I want to see if you can beat Amberley blindfolded."

"But she's—" Maverick cleared his throat, clearly struggling to be tactful. "She can't—"

"Afraid you might get beaten by a blind girl?" Amberley challenged, keeping her voice light, to help a faltering Maverick. Then something amazing happened. A flare of adrenaline spiked inside at the prospect of a real competition, a feeling she hadn't had in a long, long time. It felt good.

Jared lifted her free hand and high-fived it.

"How's this going to work?" Maverick asked.

"Tie this bandanna around your eyes and pick someone to guide you as you play," Jared said. "I'm Amberley's partner."

Her mouth dropped open in surprise. Jared helping her? If she won, she'd win his stake in Harley. He'd be working against his own interests.

"Daryl!" Maverick shouted above the din of chattering patrons and a blaring country-rock tune.

"I'll signal where the ball is and you'll sink it," Jared said in her ear as she chalked the end of her stick.

"That easy, huh?"

"You're a winner, Amberley. Maverick won't know what hit him."

She laughed, the remembered joy of working with Jared when they competed swelling her heart to bursting.

"Heads or tails, Amberley?" Daryl asked, joining them.

"Heads."

"Tails, it is," Daryl called a moment later.

Nerves fluttered in Amberley's stomach as the crack of a ball smashing into others sounded. She squinted at the table, but the mangle of colors jumped and spun.

"Did I get one in?" Maverick asked.

"Nah. Pretty pathetic, dude," Daryl said. "Amberley, stripes or solids?"

"S-stripes." She pressed her shaking lips together. She didn't have to see to feel the collective weight of the patrons' gazes on her. She hated losing and was about to go down in flames.

"You've got this, Amberley," Jared urged in that fired-up voice they'd always used to hype each other up. "There's a striped yellow about three inches from the corner pocket diagonal to you. The cue ball's in front of it. Can you see it?"

She shook her head. This wasn't going to work. She'd lose the game, lose the last of her dignity and, worst of all, lose the chance to sell Harley so he could have the opportunity to be a champion.

Jared reached over her and put his hand on top of the one that gripped the cue. He then positioned the fingers of her other hand on the wood before lightly gripping her wrist. To Amberley's dismay, her face became warm and her heart did strange things. She wasn't sure if it had sped up to a single hum, or if it just wasn't beating anymore.

"Close your eyes," Jared urged, letting her go. "Picture it."

She mashed her eyes shut and tried imagining the shot the same way Jared helped Emily "see" her flight to the sun. She envisioned the yellow-striped ball resting on the green felt. Three inches from the corner. White cue ball nearly touching it. Her jaw set. Now or never.

Cowgirl up.

Brow knitted, she aimed the cue where she pictured the white ball. The pole slid easily between her fingers as she steadied her hand on the felt surface of the table.

Not too hard, she cautioned herself, easing her grip on the pole slightly and adjusting it to keep it level. With a lurch of her arm, she jabbed the rod forward.

The hard crack of ball meeting ball sounded. The crowd whooped.

"Nice!" Jared crowed.

Elation nearly lifted her off her feet.

"Now don't get cocky," Jared warned, bringing her back down to earth the way he did during competitions. Positivity. Steadiness. Focus. They were experts at that and with each other. Who knew her better than Jared? No one save her mother.

And your father! piped up the angel on one shoulder.

He only cared about you when you won, groused the devil on the other.

She ignored the voices within. "Where's my next shot?"

Jared described two possibilities.

"Which is the easiest?"

"That's your call."

She opened her mouth to object, to ask for more help, then shut it and nodded instead, striving to portray serenity. Confidence. In reality, something slow and unsettling was happening to her body: she was seeing tiny black dots, her head was featherlight, her palms were clammy and her heart was beating hard.

Jared was right. She needed to call the shots, not just here but in all areas of her life. For the next few minutes she sank one ball after another, each eliciting claps of approval from the growing crowd surrounding them.

"This next one's tricky. You've only got a bank shot." Jared described the angles and position, and she closed her eyes to picture it.

Leaning down, she jerked the stick forward and heard it gently knock into a ball.

A groan rose from the group.

Shoot. Humiliation stung her, but not as badly as she'd feared. After watching the kids at Spirit Ranch fight to overcome their challenges, she now understood the dignity, the strength in simply trying, in moving forward, no matter how far you got. Effort mattered more than winning.

"Sorry, Amberley." Jared's hand settled warm and firm on her shoulder.

"I'll get it next time," she vowed.

"Not a doubt in my mind," he said, and his confidence built hers as it always had.

"You're up, Mav," she heard Daryl say, followed by a string of directions.

"Describe the table to me."

She listened closely to Jared's narration of the balls remaining on the table. Their relative positions swam in her mind's eye. A jolt snapped through her. She could see it. She could see the whole thing without even looking.

After a couple of clarifying questions, Maverick sank his first ball, then missed the next.

"Your turn, Amberley."

She and Jared fell into a rhythm, and in short order she dispatched all but the eight ball.

"This is it for the win, Amberley!" Jared wrapped an arm around her and gave her a quick squeeze that fogged her brain for a second. Why did he have to feel so good and why did she have to notice it?

She lined up her stick and imagined the spot on the side of the table she needed to hit with the cue.

"How close is that eight ball again?"

"About five inches and just to the left of the second pocket."

Tendrils of hair stuck to her damp forehead and she wiped first one palm, then the other on her jeans.

Please, please make this for Harley...

"Go for it, Amberley!" she heard someone say. A woman.

"You've got it, girl!" hollered an unidentified cowboy.

"Yeah!" roared another.

She swallowed the lump in her throat and lifted her chin. It'd been a long time since anyone had cheered for her, and it felt darn good.

Closing her eyes to blot out the distorted world, she relied on the picture Jared wove and struck the cue.

A rip-roaring holler nearly tore the roof off the pool hall. Jared caught her around the waist and twirled her until she lost her breath and pounded on his broad chest.

He let her down gently but kept a possessive arm curled around her waist. He pressed something crisp—paper—in her hand.

"A hundred dollars," she heard Maverick say. "You earned it. Sure kicked the pants off me."

"And you said you'd have beaten me blind-folded," Jared taunted.

She could practically hear the shrug in Maverick's voice as he said, "Still believe that to be true. Losing to Miss James here, now, that was a revelation."

"Didn't surprise me," Jared said, stout. "Amberley's a champion through and through."

The crowd agreed with loud, lusty cheers.

Amberley waved the money. "How about a round on me?"

An hour later, she and Jared exited the pool hall, laughing. She placed a hand to her aching cheek from smiling so long. Her cell rang.

She hit the answer button in the position she'd been taught, and her mother's voice came over the speaker. "Honey, the town board meeting's running late. Would you mind staying at the bar a bit longer?"

"I can see her home," Jared assured her. "If it's alright with Amberley."

"Fine by me."

"Oh. Mr. Jenkens asked me about Harley," her mother continued. "He's wanting to know if you're still selling him. His granddaughter's interested. A talented racer by the sound of it."

"I won a pool game tonight," she heard herself say, avoiding the question.

Why was she stalling?

"Pool? How?"

"Jared talked me through it." She leaned her head on his broad shoulder and smiled up in the direction of his face. Once again, they'd made a good team. She'd trusted him, and just as he always vowed, he hadn't let her down. Should she trust his crazy idea to get her and Harley back into competitive barrel racing?

"I'll be," her mother murmured, then, "So about Harley…"

Working with the children this week showed her that her life still had a purpose. Tonight proved her career might not be over either.

She'd never know unless she tried.

"Tell Mr. Jenkens…" She hesitated and Jared seemed to freeze beside her. "Tell him, Harley's not for sale."

Jared let out a wild whoop and danced some kind of crazy jig.

"Don't get ahead of yourself, cowboy," she teased after she finished her call. "You still lost your bet."

Jared quieted, cupped her face and leaned down to rest his forehead against hers. His warm breath rushed across her lips.

"Did I?"

CHAPTER NINE

"CAN I OPEN my eyes now? It's not like I can see anyway," Amberley groused, more intrigued than annoyed by Jared's silence on today's mysterious outing. Since their winning pool game two days ago, Jared had been acting cagey and furtive, hurrying to some unnamed mission after therapy sessions.

What was his secret?

Her boots crunched on a pebbled road somewhere on Cade Ranch. The scent of manure signaled they passed a pasture, an unoccupied one given the relative silence.

"You can see some," Jared's deep voice rumbled beside her ear. Instantly, her pulse ratcheted up several notches. "I want to surprise you."

"I hate surprises." Her palm slid on Petey's halter handle. He'd been training hard, Jared reported, and would most likely pass his certification test next week. Amberley didn't doubt it. The rambunctious dog calmed instantly at Jared's signal and now walked sedately ahead of her. His wagging tail brushed her bare knees as he guided her down the lane. It surprised her how easily she'd put her trust in Petey.

Could she do the same with Jared and his crazy scheme to return her to competitive barrel racing?

"You'll love this surprise." His calloused fingers mingled with hers and tightened.

Her heart leaped into a gallop. *Let go*, she warned herself, then released his hand and drew off her hat. The warm late-afternoon sunlight warmed her face. A balmy breeze rushed through her unbound hair. "You said that before you tried making me bungee jump."

"It's still on our bucket list."

Long ago, they'd listed everything they wanted to do together before they died. It'd never occurred to them that they wouldn't be friends forever...until one kiss changed everything. Now she didn't know what to call their status.

Was there an emoticon for friends with momentary lapses in romantic judgment? Maybe a fallen Cupid clutching his spinning head?

"It's our last entry for a reason—possible death. Plus, I can't do half that stuff anymore."

At Jared's snort, her drooping head lifted. "Yes, you can, and I'd never let anything happen to you. Ever."

The taut muscle of his bicep brushed against her bare shoulder, raising goose bumps. She wore a pink lace-edged tank top today—a birthday gift from a friend. She'd thought it way too girlie for her taste, but when Jared called to make plans, it'd seemed like exactly what she wanted to wear.

Which didn't bear much examining...along with her mixed-up feelings for Jared.

She loved him, had always loved him, but was she *in* love with him now?

A groan swelled in her throat, and she swallowed it back. No girl should entrust her heart to a lady-killer like Jared. Besides, she needed him in her life long term. Now, more than ever. It'd be the dumbest mistake in the world to get involved with him.

They passed the next few moments in silence, then Jared said, "Hold."

Petey stopped. She knelt on one knee, cupped his furry head and stroked his wiry hair. Large paws landed on her shoulders, and

Petey's sandpaper tongue rasped over her fingers and face, his tail slashing the ground like a whip.

"Down," Jared commanded, and the obedient dog flopped to the ground and let loose a sigh so human it made her laugh.

"You little sweetheart," she said with a chuckle. "Such a good boy."

If Jared didn't work out, she'd always have Petey, she thought, mouth twisting sideways. He lent her confidence in navigating the world. Freedom. Independence. Her lungs expanded in a deep breath.

The air smelled of wild irises. She could practically feel the scent float into her nose, her lungs, her blood. Her veins would smell of purple. Funny how her other heightened senses had rushed to fill the void left by her sight. She could identify flowers by scent, horses by their gait, women by their perfume... As for Jared, well, she had a special sense for him. She seemed to know, intuitively, whenever he was close.

And then she heard it.

A high-pitched whinny cracked in the humid air.

Her eyes flew open. "Harley!"

A blur of black and silver rushed to what must be a gate.

"Easy there, boy," Jared called, pitching his voice low and firm.

A moment later, the metallic latch clicked open and Petey led her through the opening. A carpet of greenish-brown appeared beneath her feet. The burnt-straw smell of dead grass reached her nose. She peered all around and made out the faint horizontal white of what must be a fence encircling a large space.

Her stride faltered, then stopped. "Where…?"

"Let me show you." Jared's voice sharpened with urgency.

Her lips hooked up in the corners as she pictured his kid-on-Christmas-Day expression, all bright eyes and flashing teeth, the mental image making her feel ridiculously warm and tingly. Funny how, despite her inability to "see" him, her mind, her heart, kept Jared in sharp focus, deftly recalling images like now. In some ways, she saw him clearer than ever.

He nearly dragged her off her feet to a bright yellow object, about five feet high. Round.

Her fingers slid over the hard, metallic surface.

"A barrel?" she gasped.

"Yep. Three of them. They're in the WPRA pattern using standard spacing."

"You made me a practice rink?" Her heart dropped and rose inside her like a buoy. "And trucked Harley over?"

"One hundred and thirty by two hundred foot," he pronounced, each word swelling with clear pride. "Professional. I did it for you *and* Harley."

"Jared…" She didn't know whether to smile, laugh, nod or cry and dance. "That is the kindest, the sweetest…"

His scoffing noise interrupted her. "Aw. Don't get all sentimental, Amberley. This is about winning. One of us needs to start doing it again."

"Winning, huh?"

Her elation popped and withered. She'd never be a winner again.

The tips of his boots nudged hers and his cowboy hat brim brushed the top of her head. "And it's about friends."

"Okay," she said, a breathless catch in her voice, her stomach jumping. She'd told him to stop flirting, but lately she'd stopped objecting as much. What did she want from Jared? From them?

A heavy silky neck dropped over her shoulder, a long head nudging between them.

"Hey, boy." She hugged Harley and tried ignoring the worry that'd slipped into her stomach. Walking him around a small rink posed little risk, but a real barrel racing course? What if Harley took off on her? What if she steered him into a barrel? Or a fence? What if...

"Let's get you up on Harley and give this a go."

She set her jaw and swung herself into the saddle. Jared led her back the way they'd come, toward the open gate.

"This here's your score line. I spray painted it."

She peered down at a waving streak of fluorescent orange as she turned Harley back around. "I see it."

"Good. So now look at the barrels."

She squinted into the field, and for a moment she heard it, the sound that haunted her dreams. Cheering crowds. Hooves pounding, thunderous hooves, just as fast as her heartbeat and a win, a championship, a spot on the ERA Premier touring team in her grasp, burning like a brand on her heart. Amberley shook her head and the sound stopped. Her breath whooshed out of her, and she shoved the memory down so deep it couldn't hurt her anymore.

Those days were done.

She was crazy for even trying this. Honest to goodness, she didn't know if her heart could take another failure.

Her head dropped to her hand. "I can't do this."

"Yes, you can," Jared's voice urged, static-filled. Close.

Where?

Her groping fingers landed on a walkie-talkie affixed to the side of her saddle horn.

"I can't," she whispered into it.

"Prove yourself wrong."

She peered in Jared's direction. A black-and-white blur clung to his side. Petey. Jared had trained the abandoned stray to become the ranch's top herder and now a guide dog. He could train anyone. Did he see her as just his latest project?

Or more?

And did she even want it to be more…?

"I don't have to prove anything."

"Then prove to me you're a quitter, because I don't believe it. I don't believe that about you," Jared declared. Staunch. Always her loyal defender.

"What if it's true?" She was sweating, and felt dizzy, nauseated, too small and too large all at once.

"It's not. Please don't make me beg, or do my Elvis impersonation—whichever annoys you the most."

Despite everything, a smile crept across her face. "Definitely Elvis."

He crooned a classic tune over the walkie-talkie, making Harley sidestep and nicker. And just like that a bubble of laughter escaped her, their age-old pre-competition ritual of tough love and slapstick working its usual magic.

She clamped hands over her ears. "Please make it stop!"

"Some people don't appreciate good music," he huffed, sounding so goofy that her chuckle turned into a full-on belly laugh.

Jared scrupulously maintained his reputation as the local legend and heartthrob, dressing and acting the part in public. Those who knew him best, his family and her, however, saw his silly, sometimes flat-out weird side, which made her special...a friend, sure, but maybe, just maybe they were becoming more than that.

Did she dare slide a toe over the line they'd been dancing on these past couple of weeks?

"All set?"

"You bet," she said, realizing her readiness in that instant.

"Close your eyes and picture those barrels just like we did those balls at the pool hall. Your first one's sixty feet starting at a forty-five-degree angle to your right. The distance between the first and second barrel is ninety feet, and the distance from the second barrel to the third barrel is one hundred and five feet. Got it?"

She nodded, unable to speak, as she struggled to see those barrels in her mind's eye. After hundreds and hundreds of runs around them, she'd sometimes thought she could ride a course blind. Not that she'd ever been dumb enough to try it.

Until now.

Lord help her.

"Start with walking Harley through the course."

She nodded, resolved, and tapped the top of her black Stetson for good luck.

Daddy. If you're watching. Uh… Please don't.

She squeezed her legs, and Harley moved forward a mite too quick. Tension flowed up the reins.

Keeping her hands light, but firm, she held him in check as she squinted for the first barrel. Sixty feet had never seemed so far before at this snail's pace.

"Coming in on it now, but you're crowding, ease off," Jared advised through the walkie-talkie.

A yellow blob emerged from the dim. Amberley felt each of her heartbeats hammering in her veins as she pulled Harley's head slightly to the left, away from the barrel. Dismay rocked through her when he dropped his shoulder right into the metal container, knocking it slightly.

She bit her lip, wincing for Harley, who, unable to see with his head pulled sideways, trotted too far. A groan escaped her. She'd just made one of the worst rookie mistakes. A thick knot filled her aching throat.

"Turn him around. The barrel's right there," Jared said, his voice steely, full up of no-back-down.

It prodded up her chin.

Right. Jared dared her to prove herself a quitter because he predicted she wouldn't. No one knew her better than Jared, even herself.

She guided Harley around the barrel, then rose in the saddle, giving him his head several paces later. In an instant, he took the bit and kicked into a trot that rapidly carried them across the empty space toward the second barrel.

His silver mane flew behind his lifted head, his pace, his bearing oozing confidence. Excitement. He knew this course as well as she did. Centering herself in the saddle, she counted his strides and prepared herself for the second barrel.

"Almost on it," she heard Jared say, "Rate Harley!"

Without warning, yellow burst before her, quicker than she'd expected. Alarmed, she tried gathering Harley, but he strode a length too far, their rhythm out of sync. When he caught sight of the fence, he balked, then jerked to a stop so abruptly her teeth bit her tongue.

She leaned down and stroked his quivering neck. "It's okay, Harley," she murmured over the thumping, the banging of her heart. "It's okay."

What a miserable mess. A failure.

"You quitting?" Jared's holler was so loud she could hear it through the walkie-talkie and in the clear, warm air.

"Nope."

"That's my girl."

Locking her jaw, she brought Harley around.

"Barrel's a hand's length away as you go past," Jared said. "Position him for the last one, now."

She closed her eyes, pictured that final barrel, then gave Harley his head. His legs flashed forward and back in a familiar gallop. At that speed, she instantly knew their position and how long before the last turn. Her body relaxed and rocked in time with Harley's, the familiar rhythm returning at last.

One, two, three...

She opened her eyes, and sure enough, the yellow loomed. Instinctively, she eased back into her pocket the moment her thigh flashed by the barrel, then rotated her body through a turn she felt more than she saw. Harley responded to her cue and executed a tight turn.

They thundered back in the remembered direction of the starting line.

In a second, they swept through and past the gate.

"Whoa! Hold up!" hollered Jared as they flashed by him and a barking Petey.

Oh, but it felt too good to stop! Jared jogged beside her and snagged Harley's bridle just as she pulled him up. Her breath came in short, hard pants, her pulse thundering against her eardrums. She'd done it. She'd raced a course.

"What was my time?" she gasped.

"Wasn't clocking you."

"Will you next time?"

"So, you're not quitting?"

"Never!" She laughed, exhilarated, pumped with enough adrenaline to lift her right off this saddle and into the sky. "Let's go again."

A couple of hours of hard work later, she flung herself from the saddle and into Jared's waiting arms, euphoric.

"We did it!"

One large hand stroked down her back. The other cupped the curve of her hip. "*You* did it!" His deep, soft voice held an unfamiliar note. If she had to name it, she'd say uncertainty. Did she rattle Jared's infamous confidence?

Harley whinnied.

"Okay, fine, diva, *you* did it," she joked, finding it hard to breathe this close to Jared.

They laughed, but silence soon crept over them. A smile still played about her lips, and he reached for her hand. She wanted to pull it away but couldn't bring herself to do so. He held her hand against his, flattening their mismatched palms against each other, interlocking his long fingers with her smaller ones.

"You proved me right. You're no quitter," he said, his eyes downcast, she supposed, fixed on their hands.

"Not me," she avowed, her heart raw and trembling.

Her nostrils flared as she inhaled his fresh-laundry scent, now tempered with an edge of sweat. Drawn to him, she inched nearer still, close enough for the curls of his breath to touch her face. Her pulse thundered in her ears. Oh, how she wished she could see his face. Never had the ache of her disability struck her as hard as it did in this moment.

"You looked good out there. Except for all these tangles."

As if he were handling the finest gossamer, he released her hand and swept her hair to one side of her neck, then gathered the messy strands. Not into a bun, like she sometimes did: a loose braid that drew together over her shoulder. His work-roughened fingers ran over her scalp and throat, alternating one group of hair with the other. The softest tremor ran down her spine.

Jared released her hair, then tucked a stray curl behind her ear. His other hand came to rest on the small of her back, pressing her to his chest. The warmth of him comforted her. And she could feel the exquisite tension in his muscles, the thunder of his heart.

Did he want to kiss her?

He nuzzled his head against her cheek. His fingers traced her collarbone. Her blood turned gold and glittery.

"Your skin is warm," he said throatily. "I never—" He stopped.

Her fingers pushed between his knuckles. She kept her eyes open. His lips moved to her jaw. She guided his hand to her waist. The excruciating lure of his touch hypnotized her; she couldn't flinch or refuse him. She wanted this. Today reminded her of who she used to be—a no-guts, no-glory kind of gal. She'd relived their kiss every time she'd looked at him this week and suddenly she needed to know, right here, right now, if it'd been a fluke.

"Are you flirting with me?" His teasing tone came off wrong, more serious than light.

"Could be."

"Amberley," he began, but she surged forward and kissed him. She almost knocked him to the ground. But he shot out an arm to Harley's side and braced himself as his spare arm wrapped around her middle. She let the touch, the taste of him fill her senses. His breath filled her lungs. She twined her fingers in his crisp hair, and as he kissed her fiercely, she let everything fade away.

Don't stop, don't stop.

His hands ran up her sides, her back, and clasped her. She placed her hand against his neck. She felt the thick beat of his heart. His rhythm. Her rhythm. She'd never felt anything like this in her life—this rising in her chest, this thirst to touch. She burned.

His lips nudged hers apart as he held her face in his hands and traced her lips. His thumbs brushed over her cheeks. Their foreheads touched.

Don't stop, don't stop.

His lips sampled her mouth, her cheek, her

neck, and the hollow of her throat. He slid his palms over the curve of her hips and the dip of her waist. Firm, bold strokes, brimming with rising confidence. Awakening. She undid the top button of his shirt. Her fingers slid over his collarbone.

She kissed his corded neck, and he grasped a thick handful of her hair. *Don't stop.* She'd never touched him here before. His hot smooth skin made her want to be closer still. Her hands slid farther inside his shirt.

He tensed beneath her fingers. "Amberley," he said softly, but she didn't stop. He made a low sound in his throat.

"Sweetheart." He lightly pressed his nose to hers. A slow, sweet ache rose inside her, and she didn't know what to do. Jared didn't take his eyes off her face, so she looked down at their hands, his larger hands on hers: chaffed and rough, same as hers. A match in every way but size.

Were they a match? It shocked her how much she wanted the answer to be yes.

"Sweetheart."

That single word sent a tremor through her skin. "Sweetheart?"

"You don't like darlin'." She could feel the

smile in his voice and wondered if her heart might explode in her chest.

"You've never called me sweetheart before."

Jared's strong hands cupped her shoulders, and he released a breath. "Plenty of times. Just not out loud."

A breathless silence descended, then—"What are we doing, Jared?"

The brown of his eyes vanished, and he averted his head. "I don't know."

Her heart squeezed out a sickening thump. "Do you want a relationship?"

He placed her palms on his damp cheeks and shook his head.

Disappointment rolled inside her, a thick, cold fog smothering everything. She'd wanted to know if their first kiss had been a fluke, had taken this chance and…failed. Jared wasn't a relationship kind of guy. She shouldn't have believed, even for a moment, that their friendship gave her a different status.

Stupid, *stupid* girl.

Now they'd crossed the line, twice, and they couldn't go back. At least, not her. "Then why'd you kiss me?"

"I don't know."

Her body trembled, absorbing the blow of those words.

"How come you kissed me?" he asked, his voice so hoarse she could barely hear it.

She groped for Petey's handle. "Because I wanted to know if this—" she gestured between them "—was real."

"And...?"

"Guess I was wrong."

"Amberley."

"Do you want a relationship or not?"

She spied the flesh-toned flash of his fingers as he must have run them along the brim of his hat, silent. "That's what I thought."

And with that, she trudged up the lane to his house, determined, from now on, to go it alone. Her dreams were shattered, her heart in just as many pieces.

Jared made her believe she could fly—all the way to the sun. But the sun had burned her wings clean off and sent her tumbling back to earth. At least now she knew where she stood. Where they stood.

No more Jared.

No more confusion.

No more best friend.

Another loss. What should one more matter?

But it did.

Her stinging eyes screwed shut and her mouth worked.

It did.

CHAPTER TEN

A SHRILL WHISTLE BLASTED, and Jared exploded off the painted line on a practice field beside the Cade homestead. Peering through the dim, predawn light, he bolted to an old tractor tire, heaved it over, jumped inside it, then sprang out again and dashed to the rope ladder atop flattened grass. His feet weaved, in and out, as he navigated the rungs, and his heart bashed madly against his chest. Sweat dripped from his hair, trickled down his cheeks and slicked his steaming torso.

Clear of the rope, he blasted to a stack of hay bales, spun, reversed course, dodged around them, then repeated the maneuver when a second, then third group loomed. His cleats churned up the soft earth as he sprinted to the marked "end zone," pushing his screaming muscles to keep working, despite the grueling workout he'd begun an hour and a half ago.

He slowed to a jog, then a walk, then a stop.

Bent at the waist, he heaved air into his burning chest. He'd pushed himself hard today, and every part of his body felt broken, including his heart.

He blinked hard in the dawn light, allowing the events of the previous day to seep slowly into him. Amberley hadn't let him drive her home and was blocking all his calls. It stung hard that he'd left her feeling confused and wounded. He hurt, too. And his head buzzed, his thoughts muddled. Grabbing the toe of his cleat, he pulled his heel up behind him and stretched.

Yesterday's kiss had knocked him flat. Every emotion he'd ever had for her, ones he didn't know he possessed, had bubbled to the surface. He loved Amberley, always had, always would. Only now those feelings felt deeper, fiercer, harder. Like he could conquer the world with just one hand as long as she held the other one.

Was he *in* love with her?

He'd never been in love before and didn't know what it felt like. It'd be every kind of wrong to mess with Amberley's heart while he tried figuring it out. Was he ready for a real relationship?

He'd never done anything by half. When he loved a woman, he'd love hard, with everything that he was, with all that he had. But what he had right now wasn't much. Until he achieved his goal to return to a starting football position, reclaimed his hero status, he'd never have a worthy life to offer another, especially someone like Amberley.

"A minute forty," his mother called, interrupting his thoughts as she hurried his way. "You shaved off six seconds!" The pinkening light gleamed on her silver hair and set her frameless lenses aglow. She wore a light pink sweater buttoned over a flowered house dress and white sneakers with a matching pink swoosh decal. "Very good."

"Not good enough," he muttered, twisting side to side, elongating his lats.

A soft hand fell on his shoulder. "You're trying, honey. That's what matters."

He bent at the waist and touched his toes. "Dad wouldn't agree." Pa wanted a winner, a hero. The real world didn't award points for effort.

"Your dad's gone."

"And now you're dating Boyd Loveland,"

he said as he straightened, instantly regretting the bitter words the moment they left his lips.

The corners of her mouth drooped and her brow furrowed. "We're not seeing each other. Not anymore."

"How come?" he asked, though he could guess. Without Boyd knowing, his children had blocked his mother's number on his cell, and Jared and his siblings did the same to their mom, cutting off communication…phase one of the plan.

Phase two started next week.

Instead of answering, she whirled and marched away, her stride brisk, her shoulders hunched as if she faced a strong headwind. "What can I get you for breakfast?" she called over her shoulder.

"Eggs and bacon. But I can get it."

In the distance, Mount Sopris's bald top glittered, the rising sun peeking over its crest. Its first rays sliced through the chill, and pure air and dew-soaked grass brushed his calves as he followed his mother back to the homestead.

"Let me. Makes me feel useful."

A sigh heaved out of him. Was waiting on him and his siblings all that gave Ma's life purpose? She had her new grandson, plus her church group. She also chaired the annual garden gala. Those counted...but were they enough? There had to be other ways to fill her time besides Boyd Loveland.

"Alright, then," he muttered, thinking hard, for the first time, about his mother's life, or lack of one, outside of her children... "Much appreciated."

Petey bounced up and nudged his wet nose into Jared's hand. "Ready for more training, boy? Your test is coming up quick."

"Was Amberley impressed with him?" The hem of his mother's housecoat belled around her ankles as they mounted the rear porch steps. Petey streaked off after a chittering squirrel.

"I reckon." He held the door for her, kicked off his dirt-crusted cleats and followed Ma into the kitchen.

She grabbed a frying pan from the wrought-iron rack above a large granite-topped island. "She seemed to leave awful quick yesterday."

"Uh-huh," he murmured, noncommittal. After grabbing eggs, bacon and a bottle of orange juice from the fridge, he joined her at the island.

His mother cracked an egg and dropped it

into a bowl. A thick white square of paper, his brother Jack and Dani's wedding invitation, dated just a week away, rested on the brown-and-white-speckled surface. It struck him suddenly that Jack would no longer just be his brother, he'd be Dani's husband, and someday, a father, too. A strange yearning opened inside him, the wanting for something previously unknowable. The same sensation that came over him whenever he witnessed James cuddling with Sofia and Javi.

A family.

A love of his own.

Was he ready for all of that with Amberley?

After dropping eggshells in the garbage, his mother turned. "Did she like the training rink?"

"Seemed to." He perched on a stool, picked up his cell and scrolled through a screen of baseball stats.

"Jared William Cade."

Hearing his full name spoken by his mother meant only one thing. Trouble. He lowered his phone quickly.

"I'm talking to you."

"I'm listening."

Her elbow jerked as she whisked the eggs,

her steady gaze on him. "What's going on with you and Amberley?"

Shoot. "Nothing. Want me to put on the bacon?"

She nodded. "You two fighting?"

He flicked on the stovetop, placed a pan on the front burner, then peeled back the top of the package. A smoky, apple wood scent rose from the cured meat. "*I'm* not."

His mother clucked. "What'd you do?"

His lips burned as the memory of the kiss returned, so real he could taste and feel Amberley, sweet and spice.

"*K-I-S-S-I-N-G!*"

Javi sashayed in the kitchen wearing Batman pajamas. "I saw them, Grandma!"

"Javi!" Sofia smoothed his tangled dark hair from his face. "You didn't brush your teeth yet." She met Jared's eye. "Sorry. Kids and their imaginations…"

He didn't need a mirror to know red now stained his cheeks. If Javi knew, then James knew…

"Well. It's about time," his mother exclaimed once they were alone again. She elbowed him out of the way and set another pan on the stove.

A bacon slice dropped from his numb hand, landing half in, half out of the skillet. "What?"

"You and Amberley are made for each other."

He placed ten more slices in the fryer, mulling that over. "How do you know if you're in love?"

A sizzling sound rose as his mother poured the eggs into her pan. "It's more a feeling than a knowing."

Small bubbles appeared around the edges of the bacon, and he nudged them with the fork. How did he feel? He saw her face each time he closed his eyes. She haunted his thoughts, made him wish to do grand and wonderful things in her name, made him want to be a man who deserved to be by her side.

But would those feelings last forever?

He had no experience with permanent and wouldn't start something he couldn't see right through to the death-us-do-part end. Heroes didn't fail their women, and he didn't have a crystal ball telling him if he and Amberley would make it.

"How'd you feel about Pa?"

Bacon fat splatted in the silence as she stirred the eggs. "Comfortable," she said after a moment. "Like I'd been lost and just found my way home."

He turned the darkening strips. "Doesn't sound exciting."

"It doesn't have to be. It just has to feel right."

"James said you dated Boyd Loveland in high school."

Her spatula scraped the side of her pan. "True."

"Did that feel right, too?"

"I thought so."

"What about now?" He clamped his lips together. He shouldn't be encouraging her to talk about a man they needed her to forget.

"I thought…maybe…" She slid the eggs onto two plates and he added bacon. "Guess I'll never know."

Glasses in hand, he joined her back at the island. "Why's that?"

A twinge of guilt turned his stomach, and he pushed the eggs around on his plate with his fork. He knew why she'd never know… he and the Loveland gang wouldn't let them.

"He hasn't called in a week. I guess I'm just an old fool for having a young woman's dream." Her stool scraped back as she stood.

"I'm not as hungry as I thought. Just leave the dishes in the sink for me when you're done, honey."

He watched her slumped shoulders as she retreated to her room, and his heart squeezed. His mother wasn't an old fool. He grabbed her cell phone, unblocked Boyd's number and slid it back next to her purse before he changed his mind.

He speared his fork in his eggs and shoved a big bite into his mouth. Suddenly ravenous, he chewed furiously, in a hurry to get to Spirit Ranch and Amberley.

His mother deserved a chance to figure out her feelings.

And so did he.

AMBERLEY SWAYED ATOP Harley later that afternoon as he followed the string of horses traveling on Spirit Ranch's beginner trail. The sunlight warmed her skin, and the weight around her shoulders drifted away momentarily as she lost herself in the moment.

Carbondale in summer was the most beautiful place on earth. With her eyes closed, she pictured the scene her senses relayed. Songbirds flitted overhead, calling out their territory. A soft breeze carried the sweet smell of wildflowers and rustled the leaves of cottonwood trees arching overhead.

When she opened her eyes, she peered at the smears of sunlight filtering through the canopy. Harley threw his head back and opened his mouth in a huge yawn that mirrored her boredom. With the reins loose in her hand, Harley on autopilot, she felt more like a burden than a rider. What a difference a day made. The exhilarating rush of yesterday's barrel racing practice, followed by a shattering kiss, looped in her brain.

Bitter heat rose inside. She'd acted a fool to fling herself at Jared. What had she been thinking? Doing? She should have known he'd get squirrely when she pinned him down about a relationship. Yet she'd gone ahead and done it anyway.

You wanted to know, soothed the angel on one shoulder.

You looked like an idiot, bit out the devil on the other, savage, sulking.

Her shoulders slumped and her head dipped. For once her vision loss worked to her advantage. She couldn't see Jared, riding in the lead. It'd been easy to avoid catching sight of him for much of today's therapy session. Whatever expression he wore, she didn't want to see it: pity, regret and, worst of all, concern. She'd done her best to pretend she didn't want him anymore. She would just have to pretend hard enough to make it come true.

The trees must have thinned because she could hear Crystal River where it raked over the shallows to her right. The tangy smell of horsehair crept into her nostrils. She bent down and patted Harley's velvet-soft neck.

"Sorry, boy," she whispered, and he bobbed his head, shaking the silky strands of his mane over her hand. This morning, he'd greeted her with a high-pitched whinny, raring to go, she supposed, back to the practice rink. Now she'd ruined not only her chances, but his, as well. That hurt worse.

The hard edge of a folded-up flier dug inside her pocket.

The ERA Premier touring group was pleased to announce tryouts in Denver next month, her mother had read out loud over breakfast.

Four weeks.

If she hadn't messed up with Jared, she could be training for it. Maybe she didn't have much of a chance, but it would have been a shot. Now, she'd lost her friend, her heart and this opportunity.

For her and for Harley.

"Everyone pull up in the clearing," she heard Jared shout up ahead.

A moment later, the brown-green of the trees parted as she passed through them, and the open field surrounded her in an explosion of space and green grass and blue sky. She swung down from the saddle and waited for someone to guide her to a tie-up spot for Harley.

"Want me to take him?" she heard Maverick ask.

Her gaze traveled up, up and up to reach where his face must be. Corn-fed and stalk-high, her mother always said about the Loveland boys.

"I'd appreciate it, thanks."

After accompanying Maverick and securing Harley beneath a copse of trees, she groped forward and helped a few of the other children. Their happy chatter eased the strain inside her, and she found herself smiling when one of them thrust what felt like a bouquet in her hands.

"For me?" she buried her nose in the fragrant flowers. Honeysuckle. Her favorite. And not easy to find.

"It's from Jared." Emily giggled. Then Amberley noticed the tall, broad-shouldered shape behind the child's wheelchair.

"Please tell him thanks," she said, keeping her voice steady despite her jumpy heart. Flowers? Why? What did they mean?

"Jared," Emily twisted around and shouted, "Amberley says thanks."

He chuckled. "I heard."

"There you are!" a woman exclaimed, Emily's mother if Amberley recalled the voice correctly. "The peanut butter and jelly sandwiches are going fast. Best hurry."

A moment later she found herself alone with Jared. Her lungs expanded, dragging in the subtle spice of his cologne.

"Can we talk?"

She shook her head. "You said everything yesterday."

"Not everything. Would you hear me out? Please?"

She wanted to sink through the ground and escape this agonizing moment. No doubt he'd prepared one of the gentlemanly breakup talks he gave infatuated ladies. Jared embodied old-school cowboy cordiality. He couldn't bear to hurt a woman, and now she'd become just another one to let down gently.

Her back teeth clamped together.

Fine. Get her done, then.

"I'm listening." She leaned against the tree behind her, and its rough bark scraped through her T-shirt. In the distance, the children shrieked and the horses nickered quietly to one another beneath the cool shade trees.

"I was wrong."

She dropped her crossed arms. That didn't sound like a "let you down gently" speech. She lifted her head and tried focusing on his face. He'd swept off his hat. She discerned that much. As for the rest, his exterior remained as mysterious as the inside.

"Wrong about?" she prompted.

"Us. Look. Yesterday, well, I wasn't expecting that kiss…"

The swish-hiss of Harley's tail, slapping at a fly, snapped in the clear, dry air.

"You think I planned on it?"

Heat crept up her neck at his silence. Of course he'd believe that. Practically every red-blooded, single female in the county schemed to nail down Jared Cade. But she wasn't one of them…or she hadn't used to be.

"I'm hungry, Jared. If you don't mind, I'd like to grab lunch before we head back."

His strong hands slid into hers, halting her. "I have feelings for you," he blurted.

She went cold and hot at once. "What kind of feelings?"

"Kind of sickish, sometimes."

She yanked her hands free. "Sick? *I* make you sick?"

"No. It's just. Aw. Shoot. What I mean is lately, whenever you're near, my heart pounds so hard it hurts. And my stomach jumps and twists."

"And that's a good thing?" She had never felt so feverish, so incapable of efficiently gathering her thoughts. What did he mean?

A warm rush of air escaped him. Then— "I never felt this way around a woman before. Swear."

Oh.

The petals of her heart unfolded. If she affected him unlike any other gal, she must be special, right?

Then the memory of Jared's indecision yesterday, his rejection, returned in a stinging rush. Jared needed to prove he wanted her for certain, for the long haul, before she'd risk opening up to him again.

"I should be pleased you're nauseous around me?"

"You're not making this easy on me." Jared trailed a finger down the side of her face.

She eased away. His touch lingered on her skin and made her insides giddy. "Why should I? Because everyone else does?"

Widening her stance, she planted her hands on her hips and squared off in his direction. "I always thought we were the lucky ones, people who achieved things easily, champions others admired, but now, now I don't see it that way," she said. "There's something special about working hard for something, giving it everything you've got even when you don't think you've got a chance, because then it's not about the win, it's about the effort, which, I'm discovering, is more important."

The blur of movement suggested he shook his head. He didn't get it. For the very first time since her disability, *she* actually felt a little sorry for Jared. They were no longer kindred spirits.

"Amberley, please," he pleaded, his voice

as raw as a bruise. "I've got two left feet and a swollen tongue around you lately. Nothing I say or do comes out right. I don't know if we're coming or going, but I know I want to find out. Give me a chance."

He framed her face with his hands then leaned over and kissed her. Thoroughly, sweetly, wonderfully. For a moment, everything stilled: her breath, movement, her heart. The world, possibly.

"No!"

She shoved his chest.

"No?" His eyelashes blinked rapidly, brushing against her temple.

"It's not that easy." Her breathing slowly returned to normal, though her heart still pumped overtime. "You don't get to decide when and where and how."

"But I thought…"

"If you want me, you're going to have to work for me." She ducked under his arm and strode forward with her arms reaching for the tree she glimpsed in front of her. She mustn't stumble or fall. Time to declare her independence. Stand tall. When she reached the tree, she rested her boots on its protruding roots and raised her chin.

Jared advanced. "We care about each other. Why make this complicated?"

"Because I deserve to be wooed. Chased. Convinced. And you don't get to know if you'll win in the end."

She didn't have to see to imagine his mouth dropping open, his brows meeting over his nose. Had a woman ever talked this way to Jared before? She doubted it. Or if they had, he'd have moved on quickly.

Well. So be it.

"Woo you?"

She would have laughed at his utter bewilderment if not for the emotion jittering inside. Did Jared even know how to woo a woman? They usually chased him. It'd be interesting to see him try. For the first time since her vision loss, she felt like her old self...no, *better* than that. She'd been tested by adversity and respected herself now more than she did after winning any of her world championships. Jared, on the other hand, had never had to struggle for a thing in his life, and it showed.

"I deserve it," she continued, "just like any woman." Her lack of vision didn't make her less than others.

A tense silence descended and beads of perspiration rose on her forehead as she waited for him to speak. Maybe she'd scared him away… and maybe that wouldn't be a bad thing, no matter what her aching heart told her. She didn't need a man who wouldn't move mountains to win her heart.

"You deserve everything," he breathed, sliding his fingers down the length of her arm.

"Then show me."

"How?"

She yanked the flier out of her pocket and held it out. "Let's start here."

CHAPTER ELEVEN

"THANK YOU, KIDS."

Jared returned his mother's hand squeeze and averted his gaze. How much longer before Boyd, and his "date," arrived at the restaurant and spoiled her happiness?

He shouldn't have come tonight.

Last week, Justin called him a traitor after he'd intercepted Boyd's call on Ma's unblocked phone. Cades were men of their word, Justin reminded him, fuming. They wouldn't back out of their pact with the Lovelands. Plus, Boyd's motivations for wooing Ma hadn't changed. Rumor had it his town credit ran out, something he'd fix by marrying a well-off widow like Joy.

Jared could either get with the program, Justin warned, by blocking Boyd's number again, or stay out of the loop like James. Neither choice sat well with Jared. He'd find a way to help his ma tonight without breaking his oath to his siblings.

"It's your anniversary." Jewel leaned forward and grabbed kettle chips from a bowl in the center of their table. "We didn't want you to forget *Daddy*."

He and Justin exchanged a swift look. They'd picked today for the second part of their plan so she'd remember how happy she'd been with their pa. He rolled one tense shoulder, then the next. But if Boyd made her happy, too, she deserved another chance at love.

"Today would have been thirty-five years." She pulled off her fogging glasses and polished them with a bright blue scarf that matched her handbag, eye makeup and earrings. "He loved this place and especially those." She gestured to a bowl of bread-and-butter pickles.

"He loved you best," Jared said.

Someday, he'd give Amberley the same devotion…if she'd let him. He slipped a finger inside his shirt collar and yanked it from his neck.

It was dim and warm outside beneath Smokey's red-and-white-striped awning. Locals after tonight's baby back ribs special packed the picnic tables. Grills ran the length of the tented space, dishing up foil-wrapped corn on the cob and baked potatoes from different ends. Beneath the smell of tangy sauce and roasted meat lay a foundation of cigarettes, barn and sweet tea. In a corner, Heath Loveland crooned a Toby Keith song while Maverick played drums.

Jared waved back at a couple of gals, pulled down his hat, then slid lower in his seat. Wanting something and getting it weren't guaranteed, he'd discovered this week. Amberley had been single-minded while practicing for the upcoming tryouts. It'd been disorienting spending time around a woman who barely seemed to notice him.

But Amberley wasn't just any woman, and he'd been doing his best to woo her the way she'd asked. He'd picked flowers, made her a playlist of their favorite road-trip songs, gave her a bag of Lucky Charms—marshmallows only, the way she liked—heck, he'd even fried up bacon in the shape of a heart and earned a belly laugh from his brother James for his troubles. None of it, however, won him more than a smile from Amberley.

Turned out, his reputation as a ladies' man was a sham. Catching the ones who jumped at you didn't take much effort. Catching those who stayed out of reach, like Amberley, required a new level of tenacity. Once he won her heart—if she gave him a second chance—it'd be all the sweeter for the extra effort. He wasn't as big a fan of "easy" as he used to be.

Another sign he was changing? He hadn't quit his grueling workouts, despite little progress and an agent who'd stopped returning calls. He had no team, and no prospects, yet he pushed himself harder than ever, just like the Spirit Ranch kids and Amberley. Effort meant more than the win, she'd said.

He might have to content himself with that, he thought, sliding a toothpick into his mouth.

"Boyd!" someone called, and his ma's head snapped around. The older man sauntered in, his lean, wide-shouldered frame belying his age. He snagged many of the ladies' attention as he searched out a table.

Joy half rose, then dropped back in her chair when Boyd gestured for a diminutive woman to precede him. Must be his cousin, Jared pondered, noting that same deep blue eye color. When the Lovelands heard she planned on visiting, they'd coordinated the "accidental" meeting with the Cades.

The plan hinged on Joy believing Boyd hadn't returned her calls, or attended line dancing, because he now dated someone else. His kids had found one excuse after another to prevent Boyd from leaving home Thursday nights.

"Could we get the check?" Ma whispered, staring down at her lap and blinking fast as Boyd and his cousin sat at a nearby table. A paper napkin came apart in her fidgeting hands.

"Ma?" Jared slid an arm around her trembling shoulders.

"Guess I'm not hungry anymore." He had to lean down to catch her words.

"Cake's coming!" Jewel announced heavily, her eyes on their mother, her lips turned down in the corners. Looked like his siblings shared Jared's regret. Talking about a plan in the abstract and witnessing the real pain it caused were two different things altogether.

A crowd of servers descended on their table and lustily sang "Happy Birthday" to Joy, oblivious to the frosting that spelled out Happy Anniversary. The crowd whistled and stomped their feet, all except Boyd Loveland, who'd grown pale when his eyes locked with

Joy's. His mother's mouth worked, then she yanked her gaze back to the family and forced a shaky smile.

"Why, thanks, everyone. This does my heart good." Joy leaned over to pat Justin's and Jewel's hands. Jewel blinked fast, and Justin pressed his lips together so tight they blanched.

Enough. This farce had gone on long enough.

"Boyd!" Jared called. The older man tore his gaze from Joy and regarded him. "Join us."

"Don't have room," Justin said, sliding down to occupy the empty spot at the end of their table.

"Course we do." Jared ignored his mother's small head shake and squeezed her knee under the table.

"Wouldn't want to put you folks out." Boyd stood to his impressive height, tall enough that Jared had to crane his neck a mite. What did they feed those Lovelands?

"We were just leaving anyways." Jewel signaled for their server. "Ma's feeling poorly, so we're taking this to go."

In a couple of strides, Boyd squatted beside Joy and swept off his hat. "You alright, darlin'?" he asked, his voice gruff and tender.

She lifted her chin slightly. "Looks like *you're* doing just fine." She nodded at Boyd's companion. "No need to bother yourself with me when you're on a date."

"A date?" The petite lady joined them in a cloud of choking perfume. "I'm his cousin, Michelle. Was coming through town and Boyd offered to treat me out so we could hear my nephews play." She pointed at Heath and Maverick.

Justin gulped half a bottle of pop while Jewel crushed chips in her hands. Jared bit back a smile. *The truth will out.*

"Cousin?" Joy twisted her pearl necklace. "I thought…"

"Hey, wait." Michelle's eyes narrowed on Boyd. "Is this the lady friend you've been talking about?"

His mother stilled. "I don't know. How many does he have?"

"Only one's taken his fancy since he lost Grace. I'm thinking that's you. Am I right, Boyd?"

He nodded slowly. "Not sure if the lady welcomes my attention, though."

"The lady in question hasn't received your attention since you don't return her calls." Joy tossed her napkin onto the table.

"What calls?" Boyd cocked his head. "I've rung you every day for the past couple of weeks. How come you don't answer?"

"I don't understand." Joy pulled her phone from her purse, and her thumb brushed over the screen. "There aren't any messages from you. No record you called."

"Same here," Boyd said without looking up from his cell.

"But how could that be…?"

"Blocked," Michelle cut in, helping herself to a square of corn bread from Justin's plate. "You blocked each other's numbers. My son taught me how to do that so the credit card companies would stop phoning."

"But I didn't block you…"

"Neither did I…"

Jewel sliced a finger across her neck while Justin dropped his chin to his chest.

Joy held out her phone. "Could someone explain?"

Heath ended his set and the restaurant quieted. Jared accessed Boyd in her contacts and clicked on his name so his information filled the screen.

"It says blocked," Joy breathed, peering over Jared's shoulder. "But how?"

"You didn't block me on purpose?" The lines on Boyd's forehead smoothed.

Joy beamed at him. "Must have been an accident." Then her smile faltered. "Why did you block *me*?"

"I didn't..." Boyd's steely gaze leveled on them. "Are my kids involved in this?"

"Yes," said Maverick, joining them with his younger brother, Heath. "We all were."

"You wanted to keep us apart?" Boyd demanded.

"Yes, sir." Heath raked a hand through his hair, making it stand up every which way.

Joy's wide eyes swept round the table. "I'll be." Then she started to laugh.

Boyd's deep chuckle wove with hers, leaving the rest of them dumbfounded. When Joy scooched over, Boyd slid in beside her. "History repeating itself."

Michelle plopped down next to Justin, and Jewel blushed scarlet when Heath settled close to her. Maverick remained on his feet, rocking back on his heels.

"What's that mean?" groused Justin, never gracious in defeat.

Michelle grabbed a rib from Justin's plate, undeterred by his glower, and pointed it at Boyd and his mother. "It seems people have been trying to break these two up for years."

"Still haven't succeeded." Boyd chucked his mother gently under the chin, eliciting a growl from Justin.

"Down, Justin," hissed Jewel. "I want to hear this."

Michelle nodded as she chewed, clearly relishing the attention. "You see," she mumbled, swallowed, then said, "apparently your mother's folks thought my cousin was no good for her."

"Sounds right," muttered Justin, then— "Ow!"

Jewel lowered her fist fast at Heath's astonished expression.

"Anyways," continued Michelle, tucking into some beans. "Joy got hurt when Boyd took her to Deadman's Drop."

Justin jerked his chin at Boyd, approval flashing in his eyes. The dangerous spot, notorious for causing endless injuries and even one death, made it Justin's favorite swimming hole, of course.

"While she recuperated in the hospital, Joy's parents told the nurses to refuse Boyd's gifts and to stop him from visiting."

"Couldn't understand why he'd abandon me," Joy mused. Jared noticed her hand now rested close to Boyd's on the table.

"I figured she was mad at me for dragging her there. Broke my heart when she returned my gifts. I enlisted in the army hoping to forget her." Boyd shook his head. "Didn't work."

"You must have come back on leave…" Jared prompted, fascinated like the rest of the group. Jewel leaned so far forward, her braids dangled above her applesauce. Heath drummed his nails on the table, knee jittering. Even Justin sat straight for once. Maverick paced around the table.

"Yep. We met and cleared everything up then." Boyd and his mother exchanged wistful smiles.

Jewel stopped biting her nail and lowered her hand. "So why didn't you get together?"

"I came home seven months before your brother Jack was born," Boyd answered.

"So. Wait." Jewel frowned down at her

watch, then peered up again. "Ma was married and she still snuck out to meet you?"

Jared's eyebrows rose. His mother would never betray his father.

"No." Joy cleared her throat, then met their stares head-on. "Truth is, this is actually my thirty-fourth anniversary. Your father and I married *after* we had Jack. We didn't want Jack to know..."

"That he was born out of wedlock," breathed Jewel, her eyes wide.

"Did you marry Pa because you had to?" Justin practically fire-breathed.

"No." Ma paused and her lids lowered. "I loved your father. Boyd and I agreed we just weren't meant to be."

"Until now." Boyd gathered her hand in his and turned it over gently, as if examining a precious artifact. Ma's lashes rose, and they exchanged a long look, anguish mixed with hope tangled in something Jared struggled to name, but felt: wonder.

Was this what Ma meant when she said love was more a feeling than a knowing?

"Then *we* tried breaking you two up again." Heath's lips vibrated with the force of his exhale. "That's not called karma… It's…what's the word? It's…"

"Rotten," Jared supplied, firm. "Sticking our noses where they don't belong." He stuck a hand out to Boyd. "Sorry, sir."

Boyd pumped his hand, then released it. "According to Maverick, you've been doing a good job at Spirit Ranch."

"Maverick said that?" Jared's eyes swept to his nemesis.

Maverick shrugged. "I call it like I see it."

"Thanks, man." Compliments flowed in Jared's direction regularly, but hearing one from taciturn Maverick somehow meant more.

He wasn't going soft and getting friendly with a Loveland was he?

"Does this mean we get to call Jack a bastard during the wedding toast?" Justin's dark eyes glinted with either humor or menace… never easy to decipher with him.

His mother sputtered on her drink and lowered her glass. "No—" Cough. Cough. "I—"

"Kidding, Ma. Jeez." Justin's teeth flashed white against his dark facial scruff.

The group breathed a collective sigh of relief.

"How about we let these two finish their

dinner?" Heath stood and assisted Jewel out of the bench seat.

Justin angled his head at the pair, caught Jared's eye and mouthed, "Whaaaaat?" Jared rubbed his eyes to be sure his vision worked correctly. Since when had Jewel *ever* needed help, let alone accepted it?

"Anyone for pool?" asked Maverick. His gaze swept over the group, then stopped on Jared.

"Only if you're in the mood to part with some money."

Maverick grinned. "You're on."

"Does this mean the feud's over?" Jared grabbed a pool stick a moment later and began chalking it.

Maverick dropped the balls in the holder, then straightened, one side of his mouth lifting.

"Heck, no."

"FIFTEEN, TEN!" AMBERLEY heard Jared holler as she and Harley thundered by him in a choking cloud of dust. She wheeled her black stallion around and trotted back to the fence, breathing hard. Sweat streamed down the back of her shirt, and the reins slid inside her slick fingers. She brushed the grit from her mouth and eyes.

"Pull up!" Jared called, but she'd already anticipated the distance and reined in Harley a yard from the gate. Harley's steaming sides heaved beneath her legs. Flinging back his head, he shook his silver mane, and she heard him blow hard. The pungent smell of his lather filled her nose.

What a champion. They'd been practicing for hours in the relentless summer heat, and he'd responded to every cue without hesitation, his trust, his determination to please her unfailing. No horse had more heart, more grit than Harley.

It was hard explaining the connection between a rider and a horse to someone who wasn't a horse person. The bond grew out of constantly taking care of each other, making sure the other one felt supported and loved. Harley gave and gave and gave. No matter what, he'd always been there for her—in the rink, in the stable—and he provided the same support to the Spirit Ranch children. His affectionate nature made him beloved in their small world, as much a star as he'd once been on the rodeo circuit.

"I'll get you back there soon, boy," she whispered, her voice hoarse, her throat raw. Leaning forward, she stroked Harley's wet neck.

She rolled her eyes up to Jared's blurred shape as he approached, Petey by his side. He'd donned a white hat today, she made out, and she pictured how it must be bringing out the golden brown of his eyes and contrasting nicely with his tan skin. Despite her resolve to focus only on riding this week, a flutter of awareness skittered over her skin.

It'd been a week since he'd held her, kissed her, and she missed his touch with a bone-deep ache. Her need for him shocked her, but she'd stayed strong, wanting to be sure he wouldn't take what she offered just because it came easy. If he worked to win her, he'd prove his feelings were real and meant to last. She'd accept nothing less.

"Fifteen ten?" she croaked out, repeating the time, hoping she had it wrong.

"You shaved off a tenth of a second." Jared's approving tone broadcasted "good enough."

Amberley laid her cheek atop Harley's head as he shifted on his hooves and tucked his nose into his chest. "I need to be in the fourteens for the tryouts."

"You'll get there."

She buried her shaking fingers in Harley's damp mane, hiding the tremble that seized her exhausted muscles. Pain wrapped around her spine and knotted in her shoulders. She rolled one, then the other, hoping to ease the gripping tension.

Jared sauntered closer and pressed what felt like a water bottle in her hand. "Let's call it a day."

She shoved herself upright. "We can get under fifteen. One more run."

"Nah. Save it for tomorrow."

She brought the water to her lips, and the cool fluid splashed down her throat, easing the burn. "We practiced an hour longer yesterday."

"It wasn't ninety-five degrees yesterday."

She nodded. Still, she had to push herself or she'd never make the ERA Premier touring team. Winning consecutive world championships hadn't guaranteed her a spot in the past. She doubted this time would be any different. Still, she'd give it her all. In fact, the stacked odds only drove her harder. The children planned on attending the tryouts; she wanted to show them having a disability never stopped you from chasing your dreams.

She passed him back the half-empty bottle. "Give the rest to Petey. We'll quit right after this last run."

A frustrated sound, half groan and half sigh, escaped Jared. "Stubborn woman."

She tapped the top of her Stetson and squeezed Harley's billowing sides to get him moving again. "I'll take that as a compliment."

"It is," he shouted after her, his voice warm.

Daddy, if you're watching, maybe just use one eye...okay?

Harley jerked into a gallop at her signal and veered toward the first barrel, its position so familiar to her now, she could almost close her eyes.

"Too wide, angle in ten degrees," she heard Jared say through the walkie-talkie.

Harley didn't adjust when she tugged on the reins. A beat of concern fluttered inside. She pulled harder and breathed a quick sigh of relief as he swerved last minute. Then they flashed by and swept around the first barrel. Wide.

She leaned low over his neck and gave him his head. "Come on, boy," she urged. They'd lost precious time there. Harley elongated his stride, and his hooves churned up the rink as they hurtled to the second barrel…his gait a bit jerky.

A trickle of fear formed in the back of Amberley's mind. Was Harley flagging? Horses made mistakes when they were overtired. Dangerous ones.

"Coming on the next barrel. Angle back," Jared called sooner than necessary, she judged, based on her counting. He must be worried Harley might balk at the approaching wall.

She held her position a beat longer, wanting to give Harley maximum speed going into this turn. They had to get under fourteen seconds.

Yellow flashed as they dashed by the second barrel, then past. Too far! Cold-hot shock swarmed inside when Harley sprinted headlong at the wall. She leaned, struggling to turn him, but he responded a beat too late and his hips slid out from under him. The ground rose to meet them, then dropped as he reared, squealing, attempting to jump over the barrel to keep them upright. To save her. To save them both.

His hooves flailed and then he stumbled, tripped by the obstacle. She heard Jared holler and then a pop, a sickening sound like a gunshot, before Harley dropped to the dirt, kicking and jerking.

Her pulse slammed in her veins and her harsh breath sounded in her ears. Harley! He rolled side to side, his tail lashing. His agonized cries tore right through her chest and ripped her heart out.

Strong hands grabbed her beneath her arms and hauled her out from under Harley's crushing weight. Petey raced around in a black-and-white streak barking frantically.

"Are you okay?" Jared choked out, clasping her tight. Petey butted her legs, sniffing and woofing. "Petey, down!" Jared ordered. The dog quieted and Jared's fingers ran the length of her, but she jerked free and fell to her knees beside her injured horse. "Harley!" Tears streamed down her face, the world a waterfall, a deluge of agony.

Jared kneeled beside her. "What happened?"

Panic closed on her tongue and refused to surrender even one word as Harley continued struggling to stand, neighing wildly. She felt his eyes on her, pleading for her help, confused and full of pain. When she reached for his thrashing limbs to assess his injuries, Jared yanked her back.

"Put this over his eyes and stay clear." Something soft, his T-shirt by its laundry-soap smell, dropped in her hands.

She scrambled to Harley's head, draped the cloth over his eyes, then pressed her face to his, her heart pounding erratically. "It's okay, boy," she crooned, trying to calm him so Jared could check his legs. Harley stilled, listening close, trusting her like he always did. "You're going to be okay." Her voice cracked, because he might not be okay…she'd heard a popping sound.

"His front left leg isn't bending," Jared said, grim.

Her thoughts skipped and skidded and skittered. No. Not Harley. A broken leg sentenced horses to death. A black tide of fear overwhelmed her.

"Shhhhhhhhhhhh," she crooned to Harley, her chest aching. He pulled back his lips and pressed his teeth against her neck. Tears splashed down her face at his familiar, loving gesture. Even in this horrible, horrible moment, he wanted to reassure her. To take care of her.

She had to save him.

"Saw what happened," she heard someone huff, out of breath. James, Jared's older brother, she guessed. "Can he get up?"

"Not on his own. His leg could be broken."

Silence fell as she continued stroking Harley's quivering nose. Then he squealed in pain again and heaved. Petey howled, then hushed. Her pulse thundered in her veins.

"He won't let me touch it long enough to be certain," James uttered. "But it's paining him like a break."

"I just called Dr. Cooper," gasped another voice. Female. Jewel, Amberley guessed. "His wife says he's out on an emergency call. Stable fire. She's not sure how quick he'll be able to come. Could be hours, but she said she'd try to find someone else."

Harley's jerking movements slowed, his strength ebbing. "Hang in there, Harley!" Amberley whispered in his ear.

"He's suffering," James said heavily. "Amberley, what's your call?"

In the sudden silence, Harley's breathing labored.

"Amberley?" Jared smoothed a hand over her brow.

She lifted her head slowly. It weighed a million pounds. "He's not getting up on his own steam."

"What do you want to do, sweetheart?"

Do? She wanted to reverse the clock, back to the time when she should have paid attention to her exhausted horse, not her racing time. She'd failed Harley completely.

"I can take care of," James cleared his throat "things, if you all want to head back to the house."

"No!" she wouldn't leave Harley just like he wouldn't leave her. Ever. She didn't need to ask James how he'd "take care of things." On the rodeo circuit, she'd witnessed animals put down when euthanasia wasn't available.

And maybe a bullet equaled a humane solution, but she couldn't let Harley go this way. He was a fighter. They'd battle through together. But if he stayed down too long, his temperature would drop and his organs fail. Plus, the pressure of his body on the hard ground might damage the nerves on that side of him.

"I've got an idea. Come, Petey!" Jared pressed a kiss to her forehead and hurried off.

She buried her face in Harley's neck and threw her arms around him, giving him as best a hug as she could manage, knowing how much he loved them. Would this be the last one they ever shared? She could. Not. Bear. It.

He lifted his head, then dropped it again, and a female hand slipped into hers. "We're here for you, Amberley," Jewel said.

"We'll do everything we can for him," James added. "Whatever you want."

"Thank you."

Minutes felt like hours as she stroked Harley, over and over, murmuring to him, telling him how much she loved him, what a great horse he was, the best horse, how happy he made her and how she was right here so he shouldn't be afraid. She wouldn't let anything bad happen to him.

You just did, hissed the devil on one shoulder.

The angel on her other shoulder didn't speak a word in her defense. There wasn't any.

The mechanical hum of an engine burbled in the distance a while later. It grew louder and louder as some kind of vehicle approached.

"Jared!" she heard Jewel exclaim. "He's got the skid loader."

"He's attached the crane," James observed.

"How many pounds will it lift?" Jewel asked.

"Could be enough for Harley." James's shadow fell on her as he stood.

The engine snapped off, then Jared asked, "Who's ready to be a hero?"

Hope sparked beneath her heart, lifting it like a Chinese lantern in the dark. Jared. Her champion and hero. She didn't need to put him through any more tests. He'd more than proved himself.

The Cades hustled around Harley, sliding something under one side of him, then rolling him over to pull it the rest of the way beneath him. Petey's shape flew back and forth, from one end of Harley to the other, supervising, his innate responsibility to protect other animals kicking in.

"Slide that bar through there," she heard Jared order, then chains rattled and the winch whined.

"Careful!" James shouted. Then "Hold." Followed by what must have been a thumbs-up or some other signal that started the process over.

She held her breath, straining to see. Slowly the black blur of Harley on the ground rose and rose and rose until he stood, held upright in the sling.

"Okay?" Jared called.

She nodded, beyond words grateful to him. He'd given Harley a reprieve until a veterinarian arrived.

Would help come in time?

CHAPTER TWELVE

"Is HARLEY GONNA be alright?" called a young girl's voice from atop her mount. Amberley recognized Emily's slight lisp.

Like the rest of the children, she'd stopped by every day this past week to check on their favorite horse. Some, like Emily, visited even during their non-therapy program days. Homemade cards festooned the stall's doorway, overlapping one another to fit the space. Treats, including oat, molasses and berry bars Jared concocted with the group, overflowed the back shelf. A large Get Well Soon, Harley sign, decorated with glitter glue and horse stickers, hung from his stall door.

"We're sure hoping so."

Amberley snapped off the hose wand. The spray of cool water, aimed at Harley's injured leg to reduce the inflammation, slowed, trickled, then stopped. Uncaring about the wet, Petey huddled at her feet. Since the accident, he'd acted more protective than ever, refusing to leave her side except when he'd taken, and passed, his therapy dog test yesterday.

"He'll be just fine," said a woman, joining them. "He's going to need some TLC for a few months, but eventually he'll be nearly good as new."

"He's good no matter what!" Emily cried, staunch, then her parent led her away. Deep down, Amberley knew she and the rest of the children identified with Harley's lameness.

As wounded warriors, their common cause, the battle not only to survive, but to thrive, united them. They succeeded by their own measures and accepted themselves as they were designed. Flaws, injuries, illnesses represented badges of honor worn with pride. They marked you as someone whom life tested, an individual facing constant challenges, a survivor who'd never quit fighting, just like Harley.

Just like her.

"Hi, Dr. Loveland." Amberley smiled in the woman's direction. Luckily Dr. Cooper's wife had reached Sierra Loveland, Maverick's sister and a wildlife vet, to fill in for her husband. Sierra's quick action, as well as Jared's clever maneuver to keep Harley vertical while awaiting help, saved Harley's life.

An on-site ultrasound revealed he'd torn his deep digital flexor tendon, the most serious soft-tissue injury a horse could get. Harley couldn't bend or bear weight on it because the tendon stabilized the leg and flexed the lower joints.

After Sierra applied a splint and administered anti-inflammatory and pain medication, they'd carefully led Harley back to the Cades' stable for an overnight watch. It'd been the longest twenty-four hours of Amberley's life, filled with misery, panic, fear and exhaustion.

When he'd stabilized enough, he'd transferred back to Spirit Ranch the next day for stall rest. Ever since, Amberley had been by his side, sleeping, eating, reading out loud to him, even playing his favorite music—banjo-heavy bluegrass tunes that made his ears twitch and his tail swish.

"Call me Sierra," the petite woman said.

Amberley searched her memories for a mental picture of Sierra. She'd always reminded Amberley of a fairy—delicate features too perfect to be human and beautiful, long blond hair. Her down-to-earth, friendly personality tempered the jealousy she aroused in others. Oh. And she snorted when she laughed. Not even a cute, dainty snort. It reminded Amberley of a Canadian goose. It was a loud honk that'd landed her in trouble in school whenever her classmates got her giggling—something everyone liked doing since Sierra's laugh-snort was uncontrollable and infectious.

"And how's my patient today? Behaving himself?" The changing direction of Sierra's voice suggested that she circled Harley, assessing him for signs of strain on the other limbs now carrying more of Harley's weight.

"Mostly." Amberley grabbed Petey's collar. She crossed to the hose reel, dragging the heavy line. "He's becoming a little spoiled with all the treats. This morning, he turned his nose up at the cornmeal mix."

Sierra's snort carried on the cooling, late-afternoon breeze. "Can't let him turn into a diva."

"Too late for that." Amberley wound the hose, then bent to turn off the spigot. "But he deserves pampering."

And her apologies…which she'd given him nonstop. Her mind replayed the accident on constant loop, lingering on all the signs she'd missed, the ways she could have prevented his career-ending injury. Most likely, Harley would never barrel race again.

Given how he perked up around the children, though, she hoped he'd find happiness spending his days on Spirit Ranch. He couldn't compete, but he could love. No disability on earth could stop you from doing that...

And maybe, maybe it even let you love just a little harder, appreciate others more, be extra grateful for the time you have and what you give instead of take. That was Harley. Now he'd bestow his big heart on children who needed him more than rodeo crowds. They'd always cheer and hug him, and she hoped it'd be enough.

"Any preference on color for his elastic wrap?" Sierra called.

"Purple?"

"Got it."

Petey guided her around a puddle, left from last night's rainstorm, and back to Harley. After the deluge, she'd woken to silence and the earthy smells of washed greenery. Her lungs drew in breath after breath, the freshly scrubbed air tasting like a new start, a second chance, hope.

"Hey, Amberley. Sierra. How's Harley?"

Her heart sputtered at Jared's baritone. While he'd stayed with her all week, sleeping outside the stall, fetching her food, water, fresh clothes from home, he'd kept his distance romantically. Was he respecting her painful situation with Harley or, now that her chance at competing, at winning, ended with Harley's injury, had his interest in her waned?

"Swelling's going down and I'm seeing a bit of range of motion," Sierra answered.

Petey halted her beside Harley and Jared. She peered his way, but Jared didn't turn his head or otherwise notice her.

Had her decision to keep him at arm's length backfired?

Was he waiting for Harley to improve enough, for her sake, before moving on to greener pastures? The Cades celebrated James's wedding this weekend. Considering Jared's silence about the big event, she guessed he already had a date.

"Prognosis?" Jared asked. The blur of flesh color suggested he stroked Harley.

And he still hadn't looked at her.

Sierra's shape straightened, and purple now covered what Amberley knew must be Harley's front leg. "I'd say another few weeks of stall rest, then some supervised grazing, small pasture for a month before we let him loose."

Amberley's shoulders loosened. It'd be months of dedicated care, but Harley would pull through.

"And racing?" Jared prompted, though he and Amberley had already surmised the answer.

"Not possible." Sierra clucked at Harley, then held out something red he gobbled up quickly. An apple. "But he'll still be able to give the little ones a ride."

"How soon?" Amberley asked. Harley struggled to the stall door whenever he heard the therapy groups pass by, eager for a glimpse of the children.

"Three months or so. Could be earlier. We'll have to wait and see. Right, boy?" Sierra's voice rose at the end, softening as she addressed Harley. "Who's my miracle horse? Huh? You brave boy."

Amberley smiled at the dedicated vet who didn't mind indulging in a little baby talk when it came to her charges. Despite her busy practice, Sierra insisted on caring for Harley personally. She always finished what she started, she'd declared, and she wouldn't miss one step of Harley's journey back to health.

Sierra, Jared, Maverick, the children…their outpouring of love and support for Harley meant a lot. If fairies required belief and applause to fly, then horses like Harley needed affection to recover. Every hug was water on a parched plant, replenishing and restoring him.

Jared behaved especially attentive to Harley. At times, she felt almost jealous, wanting that same attention. But Harley came first. She wouldn't begrudge him anything, though she wished Jared wouldn't leave her in the dark about where they stood.

What held him back?

You pushed him away, sniped the devil on one shoulder. *Told him to prove himself instead of trusting him.*

You haven't told him how you feel yet, soothed the angel on her other shoulder, piping up for the first time since the accident.

True, Amberley mused. After nearly losing Harley, she'd never take loved ones for granted again. While Jared's romantic gestures before the accident touched her, his steadfast support and devotion to her injured horse, to her safety and well-being, proved his head and heart were in the right place.

Maybe she overthought this when she should just reach for him if she dared.

"Hey," she heard Maverick say, and she glanced up at his mountainous frame. "How's our favorite horse?"

While Sierra updated her older brother, Jared approached and bent down to pet Petey.

"He's legit now," Jared said, referencing Petey's new certification and the blue "Service Dog" vest he wore. "And taking his job seriously. He hasn't quit impersonating a pair of slippers yet, has he?"

"Nope." She chuckled, peering down at the black-and-white fur entirely covering her boots now. "It's like he doesn't want me to go anywhere."

"I know the feeling," Jared mumbled, low.

"What do you mean?"

She heard him exhale and held her own breath. If he said he didn't want to pursue her anymore she'd...

He cupped her elbow, breaking her from her dark thoughts, and steered her a small distance away. Petey followed, then dropped atop her boots with an exasperated huff.

"Seeing you fall off Harley," Jared blurted, his voice raw. "I thought you were crushed. Dead."

Her hand rose to his face and skimmed the rough bristle on his cheeks. Meticulous Jared—unshaven? And he wore the same wrinkled shirt he'd donned yesterday and the day before that. This from a guy who ironed his T-shirts. He turned his face into her palm and pressed a small kiss in its center.

"You've been distant this week."

"Every time I looked at you, I pictured the accident and how close you came to dying. I should've stopped your last run."

She opened her mouth to agree, then closed it and shook her head instead. "Have you ever been able to stop me when I'm set on something?"

A beat of silence and then a short guffaw. "No."

"I'm to blame for chasing a fool's dream instead of accepting my disability. I could have killed Harley."

"It was an accident. Plenty of sighted riders have them."

"But—"

"And never give up your dreams," he insisted. "If not for Harley's injury, they might have come true."

"Guess we'll never know."

"Never say never," Maverick drawled, joining them. "I've got a trained barrel racer if you want her."

Her muscles seized. "What? Who?"

"It's Calamity Jane."

"Calamity?" she echoed… "That's Ella Parks's horse. Why would she lend her to me?"

A ten-time world champion barrel racer, Ella toured with the ERA premier group. Amberley beat her for the last three titles, but Ella was a legend and still at the top of her game.

"She married last year." Maverick's voice dipped, and suddenly Amberley remembered that he and Ella once dated. Dubbed Rodeo's golden couple, they'd reigned as king and queen of their sports. What'd broken them up.

"Anyhow," Maverick continued after a gruff throat clearing, "she's expecting and when she heard about your accident, she called and offered her horse. She said it'd be good exercise for Calamity since Ella's on bed rest."

"That's an incredible offer," Jared cut in. "What do you say, Amberley?"

Hope burbled inside, welling like a spring-fed brook. Then she heard Harley's screams again and the geyser stopped. Too much risk. If not for Jared, she could have been crushed and Harley would have died. Besides, Harley and their bond made racing possible. Without him, she'd never navigate a course, let alone compete on one again.

"Please tell her thanks, but I can't accept."

"Okay, then." Maverick's head dipped, like he tipped his hat, then he ambled away.

"Courage is being scared to death—and saddling up anyway," Jared quoted. He twined his fingers in hers.

"I'm not scared!" Her heart beat double time, belying her words, as image after image—of Harley running pell-mell into the wall, Harley's slide, then fall, Harley writhing on the ground—flashed in her mind's eye. "I'm being realistic. Harley made racing possible. It'd be tough to compete last minute on a new horse, even if I had my sight."

"Tough, but not impossible."

"I'm not a Pegasus, Jared. I can't fly."

His grip tightened around hers. "Yes, you can."

Her breath caught. "You never stop believing in me, do you?"

He pressed his nose to hers. "Nope. It's kind of a habit. Say—want to get out of here with me?"

"But, Harley…"

"I've got the rest of the day off," Sierra offered, passing by as she led Harley to the stall. "I planned on keeping Maverick company anyway. He needs some cheering up. I can cover for you in the last therapy group, too."

"And I'm here," put in Benny, joining them. "Plus, Joan feels up to working a bit today, so we're covered."

"Thanks." She threw her arms around Harley, hugged him, then stepped back.

"Petey needs to stay." Jared lowered himself to the dog, and the furious tail thumping suggested an ear scratch. "Sorry, bud. Next time."

"Why?" she asked after leaving Petey in Sierra's care.

When they stopped in the parking lot, Jared passed her something round, hard and familiar. Her heart jumped. A motorcycle helmet.

"Because you're about to fly."

Amberley stuffed her hat in Jared's bag and donned the heavy helmet. Her shaking hands struggled to secure the simple buckle.

Jared brushed her fingers aside to latch it. "Stay still," he ordered, chuckling.

"Can't." She bounced from foot to foot, afire with anticipation. She hadn't ridden her own Breakout, and felt the wild abandon, the freedom of the open road, in so long.

"All set?" he asked after securing her helmet.

"You bet!" She pumped her fist and hooted.

Strong hands scooped her up and settled her on the back of the seat as if she weighed less than a thistle.

"Settle down there, cowgirl," he drawled, his voice deep and warm in the middle.

Then, without warning, Jared's lips brushed hers, a soft, dreamy pressure that tripped her pulse, tumbling it in her veins. She traced her mouth when he pulled away. Had she imagined that brief, yummy kiss?

No.

He was too much shine to not be felt.

The motorcycle tilted slightly when he hopped on board. The engine revved.

"Hold on!" he shouted.

She threw her arms around his trim waist and held him tightly. He leaned forward, trying to give her more room, she guessed, but she crushed her body into his broad back, needing to be close to him. As she shut her eyes and breathed him in, she couldn't tell where he ended and she began. Her heart beat so quickly, and yet she felt utterly calm—she could have stayed there forever and let the world fall apart around them.

The smooth hum of tires rolling on pavement replaced the crunch-gravel sound of the stable's dirt drive. Jared gunned it, and the Breakout, unleashed, burst forward with tremendous speed. The wind whipped through her hair, knotting the strands with invisible fingers. The sunlight warmed her skin, and the weight she'd carried around her shoulders since the accident drifted away.

She dropped her chin to Jared's shoulder. His muscles shifted as he expertly guided the Breakout up the winding road. Gosh. He smelled good. Fresh laundry, hung out to dry on a sweet summer day, the leather from his jacket and beneath that, a bit of spicy cologne mixed with his clean, male skin.

Through her visor, she glimpsed the world zoom by in a colorful blur. The green-brown must be fir trees, she guessed, inhaling the pine-scented air. A black ribbon of road beckoned them on. Overhead arched a watercolor of blue bleeding into purple streaming into rose and then orange before it dripped down, into what must be the horizon. Sunset.

Her heart writhed and a roar built in the back of her throat.

"Yeeeeeeehawwwwwww!" she shouted as Jared poured on the speed and ripped around another curve. Breakout bikes could comfortably handle eighty-five miles an hour or more and had enough torque to manage steep inclines. Despite the danger of the sudden drop-offs on either side of the shoulder-less road, she'd never felt safer.

Jared turned back for a quick look before whipping his head forward again, eyes back on the treacherous road. He shot her a thumbs-up.

"Wooooooooo-hooooooo!" she hollered, exalting, and Jared joined her, their primal howls echoing on this lonely back road.

Too soon, they slowed, then stopped atop a mountain. Mount Sopris, if she guessed correctly from the direction they'd traveled. The wind, harsher at this altitude, lashed her hair around her face when she pulled off her helmet. Jared tucked the strands behind her ears with rough fingers.

She felt her lips puckering, wanting another kiss. Her eyes flew open a second later when he tugged her up a small path instead, and then out onto a grassy outcropping above a dizzying, wide-open space.

"Come with me." He slipped an arm around her waist, securing her to his side, and guided her to the very edge. Far below, air currents rippled a blurry purple sea of blooms.

"Laurel Canyon," she breathed. Their special place. "I didn't think I'd ever see it again."

"Why?" he asked in a husky whisper. The silken feel of his lips moving against her ear shook the skin over her bones.

"Because I can't—I can't…"

"You can do anything. Even fly."

She turned and flung her arms around his neck. The wind lifted her hair, streaming it behind her like a sheet. Overhead, an eagle cried, and the sinking sun sent tendrils of light spiraling over them.

"Thank you, Jared." The bike ride had liberated her, down to the marrow of her bones. Right now, she felt ready to soar over this range—or her heart at least.

"I have another surprise."

He steered her away from the precipice. "No peeking."

"You don't need to say that to a blind girl," she teased.

"*Legally* blind," he corrected, sounding amused, then his boots stomped away.

She drank in the cool air, thinner and purer at this altitude, as she waited on him. A moment later, she heard the snap of fabric followed by clinking glass.

"Okay. You can look now."

She popped open her eyes and trained them on a wavering square of color with some objects on it. "That doesn't help."

"Right." Jared guided her a couple of steps, then helped her down onto a soft blanket.

"Ohhhhhh…a picnic." They'd held so many in this spot, as kids and then later, as adults. They'd unwound, vented and dreamed here, all the things you do and say with your best friend. Now it seemed extra special because Jared was more… only…they still needed to define what that "more" would be.

"Sparkling grape juice, ma'am?"

She smiled. "My favorite. And I think I like *sweetheart* better."

He lifted the glass to her mouth and held

it there as she drank the sweet berry juice. "Sweetheart," he murmured then whisked the glass away.

She almost groaned aloud. She wanted him to kiss her again. Badly. Jared lifted something soft and flaky to her mouth. She sniffed. "Ham and cheese croissant?" Her eyes closed in pleasure at the first salty, buttery bite. "When did you…?"

"This morning." He moved, gesturing to the quilt she guessed. "I wanted you to remember this place and who you are. Who you want to be."

"Without Harley, I'm not a barrel racer."

"Not true. You had Crimson before that."

She let that sink in.

"Harley wouldn't want you to give up," he added.

"Now you're playing dirty."

He laughed. "Who's playing?" She gasped with he slid a finger down the side of her face. "Let's watch the stars come out while you think it out. I'll build a fire."

He moved away and she heard a match strike. He must be lighting kindling, she marveled, picturing the old fire ring they'd built one summer. It took her a moment, as he fussed over the fire, to realize what he tried to say. He hadn't brought her out here to kiss her. He wanted her to remember who she was, the fearless woman he knew, with or without Harley.

The blanket rustled when he lowered himself. They lay side by side, talking and listening to the rise of night sounds as the sky settled into full darkness. After a while, the haze of the Milky Way, a blur of sparkling white, appeared against the black.

Jared rolled over on his side to face her. "What do you want most in this world?"

She opened her mouth to say "you" but held back, still unsure of where they stood. Instead, she spoke the other desire of her heart, the one he'd reignited and wouldn't let be extinguished.

"I want to compete again."

It seemed like he nodded, and she brought her hands to his face to feel what she couldn't see. Her fingertips traced the upward tilt of his mouth and the dent of his dimpled cheeks.

"You'll ride Calamity Jane, then?"

She nodded, and those crazy dimples of his deepened.

"That's my girl."

Was she his girl? A guy like Jared—he could have any girl he wanted. Winners, all of them. Her, well, he'd have to take her as she was.

Her dad said losers weren't much. Did Jared agree?

"What do *you* want?" she asked, needing an answer on so many levels.

His facial muscles relaxed beneath her fingertips, his expression softening. He rose from the blanket. "To dance with you."

Then he pulled her to her feet and twirled her around, nearly knocking her down. "Sorry." He chuckled. "That went smoother in my head."

"You're such a klutz."

"Only around you—you've got me off balance."

She grinned. "Good." Then she put her arms around his neck—as far as she could reach anyway—and he drew her close and swayed the way you do at junior high dances, the ones they'd always skipped in order to camp out up here. She pressed her face into his chest and reveled in the sensation of this perfect safety and serenity. The rightness of them. A jolt ran from the top of her head to her heels, unlike anything she'd ever experienced. She loved the way he felt around her. She loved the smell of his tangy cologne. She loved the way his chin rested on the top of her head.

She wanted to lift her mouth to his, but sensed he was holding back. Was he ready for a real relationship, a public one, with a girl who may not ever amount to much?

That last part sounded suspiciously like her father.

Silence fell. When he spoke, his words stirred her hair. "I have one more question."

She snuggled closer and listened to the steady drum of his heart. "Shoot."

"Will you be my date to James's wedding?"

Date. He'd said *date.*

And that meant something, right?

More than friends... Maybe even more than a casual fling...

How would he introduce her? This is Amberley, my bud, or this is Amberley, my date, or this is Amberley, my gal...

Only one way to find out.

Courage is being scared to death—and saddling up anyway.

John Wayne, you'd better not be foolin'.

She drew in a deep breath and raised her face.

"Yes."

CHAPTER THIRTEEN

A CLOCK CHIMED, interrupting Jared's idyll chat with Charlotte James. She frowned at the squawking carved bird, cupped her hands around her mouth, then called, "Amberley, Jared's here!"

"I don't mind waiting." He shoved his hands in his tuxedo jacket pockets and leaned against the kitchen's doorjamb. Underneath his dress slacks, his knee jittered. This was his and Amberley's first real date, and he still hadn't sorted out his feelings. She'd asked him to woo her, yet he'd backed off after the accident.

Why?

"I'm sorry, Jared." A line appeared between Charlotte's brows. "I'll go see what's taking her so long."

"No trouble at all, ma'am."

Jared watched Charlotte tromp down the hall, then let out a breath. Since the incident, his mind shifted into fifth gear and zoomed on unfamiliar roads, destination unknown. He loved Amberley, more than he'd ever loved anyone in his life, but the final answer to the "love versus in love" question still eluded him. His mother said it was a feeling more than a knowing, and his emotions tangled in his gut. Hopefully, tonight he'd straighten them—and himself—out.

Because of his unshaken faith in Amberley, he wanted her to compete again. But *his* confidence had taken a hit. Before Harley's crash, she'd seemed bulletproof, despite her visual impairment. Now he saw the fragility he'd ignored. A thin line separated her from disaster, and on it stood Petey, her mother and him. Holding that line was a huge responsibility. He didn't want to fail her again.

She deserved a hero, and he'd done little to prove himself worthy of that role. The promise he'd made his father echoed in his ear, a sharp, accusing sound. A rebuke.

"Out in a minute!" he heard Amberley call.

He checked his watch. They still had thirty minutes to get to the church.

"Plenty of time." He swept his hat from his perspiring brow and loosened his tie.

They'd resumed practicing this week with

Calamity Jane. After a bumpy first couple of days, Amberley and Calamity hit their stride. She'd even begun showing incredible speed on the course, reaching race times under fifteen seconds. And the faster she rode, the more it worried him that he held her life, her career, in his hands as he guided her around the barrels. Was it too much responsibility?

As he coached her through runs, he now scrutinized every crack, every weakness. Her utter dependence on him, and the real consequence of mishaps, caused him to second-guess himself, an unsettling feeling for a guy who'd always believed in his ability to prevail...until now.

Nails ticked on the wooden floor, breaking him from his thoughts, and Petey wagged his way over, sneezing in excitement.

"Hey, boy!" Jared crouched to stroke Petey's notched ears and sent a silent prayer of thanks to the forces that'd guided the stray to Cade Ranch. Without him, Amberley wouldn't have her independence. Did she need Jared, though, to be a winner again?

The hope on her face when she looked for him started to pressure him. How could he be Amberley's rock, someone who'd always be there for her, when he also needed to focus on himself, resuscitate his struggling career and follow the path he'd vowed to take? His sprint times and bench press numbers now neared his preinjury status. A comeback seemed in reach, though his agent still hadn't returned his calls.

"Oh, stop fussing, you look lovely," he heard Charlotte say, then—"Doesn't she look lovely, Jared?"

He straightened, opened his mouth to agree, then froze at the vision who'd just glided into the room.

"Jared?" Charlotte prompted.

He shook his head, cleared his throat and opened his dry mouth. Nothing came out.

Amberley was stunning, beautiful beyond reckoning in a lilac dress that skimmed her long, lean frame and fell to the tops of silver heels. Golden waves flowed around her fresh-scrubbed face, and her darkened lashes brought out the sparkling crystal blue of her eyes. The gown's spaghetti straps contrasted with her smooth, tan skin. He dug his nails into his palms to keep from reaching for her.

"S-say something," Amberley said, her eyes searching for him.

He jerked himself forward and gathered her small, strong hands in his. "I'm trying."

Charlotte laughed and gave Amberley a little shove. "You two have a good time, now."

Amberley's pink lips lifted in a smile. "We will."

Did he detect a wistful note in her voice? It pained him to cause her uncertainty. Amberley deserved a man who'd dedicate his entire life to her. His ambiguous future called his ability to do that into question.

In the past, casual dating helped him manage expectations and ensure no one got hurt. His career came first, something Amberley understood as his friend. If she became his girlfriend, how would she handle time apart if he returned to professional football?

No one was banging down his door with an offer, so it was stupid to waste time worrying about it, but he did. The accident had opened his eyes to how much Amberley depended on him, and he never wanted to hurt her. Ever. The possibility messed with his head and his heart.

"Got this for you." He pulled a white rose and lavender wrist corsage from its plastic container and slid it over her wrist.

She lifted it to her nose and breathed in the deep floral scent. "It's beautiful." Her eyes glistened. "Thank you."

"Aw. Well." He shuffled his feet, uncomfortable with all the emotion she laid out...his for the taking. Should he set his reservations aside and just enjoy this time together?

Let tomorrow take care of itself, Pa used to say.

"This makes up for the prom we never went to." Amberley didn't hesitate when she reached the porch stairs and started down them with Petey, her hand sliding with practiced ease on the railing.

"We should have gone." He held open his pickup's door, pointed for Petey to jump in, then guided Amberley onto the bucket seat.

She turned when he jumped behind the wheel, started the engine and drove down her drive. "Why's that? Our hot dog roast was more fun. And you know how I hate dressing up." She plucked at her gown's gauzy material.

"But you look good doin' it." He shot her a smile and she grinned back, as if she could see him, as attuned to him as ever.

Did she sense the underlying currents roiling in his gut? He wanted to make Amberley happy. Could he do it without sacrificing his own life? His destiny? And was that a selfish thought to have? "At least then we'd have known," he added.

"Known…?" She angled her head, and her brows rose.

"About us. If we were more." He yanked off his hat and tossed it into the space behind him. "More than just friends."

"Better late than never, right?" Her hands twisted in her lap, giving lie to her light tone.

His back teeth clenched. Enough. He didn't have a crystal ball to predict the future, but he knew what he wanted right now. What they both wanted. He slid his fingers inside hers, deciding then and there to live in this special moment tonight with Amberley. "Much better."

"Good." She tipped back her head and closed her eyes, her grin back on as she nodded in time to a country-and-western tune on the radio.

An hour later, he sat at the head table and eyed the transformed barn Sofia used in her event-planning business. Twinkle lights glowed behind sheets of white gauze fabric draped over the exposed beam ceiling.

All around, wildflowers spilled from lace-wrapped mason jar centerpieces atop round tables. The heady scent mingled with the cool evening air flowing through the windows. In a corner, a brown-frosted cake, chocolate he hoped, rose in three tiers. A harness circled layers topped by a silver-colored horseshoe and miniature cowboy hats, labeled "bride and groom."

"No road is too long when you're with someone you love," James proclaimed, standing, glass in hand, as he delivered his wedding toast. Jewel rolled her eyes at Jared, and his mouth twitched. So now their know-it-all older brother was an authority on love, too?

How much had changed in just six months. Last Christmas, his family had been ignoring the holiday since it made Jesse's loss too fresh and painful. Then along came Sofia with a child they hadn't known existed, Jesse's son, Javi. The two healed their broken family and brought love to his closed-off older brother.

Miracles did happen.

Could he expect one, too?

It seemed more complicated for him and Amberley than it'd been for James and Sofia. He eyed Sofia as his brother droned on. Seated beside Javi and Amberley, her dark eyes fixed on James, her expression rapt. Meanwhile, Javi tossed candy-coated almonds in the air and caught them in his mouth, a trick Jared had taught him.

He shot Javi a quick thumbs-up.

"Be sure to—to—" At James's fierce head shake, Javi dropped the nuts and straightened in his seat. "Be sure to hold on to each other, but also remember that sometimes you need to let go and trust that person will come back to you. Dani and Jack," James raised his glass higher. "May you have warm words on a cold evening, a full moon on a dark night, and the road downhill all the way to your door. Ladies and gents, please join me in toasting the happy couple. To Mr. and Mrs. Jackson Cade."

The crowd hooted and clinked glasses. Sofia dabbed her eyes with a napkin and her smile wobbled as she returned James's long, dark stare.

Whoa.

Control-freak James advising people to "let go"? Sofia's influence no doubt. Love changed people. Plain and simple. Had he changed enough to be the man worthy of Amberley's love? A man who could devote his entire life to her?

The din of forks, dinging on the sides of crystal, interrupted his worries. With a laugh, Jack swept off his cowboy hat, covered his and Dani's face, then gave her a long, thorough kiss. The crowd whistled. Boots thundered on the planked floor. A few minutes later, the couple emerged, flushed and laughing, their faces so bright it almost hurt to look at them.

A fiddler struck up a slow, twangy tune: Clint Black's "When I Said I Do." Jack led a starry-eyed Dani onto the dance floor.

"You forgot to call Jack a bastard in the toast," Justin drawled.

"You're a real comedian," James answered, not sounding the least bit amused.

Justin shrugged. "No accounting for taste."

"Has Ma told him yet?" Jared cut another piece of steak and popped the juicy slice into his mouth.

"Last night." Jewel shoved between them, plucked a bread roll from the basket and grabbed a knife.

"How'd he take it?" Jared passed her a pat of butter.

"Okay. He said at least the label matched his looks."

Jared's nose flared. The hell it did. Jack got that facial scar defending Jesse the night he died. It signified courage and brotherly love.

"Relax," Jewel mumbled around a bite of roll. "He laughed after he said it, and I heard him chuckling when he told Dani."

"Well," Justin said slowly, drawing the word out as he turned a knife over and over in his hand. "He's always been a son of a—"

"Little pictures," growled James as Javi and Sofia arrived at the table.

"Was gonna say gun," Justin grumped.

"You and your weapon obsession," teased Jewel.

"More of a hobby." Justin tested the knife-point against the tip of his index finger.

"How many guns do you own now?" Jared asked. At last count, his brother could arm a small militia.

Justin shrugged. "Not enough."

Jewel, who'd begun plucking out bobby pins, froze, her hands suspended in midair. "Now I'm worried."

Justin chuckled and James shoved back his chair. "How about a dance, Sofia?"

"Me, too?" Javi lifted one hand and circled it overhead while swinging his hips. "I can dance. Uncle Jared taught me."

"Don't hurt yourself there, cowboy." Jewel leaned across the table to buss him on the nose.

James swung Javi in his arms. "Jared taught you? Amateur hour. I'll teach you some real dance moves. Do you know the hokey-pokey?"

Sofia laughed, and the trio disappeared into the growing throng on the floor.

"How about you, Jewel?" Jared searched out Amberley again. She'd vacated her seat. Had someone guided her to the restroom? Outside for some fresh air? "Are you going to make some lucky guy's night and accept a dance?"

Justin's cackle cut off quickly at her shoulder jab. She grabbed James's seat and straddled it, revealing scuffed cowboy boots beneath the rising hem of her bridesmaid dress. "Is hell freezing over?"

Justin crossed his arms and dropped his chin to his chest. "My sentiments exactly. Wake me when this shindig's over."

"Hey! Is that Ma dancing with Boyd Loveland?"

At Jewel's observation, Justin's eyes flew open. "Where?"

"There. She didn't say he was coming."

"He's not staying."

Jared grabbed Justin's collar before he rose. Justin was tough, but as his older brother, Jared had authority and fifteen pounds of muscle on him. "*Yes*, he is."

"She looks happy." Jewel shoved back her tangled hair and dropped her chin into her hand, her elbow propped on the table.

"I'm getting some air." Justin shook free of Jared's hold and stalked off.

"I'd better go, too." Jewel scrubbed off her lipstick with a napkin, then stood. "Someone's got to keep him out of trouble."

"It'll find him anyway," Jared called after her. "It always does."

Alone, Jared met a hopeful-looking gal's eye, then turned away. Only one woman had his attention tonight. He'd spend it by her side, watching the rowdy fun and describing it to her.

His foot tapped in time to a fiery version of "Devil Went Down to Georgia" while he scanned the room. Who'd guided Amberley and where had she gone? Petey crouched on the hay-bale-lined dancing area, which meant…

"Yeee-hawww!" someone hooted in the knee-slapping, jigging crowd. And there, smack in the middle, stood Amberley.

He bolted upright.

Amberley?

He'd assumed because of her blindness she wouldn't want to dance, but there she was, stomping and kicking her feet in time to the music, fearless and flushed and beautiful as all get out. She knocked the wind clean out of him.

"What are you doing just standing there?" Jack scoffed, returning to the table with Dani in tow. "Go get her before someone else does."

A couple of his cousins, Lance, a Denver sheriff, and Cole, a Steamboat Springs smoke-jumper, now vied for a spot closer to Amberley.

Oh, heck no.

His long legs, trained for pro ball, now sped him to Amberley in seconds. A fierce frown at his relatives backed them off quick. The music cut and Amberley bent at the waist, breathing hard, laughing.

"What are you doing?" he demanded, not

sure if he wanted to throw her over his shoulder and carry her back to her seat, where she wouldn't be knocked down, or sweep her into his arms and hold her tight.

"I'm dancing. You?" Her smile stretched wide, loopy and infectious.

The fiddler's bow swept over his strings, striking a single, dreamy-sounding note before the band began its version of Anne Murray's "Could I Have This Dance."

He caught her around the waist, his feet moving to the beat of the song. "I'm dancing with you," he murmured in her ear. She trembled against him when he pulled her close.

Was there music playing? he wondered a moment later as he guided her over the rough floor. He'd almost forgotten. The world had shrunk into nothing, dissolved by the golden glow of candles flickering in hurricane lamps. But there were his feet, and here was his arm, and his neck, and his mouth that longed to touch hers.

His hands caressed her back, and she looked up at him. Jared saw the happiness written across her face. His heart jumped into a gallop, and his earlier worries dissolved from his thoughts.

"You look beautiful," he said quietly, running an eye over her. "I can't stop staring at you."

"I wish I could see you." Her hand rose to his jaw and slid along its length. Their bodies swayed together. "You shaved." Her fingers sifted through the short strands at the nape of his neck. "And you cut your hair. I always like it short."

"Good," he said, pleased by this simple compliment more than any of the lavish praise heaped on him before.

She dropped her head to his shoulder, and his pulse throbbed as the music carried them onward. He was lost—lost in a world of which he'd dreamed about. Her body pulsed warm beneath his hand, and her fingers wrapped softly around his. He spun her across the floor, waltzing smoothly. She didn't falter once, nor did she seem to care who or what might surround them, trusting him every step of the way. It seemed like they danced inside their own glass globe, inhabiting a world built just for two.

Could they live in this bubble forever? The skirts of her gown sparkled underneath the twinkling lights as he twirled her.

He suddenly felt the urge to kiss her—hard—upon the mouth. "Let's go outside." When they passed an open door, he waltzed her backward and stopped when they reached a private spot beneath the shadowed barn eaves.

Her fingers traced his lips. "You're smiling," she observed. "Are you happy?"

"Yes." He pressed her hand to his drumming heart, certain she could feel it through his suit jacket and understand what he struggled to say.

"Are you sure?" she asked, her voice faltering, the real question spinning between them.

"I'm sure. Nothing makes a fella happier than being out with his gal."

"Your gal, huh? That sounds serious."

"It is."

He watched the way her lips widened in a smile and her eyes burst with light. Then his lips descended on hers, needing to taste, to touch, to sample what he so desperately needed. Her mouth tasted like honey and her lips were smooth, and Jared lost all sense of time as she slowly kissed him back, her body melting against him.

He pulled away a moment later, peered into

her eyes as they opened, and then kissed her again. It was different this time—deeper, full of need. His arms were heavy and light all at once, and the world spun round and round. He couldn't stop. He liked this—liked kissing her, liked the smell and the taste and the feel of her. His arm slipped around her waist, and he held her tightly as his lips moved insistently against hers.

Amberley eased back and smiled. Jared leaned forward again, but she put two fingers against his lips. "We should go back inside." He raised his eyebrows. "Don't want to miss the cake," she added.

"You're sweeter." He tugged her fingers from his mouth and tried to kiss her again, but she swung under his arm and started forward.

When her hands encountered the barn door, she stopped and peered into the raucous party. She dropped her head back to his chest when he slid his arms around her from behind. "Are you with me?"

He turned her gently in his arms and brought her face close to his. "Always," he whispered, and she didn't stop him as he kissed her again.

An old-school Garth Brooks tune, one of their favorites, blared.

"Then let *always* begin!" she pronounced, whirling, nearly yanking him off his feet as she pulled him inside.

He struggled to keep up, wondering, hoping that it truly had begun, feeling his heart grow, and grow, and grow.

"JARED! PHONE!" HOLLERED his mother through the screen door the next day. He patted his empty pockets as he mounted the porch stairs and realized he'd left his cell on the kitchen counter at breakfast.

"Thanks." He dropped onto a stool and picked up the landline. His shoulders ached, along with every other part of him, but he'd done it, he'd beaten even his best times pre-injury. No matter what happened with his career, he took pride in the effort, the drive, that'd gotten him here...all of which he owed to Amberley.

His mouth twisted in a smile just thinking of their night together. It'd been goofy fun, cutting loose, not caring how they acted and not needing to impress each other. Falling for your best friend meant being comfortable in your own skin, and he liked who he was with Amberley—his authentic self, not the town heartthrob he now gladly checked at the door. "Jared speaking."

"Cade. Andrew Wiley here."

Jared stiffened. His agent—returning his call at last. "Thanks, but I resolved the issue I'd called you about on my own."

Last night he and Amberley had started their *always* together. He didn't have to chase after second best when he already had a star position, front and center, in Amberley's life. "Appreciate the call, though."

"Hold on!" he heard the man yell before he'd returned the handset to its cradle.

"Yes?"

"Don't know if you've been following the news lately…"

Jared glanced at the daily paper folded by the phone. "Not closely."

"Ted Reiss tore his rotator cuff."

He made a noise, something between a gasp and a groan that whipped his mother around. She slapped a dish towel over her shoulder and mouthed, "What?"

Ted Reiss. The halfback who'd taken his starting position. "So…"

"The team asked me to call. Are you in football-playing shape?"

"Yes," he said after a long beat, dragging the word from where it burrowed in the back of his throat.

"Would you come in for a workout and physical?"

Silence. His mother advanced, eyes wide. She raised her eyebrows in question, but he shook his head, thoughts whirling too fast to grab any one and pin it down.

"Jared?" prompted his agent. "Are you interested in coming back?"

CHAPTER FOURTEEN

"LET'S WELCOME MATTIE MCLEOD!" blared the ERA Premier Tour Group's rodeo announcer.

In an alley leading to the National Western Arena's entry gate, Amberley struggled to settle Calamity Jane as they waited their turn to compete for a final spot in next week's team tryouts. She pranced sideways, whinnying, pulling slightly on the bit.

"She's looking a little hot," Jared observed, the blurred outline of his face tipped up at Amberley.

"Tell me about it." She gulped down a breath of sweet, hay-scented air, striving to calm her own jittering nerves, as well. "It's okay, girl," she murmured to the restless ten-year-old bay. "Just two more horses to go, and then we'll let it rip."

Too bad they'd drawn the final spot in today's lineup. Harley had the patience of a saint, but Calamity...well, she lived up to her name.

How would she—they—do on the course? If she didn't make the tryouts would Jared still want her as his—whatever they were… They still hadn't defined their relationship exactly, but Jared said it was serious.

"She's always a little amped before she competes," a woman said with a strong Western twang. Amberley turned in the direction of the voice. Calamity Jane nickered, the sound instantly recognizable—a greeting.

"Hey, Ella," Jared said. "Good seeing you. Hope you're feeling well."

"Doctor cleared me from bed rest, but still no riding. Which is why I'm awful glad Amberley's giving Calamity these runs. She lives to compete."

Amberley reached down and patted her mount's soft velvet neck. "It shows. She's been buzzing since we arrived this morning."

"How'd your practice go?" Ella's shape moved to Calamity's head. "Hey, baby girl," she clucked. The horse's muscles relaxed against Amberley's thighs at the sound of her owner's voice.

"Great. We followed your suggestion and didn't do any fast work. Focused on structure and calm instead."

"Let the horse fly when the time counts," Ella advised. "Especially Calamity Jane. Speed isn't a problem for her."

An uneasy laugh escaped Amberley. "True. She's a little scattery, but she's got legs. I'm just about used to her now."

It'd taken a little while for her and Calamity to click. First off, Amberley had to change her riding style. The mare was lightning on legs and just as unpredictable. If Amberley got behind on her, she'd be in trouble. So far, though, no major mishaps.

So far...

She shook off the fear. It didn't belong with her in the saddle.

"Used to her? She's clocking in the low fourteens," Jared scoffed, confident about her as always.

Ella whistled. "Should be good enough to make final tryouts. There's two open positions on the team this year."

"Two?"

"Yep. One's permanent and one's temporary until I can return to touring—after the baby."

"Good to know." Her fingers tensed on the reins.

She had to win one of those spots. She

flicked up the drooping brim of her black Stetson and let out a breath. Just months ago, she'd thought her life over, her career dead. Now, here she sat, about to vie against ten world-class competitors. To even be among them was an honor.

But she wanted to—needed to—win.

Not just for herself, but for the Spirit Ranch kids who'd traveled three hours to cheer her on here in Denver.

"So, you're okay taking the left barrel first?" Ella asked. "I know you and Harley usually do the right."

"It's Calamity's favorite lead." Amberley rolled one tense shoulder, then the other. "I want to make sure she's comfortable."

"I appreciate that." Ella's voice now sounded on her left side, out of the way of the blurred shape of an approaching horse.

"Fourteen fifty-two!" shouted the announcer.

"Shoot," she heard the rider mutter after hearing her time as she passed, her mount blowing hard.

"Too bad." Ella whistled. "What's the time to beat to make the top five now?"

"Fourteen eighteen," a rider atop a gray

horse put in as she trotted by, heading in the opposite direction to the entry gate.

Amberley leaned down to Calamity's twitching ears. "We're next after this."

"Saw they switched up the course pattern a bit," Jared said.

Amberley's teeth chewed on her bottom lip. "It's angled more toward the track."

"Usually it's squared to the roping boxes," Ella said. "But this time we're trying to get the barrels in better grounds so the horses have surer footing instead of being on the track."

"I like how they centered them off the entry gate." Jared gently squeezed Amberley's jittering knee. "When you run in, it's pretty even whether you go right or left. The distance is the same. The eyes are still sixty feet off the barrel back to the alley."

Electronic timers, called eyes, were positioned on the course to record times down to the thousandths of a second. What would her time be today? Good enough to beat fourteen eighteen? Her stomach twisted. In the distance, the announcer called out the next rider's name, and the crowd hollered.

"It's still a standard set. Just keep the new

angle in mind," Jared warned once the tumult lessened.

"Got it." Her voice emerged in a squeak. She cleared her throat. "Got it," she repeated, only a bit steadier.

A new mount, a different course, legal blindness…what could go wrong? She swallowed down the bubble of fear that rose in her throat.

She still had Jared, and he'd see her through like he promised. Her jumping heart settled. Except for a one-day business trip, he'd been her rock all week, coaching her with single-minded focus. Their evenings together turned even sweeter, ending on his or her front porch, holding hands as they rocked together on the swing, talking about every livelong thing like they always had except now there was also kissing, lots and lots and lots of delicious kissing. So much of it, in fact, she worried she'd become as addicted to Jared as any of his girls, except she was different. He'd called their relationship serious at the wedding. For keeps, she hoped.

She loved him.

Was *in love* with him. And she'd tell him so tonight.

"Your comeback's incredible," gushed Ella. "It's a flat-out miracle. How are you handling this course with your—your—"

"Eyesight?" Amberley rushed in so Ella wouldn't feel awkward for bringing it up. "It's a challenge. But we practiced the pattern, so we should be fine."

She hoped.

"She'll be great," Jared affirmed in that steady voice that leveled her right out.

"Thank you so much for lending us Calamity Jane."

"You're doing me a favor," protested Ella, her voice warm and sincere. "I hated thinking of her cooped up in her stall."

"Understandable," Jared answered smoothly for Amberley, knowing, she guessed, that her mind flew to Harley and how much she missed him today. They'd competed together for the past seven years. Could she do it on her own?

She eyed the empty gate and wiped her damp palms on her thighs, thinking hard.

With most of the children here and not at the ranch, he'd have a long, lonely day. Her belly twisted. She'd spoil him rotten tomorrow and make it up to him. Sierra had cleared him for small pasture grazing, and she knew the perfect clover patch for his first venture.

"And you're okay using the whip?" Ella asked. "You barely need to tap her—just enough so she knows it's there."

"No problem." Amberley forced her fingers to unclench around the whip's handle. She hadn't worked with one much, but Calamity needed recognizable cues, signals a rider and horse developed over years...not days... As long as she rode in a similar style to Ella's, she hoped for a good, safe run with Calamity.

A winning run.

Daddy, if you're watching, I hope I make you proud.

Doubtful, yawned the devil on one shoulder, skeptical.

You're not supposed to tell her that, protested the angel on the other.

A gray horse loped down the alley from the course, blowing hard. Silver Streak. Amberley straightened her spine and squeezed Calamity's sides to move her forward. They were next.

"Fourteen eleven!" cried the rodeo announcer.

"Guess that's the time to beat now," Jared

said in her ear. "You'll take the fifth slot for the finals if you best it."

She nodded, but the motion felt jerky, disjointed. Fourteen eighteen had sounded hard. How could she beat fourteen eleven?

"Good luck, Amberley!" Ella called as Calamity pranced forward.

"Thank you!"

Jerking her head, Calamity reared slightly. Amberley worked to settle the overexcited mare. "Steady, girl," she soothed. Her own nerves hummed softly through her bones, just the tiniest of vibrations, but it sent goose bumps rolling all over her skin. "Steady."

"All set, sweetheart?"

She smiled down at the blurred shape of the walkie-talkie and tried not to let Jared's endearment throw her. "You bet."

"Here comes our reigning WPRA World champ!" bellowed the rodeo announcer. "She's a three-time titleholder making the comeback of a lifetime after losing her vision, folks. Some call her a riding miracle. Will she have one here today? Ladies and gents, this is the incredible Amberley James from Carbondale, Colorado."

Amberley tapped the top of her dad's black

Stetson for good luck, lightly applied the whip, left, right, and galloped out into the arena to a deafening roar.

Adrenaline buzzed in her bloodstream, and she bit the inside of her cheek to stay focused. She pictured the children lined up in the front row with Spirit Ranch owners Benny and Joan. What must they be feeling?

She hoped she made them proud.

Kids. This one's for you.

She bent low over Calamity's neck and rocketed forward, riding jockey style the way the speed demon liked it. Every muscle in her body tensed. She breathed through her nose, keeping her lips clamped together.

"Five degrees left," Jared urged, and she angled her mount at the first barrel, pinning her gaze where she imagined it to be. The raucous crowd muted in her mind. Every atom of her tuned only to Calamity Jane, herself and this unfamiliar course. One, two, three…she counted along with her mount's thundering hooves, her strides feeling longer than during any of their practices, faster.

Would she sense the first barrel in time?

"Coming on it!" Jared exclaimed, and she put weight in her heels and relaxed her midsection, directing Calamity to shorten her stride. Instead, Calamity dashed on and missed the cue. The barrel shimmered into view.

Too quick!

They overshot it by a stride. Amberley pressed her lips tight and tensed her core, twisting into the turn as she direct reined Calamity around the barrel.

Every bit of air rushed from her when they cleared it, clean.

Precious time lost, though.

Cold sweat broke out at the back of her neck.

No more mistakes.

"Hee-yah!" She ducked and leaned forward, centering herself in the saddle as she applied the whip and held the reins loosely, careful to stay out of Calamity's mouth when they needed speed most. Sprinting full out, her mount churned up the clay, legs pumping like locomotive pistons, freaky fast.

"Right there!" Jared cried a moment later.

Reacting instantly, she pushed down on the horn with her outside hand. The barrel flashed beside her thigh.

Find the pocket.

She turned Calamity's nose around the blurred yellow and pressured with her inside leg. Calamity responded like a champ. Her entire body bent as she flexed smoothly through and past the turn.

Nice!

Exhilaration whirled inside Amberley's tight chest, rising in her throat with a howl. She gritted her teeth and tamped it down.

Don't get ahead of yourself.

One more...

She slid forward, snatched the reins and angled Calamity for the next turn.

"Go, Calamity! Go!" she shouted, whisking the whip back and forth and giving her mount her head.

Calamity blasted into another gear entirely—another dimension, it seemed. Her mahogany-colored mane streamed over Amberley's flaming face and her short, quick blows matched each burning gasp of air Amberley's lungs dragged inside.

The blurred world passed at the speed of light. At this velocity, she was losing her bearings.

Where were they?

"Ten feet," came Jared's voice, as if reading her mind. "Pull her a hair off to the left, too close."

Her hands were sweat-slick. She could hardly grip the reins now, but she hung on, despite the dizzy, sickening thud of her heart. Amberley counted, one, two...monster strides, hustling the horse like nobody's business. Then she turned her to where the barrel should be and pressed the back of her calf into Calamity's side to keep her from leaning toward it as Jared had warned. Yellow swept by as they flexed around the turn, girl and horse, synchronized in a flawless pivot she didn't have to see to know.

Yes!

Then they burst past the barrel and the cheering crowd unmuted itself as she swept under the arena and loped down the gated corridor.

She pulled Calamity to a stop, swung her leg around and jumped down.

"Fourteen ten," the announcer crowed, and Amberley threw her arms around the horse's slick, steaming neck.

"Way to go, girl!" she whooped, dancing along with Calamity's prancing hooves.

She'd done it. Scored the fifth spot for the final tryouts next week. Last place. Still, it bought her one more day, one more try and next time she'd be number one.

Promise, Daddy.

Boots thundered behind her and strong arms whirled her around then gathered her against a firm male body.

"Jared!" Laughter and tears burst out of her.

"I knew you could do it! That's my girl!"

She lifted her mouth for his kiss, but met air instead.

"Reporters," he warned under his breath, giving her pause.

Didn't he want to go public with their relationship? Then again, they hadn't discussed an official announcement yet…

She ducked her head. "Right."

"Amberley! Would you mind answering a few questions?" someone shouted.

"Miss James, Red Carter with the *Denver Gazette*, would sure be grateful for your time…"

"How about a photo, Amberley?"

Clicking noises erupted, and she imagined the sea of cameras pointed at her and Jared. Guess he'd been right to postpone that kiss. They'd just have to make up for it later. Her lips curved.

"I'll take care of Calamity Jane while you give your interviews. Be back soon."

"You better," she muttered under her breath, then gave a toothy smile to the out-of-focus horde. "I'm all yours, fellas."

And then she'd be all Jared's, she vowed. And he'd be all hers.

Winning.

It sure felt good for a change.

JARED DROVE IN silence later that evening, his hands shrink-wrapped to the wheel. His burning eyes reached into the dark beyond his headlights as if searching for the words he'd struggled to say all week.

"You're quiet." Amberley scooched closer in her bucket seat, leaned across his pickup's divide and dropped her head on his shoulder.

The sweet scent of her shampoo, something light and floral, rose from her hair. His chest lifted as he breathed her in. He wanted her that near, not just beside him, but inside him, where she belonged, where he would always carry her.

Only now he had to let her go.

"Been thinking."

She pressed a small kiss to his tense shoulder. "About?"

"Us."

"Oh." She sighed, a warm contented sound, the kind you make when stepping into a hot shower after a long day in the saddle. Anticipation, relief, contentment. "What were you thinking?"

He weighed his words, trying to ignore the shattering din in his head. Earlier this morning, his agent had reached him with an offer to return to the Broncos as a starting halfback. He'd impressed the coach during last week's workout, passed his physical with flying colors and secured his comeback. At last, he could fulfill his promise to his father and himself to achieve his destiny, something he couldn't do as a bad boyfriend to Amberley. His demanding schedule meant he'd neglect her while on the road, unable to support her fully.

He'd hidden the purpose of last week's "business trip" to keep from disturbing Amberley's focus. The thought of causing her pain killed him. It'd be doubly cruel to break things off before she finished her tryouts for the premier touring team.

He was a lot of things, but cruel wasn't one of them.

Until now.

He swallowed the bitter bile rising in the back of his throat. The Broncos insisted he report to his first official team practice, and sign his contract, tomorrow. There was an exhibition game scheduled the same day as Amberley's final tryout for the premier team.

His hard work, his drive, his new determination to push through challenges was finally paying off. He'd regain his career, but lose his love. A long-distance relationship wouldn't work with a woman like Amberley. She deserved a man who could devote his entire life to her, not just bits and pieces of it. He'd be spending a lot of his time on the road focusing on his rebooted career. He couldn't take care of her the way she needed.

A long exhale vibrated his lips.

"Those sound like some serious thoughts…" she teased, her voice a bit woozy. Her lashes fluttered against his T-shirt. She had to be exhausted after a day of competing and interviewing. He should postpone the hard conversation.

Maybe tomorrow…

His jaw clamped.

No. He wouldn't take the coward's way.

She needed to know his mind once he'd made it up. Period. No matter how much this shredded him. They'd always been honest with each other. He wouldn't leave her in the dark another minute.

"I got an offer from the Broncos."

"Hmm…" She fiddled with the radio, trying to tune into something, usually a fruitless mission out on elevated back roads. The tires hummed steadily on the pavement, at odds with his thrashing heart.

"Did you hear me?"

"You said the Broncos?"

"They're giving me a contract to come back. Starting halfback."

She dropped her hand and whipped around to face him.

"What? How?" she gasped. "I mean. That's incredible." She squeezed his rigid bicep. "Right?"

"Yeah."

He lifted his eyes to the truck's ceiling momentarily and blinked the sting from his eyes.

"So how did it happen? Tell me everything."

She shoved back the hair that'd fallen loose from her braid. "I'm so excited for you."

How bittersweet. Of course she was glad for him...

"I tried out last week."

"Last week..." She tapped a finger against her teeth. "You mean that business trip? Why didn't you tell me?"

"I didn't want to say anything unless I succeeded."

A doe and her fawn appeared on the road's shoulder, and he slowed. Then slowed more. When they didn't budge, he braked and waited for them to make up their minds. A moment later they bounded across the lane and into the dense forest on the opposite side. Their tails flashed white against the dark, then they were gone.

He understood that kind of paralyzing indecision. It'd plagued him all week as he'd stayed silent, longing to confess all to his best friend, but needing to hold everything in to spare his girlfriend. He'd wanted both women and was now settling for neither.

"Didn't you want me to cheer you on? I could have come with you and..."

She cut off at his fierce head shake. "I needed to do it alone."

"Why? We never do anything by ourselves."

"We do now."

"What—what are you saying?"

His pulse trickled in his veins, then froze, right along with his words. They lodged in the back of his throat, choking him.

"Are you—are you breaking up with me?" Petey lifted his head from the back and woofed at her anguished tone.

"I'm going to be on the road a lot."

"I know. This isn't your first year playing pro ball. What's the difference?"

"We are. We're different."

"Us? Or me?"

He rubbed the back of his tense neck. "It was fine when we were just friends."

"We were never just friends." Her voice had turned brittle, breaking.

"Best friends, yes, but now, now you need more."

"How do you know what I need?" came the fast, fierce question.

Amberley.

Always a fighter. His feelings for her swelled his heart to aching fullness.

"I've always known what you need," he said simply.

"Not now you don't."

He shook his head. No. She was wrong. He wouldn't put her through what he saw other athletes' wives endure, the strain of time apart, of wondering and worrying about their partners. Living on their own. And it'd be even harder on Amberley. Her vision loss already challenged her confidence. He wouldn't erode it further.

Most of all, he wouldn't fail at a relationship with her. She deserved better. A hero. Something he couldn't be to her now. It'd be selfish to string her along, keep her waiting on his calls and visits. As much as it ripped him apart, he needed to end their romance and just hope—pray—she'd stay his friend.

Not having her in his life at all would be like losing a limb. He couldn't function without her.

Now, how to say any of that and make sense? He knew how to smooth-talk women. Lighthearted, playful conversations. These life-and-death stakes twisted his tongue in knots.

"So, you don't want me."

"I do," he insisted. He held so much emotion inside him, he swore he could hardly move.

"I don't understand what you want!" she cried, and Petey leaped to his feet with a growl.

"I want us to go back to being friends again." *Liar.* "That's all I can handle right now."

"Because you don't want to have to—" she made air quotes "—'handle' a disabled girlfriend. I should have known you wouldn't want someone like me."

"No," he denied, vehement. Water misted the road, the first evidence of the rain that'd threatened all day. "It's not you. It's me."

A half laugh, half sob escaped her.

"That sounds like a line, but it isn't." He eyed the caution sign and slowed as they cruised around a steep, tight turn. The road glistened, coated with damp.

"It sounds like an excuse."

"It's not. It's just… I've got a lot going on. I can't take care of you, Amberley. Not right now."

"Take care of me…" She gasped, like he'd sucker punched her. "I can take care of myself! I don't need you for that."

"Yes, you do," he insisted, needing her to see the truth so that she'd understand him, his reasons. "How will you get around without me?"

"My mother."

"She works."

"Then I'll take a cab."

"In Carbondale?"

A strangled sound escaped her.

"And you can't compete without me." His chin dipped to his chest, and his rounded shoulders slumped. "I'm sorry about this, but my first preseason game is the day you were supposed to try out for the final spot."

"I see."

Out of the corner of his eye, he caught the glimmer of pain that flashed across her face, so real and endless that he felt it in his gut. "I'm sorry."

"I heard you." She brushed furiously at her cheeks.

"Please, sweetheart, don't."

"Don't say that."

"Say what?"

"Don't call me that. Not if you're breaking up with me. That's what a break is." She held out her fists, pushed together, then yanked them apart. "No more us."

"Even as friends?" His eyes were hot. He tried to breathe slowly, but in his head, a terrible reality was dawning. He was going to lose Amberley completely.

"How can we?"

"Because we love each other, damn it." He pressed his lips together to hold back the emotion raging inside.

"But you're not *in love* with me."

Raindrops began pattering on his windshield. He clicked on the wipers. "Are *you* in love with me?"

She turned and spoke to her reflection. "What's it matter now?"

He opened his mouth to insist that it did, then shut it at the sudden chasm-opening revelation that she was right. It didn't matter. Nothing mattered if they weren't together.

Nothing except football and becoming the hero he'd promised his father to become.

The wind lashed the trees on each side of the road. The drizzle picked up, pelting the truck and the road, turning the side ditch into a stream. A hissing sound spewed from the vents as the defroster fought the white mist fogging the glass.

"Turn here," she ordered.

"That's not your—"

"Drop me at my aunt's."

"I'm taking you home."

"I decide. Not you," she choked, swiping at her cheeks harder, the gesture ripping his heart from his chest. He knew how much those rare tears cost her. "Let me out!"

Fine.

He needed to listen to her.

Minutes later he cranked the wheel and pulled to a stop in front of a small double-wide. In the tense silence, the only sounds were Petey's agitated moans and the swoosh patter of the rain and wipers.

"Goodbye, Jared," she said and then opened her door.

He hopped out of the cab and into the swampy evening air. Craggy mountaintops towered black above the fields, and he could smell the nearby river: wet rocks and moss and mud. He hustled to Amberley's door in time to grab her hand as she stepped down.

Petey leaped to her side. He head-butted her legs until she reached for the handle of his harness. A light blinked on above the garage and a door opened.

"Who's there?" a woman shouted from the top of a short set of stairs, her hand shading her eyes.

"It's me. Amberley. Be right in."

"Is Jared with you? Invite him in."

"He's just leaving."

Rain plastered Amberley's hair to her head and trickled down her cheeks. Her eyes burned into him. "Go."

He moved to touch her face, but she jerked away and Petey growled. His curled lip revealed a flash of white teeth. "I'm sorry, Amberley."

"Me, too." Her head drooped, and she wrapped her arms around herself, shivering in the chill wet. "Good luck with everything. I hope you get—get everything you want. I mean that."

"I know." His eyes blurred as he watched her turn and hurry away, Petey trotting ahead, skirting the puddles in the pitted gravel drive.

She pulled open the door, then disappeared inside without a backward glance.

For a while he simply stood in the rain, his feet rooted to the boggy ground, feeling as if somebody had pumped a numbing sensation into his arteries. His face was losing sensation. He ran a hand over it, brushing away the salty damp, not rain.

No. Not rain.

He watched the shadow shapes of Amberley and her aunt glide behind the window shades, his eyes hot with remorse. Truth stared him full in the face—now the dream had shattered—and he could hardly breathe. This woman was not his. She would never be his—as a friend or anything else. No matter how much he loved her, she would never be his.

He climbed into his truck, reversed back onto the road and cracked open the window. He breathed the night air and peered out at the shining road, at the distant mountains and at the dots of light from scattered homesteads. He listened to the steady drum of the rain, to the sudden blare of a radio channel, and felt as if he were being wrenched from his home.

Nothing left but to chase his destiny.

But what if Amberley was his destiny?

CHAPTER FIFTEEN

"JARED'S GONE, HARLEY." Amberley pulled her knees to her chest and dropped her hot cheek to them, stewing, listening to Spirit Ranch: the shouting of children, horses, birds, a tractor, the rustle of treetops stirred by a welcome breeze.

She plucked the small pasture's clover and breathed in the sweet aroma rising from the earth. A trickle of sweat wound down her back. Overnight, the rain had given way to heat that'd blossomed into a living thing, pressing its unwanted hands on her with hardly a break.

Petey lifted his muzzle from her feet and woofed. She slid clammy fingers along his back. "I'm okay, boy."

No, you're not! contradicted the devil on one shoulder. *Pants on fire!*

She'll be okay, sighed the angel on the other side. *Someday.*

Not today, though. Or tomorrow. Or ever...

Over the last couple of days, her body had become a leaden weight that needed to be dragged around from place to place. It was a tremendous effort to do anything at all. Only Harley motivated her to get out of bed. He could now graze, supervised, in the small pasture. She wouldn't let him miss out, even if all she wanted was to curl up and disappear.

Something silky and warm butted her ear. Harley. "Thanks, buddy." She reached around and stroked his nose. At least she still had her four-legged friends. Not Jared, though. Not ever again.

Her heart beat sluggishly in her tight chest, damaged, bruised, flattened. She'd thought losing her vision was the worst thing that'd ever happened to her, right after her father's passing. But this...this pain of knowing Jared didn't want her...was an unrelenting noose around her neck, tightening as she struggled against it, refusing to let go.

Harley pressed his closed teeth against her shoulder, and she lifted her head to lean it against him. "He thinks I'm a charity case. Helpless."

Harley blew, a frustrated sound that mirrored her inner turmoil.

Her eyes burned along with her tight throat. Was Jared right? Was her independence just a facade created by the others? Her freedom an illusion?

Jared had trained Petey. She couldn't have done that. Jared had coached her to the final tryouts for the ERA Premier touring team. And that wouldn't have been possible on her own either. Her mother had driven her here… transportation…another thing she depended on others to provide.

What *could* she do on her own?

Not much.

Just like her father said, if you're not first, you're last, and if you're last, you're not much. And she'd barely made last place at the initial tryouts. Without Jared to call her through another race, she couldn't even compete.

With a groan, she turned and buried her head in Harley's thick mane. She'd never amount to anything—had been foolish to believe she could. Maybe she didn't deserve love because she didn't have enough to offer anyone, especially a star like Jared Cade.

Cowgirls don't cry, hissed the devil on her shoulder.

Unless it's about her horse, insisted the angel on the other. *Then it's perfectly acceptable.*

Right.

She shoved to her feet, groped for Harley's reins, slid a hand in Petey's harness and headed in the direction of the gate. She knew better than to wallow in self-pity. Her family taught her better. Expect little. Give a lot. Her ma's credo. Amberley could still make a difference with the Spirit Ranch children, even if her own dreams, and her love, were gone.

"Amberley!" cried a familiar voice.

"Hey, Ella." Amberley swiped at her damp face with her arm, wrenched her wobbly lips into a smile and unlatched the gate. "What brings you out here?"

"Not what. Who. My little brother wanted to meet you."

"I'd be glad to." After leading Harley through, she secured the gate behind her and they ambled toward the stable. "Is he right here?" She slid her eyes in every direction, wondering.

"No. I left him with Maverick at Harley's

stall. He's—uh—he's been a bit discouraged lately, after his accident."

"Sorry to hear that," Amberley replied, her mind reaching back to a story she'd overheard at the last championship competition. Something about Ella's brother getting paralyzed in a car accident. "Is he okay?"

"Doctor told us last month that he won't walk again."

"Oh, Ella. I'm so sorry."

"Yeah. We're all taking it poorly, especially Dean. He had hopes of bull riding."

Amberley nodded, her heart going out to the kid. The opposite of a dream wasn't a nightmare. Losing it entirely was far, far worse.

"When I heard about your comeback, then your accident, I knew I wanted you to ride Calamity."

"That was real nice of you."

"No. Not nice. Well. Not entirely. I wanted to show Dean that he could still have a life after his accident, and that he shouldn't give up on his dreams. We got him to attend your race on Friday. It's the first time he's been out of the house in weeks." Ella's voice hitched at the end.

"But I—" She started to tell Ella that she

couldn't compete on Calamity, or any horse again, without Jared, but stopped when she made out Maverick's tree-sized shape and the outline of a person in a wheelchair.

What would she say to the boy?

"Howdy," she called, infusing her voice with friendly welcome.

"Hey," came a young man's voice. "Hope we're not bothering you. Told my sister we should wait till you're done working."

"Timing couldn't be better. I'm on my break."

A permanent break... She wouldn't stop working with the children, but her career was over.

"Is that Harley?" the teen asked.

Amberley stepped fast as Harley started forward without her, magnetically drawn, as always, to children. "Yes."

"He's friendly." Dean laughed. Harley's head looked like it'd lowered, and she guessed he hugged the boy.

"He knows good people."

Into the sudden silence, the only sounds were Harley snuffing Dean and the jingle of his harness.

"I'm no good no more," Dean muttered a moment later.

"That's not true," Ella cried. Maverick's shape zoomed in the direction of her voice. A protective gesture. Amberley wondered if he still had feelings for his ex. "Look at Amberley. She's still riding, competing."

Her face felt as though it'd turned to stone. She couldn't nod or shake her head.

"I saw you race on Friday." Dean's voice brightened. He sounded impressed. "How'd you do it?"

"My—uh—friend called my position to me through the walkie-talkies."

"Sick. So, you can't see anything?"

"Just shapes when I'm close. And colors."

"You're not scared?"

"I'd be foolish not to be."

"Why do it?"

"Because—because." She hesitated, stumbling over her usual answer about winning. Competing had stopped being about scoring the top spot, long ago, she realized. It was about something bigger than that—inspiring herself and others like Dean and the rest of the Spirit Ranch kids. "Because it's better than sitting home and wishing I'd tried."

"Even if you don't win?"

"Just giving it my best means I've already won," she said, the words rushing from some deep part of her. The truth. Showing up for competitions meant she was someone, not *nothing* like her father would have said.

Sorry, Daddy, but I don't believe I'm nothing.

And I don't believe you'd think that either. You promised I'd be okay after you passed. You told me I was strong.

I agree, whispered the angel on one shoulder.

Me, too, affirmed the devil on the other.

"Guts means more than glory," she heard Maverick say and nodded.

"Yeah," Dean breathed. "Guts…"

"You've got them, too." Amberley nudged Harley aside, felt for the warm chrome of Dean's wheelchair, then squatted beside it. "Never quit."

"Can I come here and ride?"

Ella gasped, a watery sound.

"Of course. Harley will even teach you to fly."

A horn honked in the distance. "It's Ma,"

Dean muttered. "I've got physical therapy, but I'll come back tomorrow."

Amberley reached out, encountered a mop of hair and tussled it. "I'll be counting on it."

"I'll take him," she heard Maverick say, followed by the rattle of pebbles under the wheelchair's spinning tires.

"Thank you," Ella choked out before throwing her arms around Amberley and hugging her quick. "And we'll be at the final tryouts, cheering you on. Count on it."

"Well," Amberley drawled, an idea coming straight from that "won't quit" part of her she'd never abandon again. "I wondered if you'd do more than cheer."

"Anything."

"Would you call me through the race?"

"What about Jared?"

"He's practicing with the Broncos." There. Short and sweet. She didn't need to spend more time, or words, on a man who saw only what could go wrong instead of believing in what could go right.

"I know Calamity Jane better than him," Ella mused, her voice rising slightly in excitement. "And the course setup, too. Not to mention, I am a world champion—or was until you came along."

Ella's rueful chuckle mingled with Amberley's surprised laugh. "You know," she said after they'd quieted again, "I think I might help you score higher than Jared did."

"That's a competitor speaking right there," Amberley observed through a grin.

"Me?" Ella exclaimed, all innocence. "Let's just say I've got a horse in this race…literally. I want to see you make the team."

"Because of your brother?"

"Partly, but also because I believe you're an amazing rider and you've earned the spot. If you make it, I'll even come on the road with you when the team tours, right up until I have the baby, and again when I take my spot back on the team."

Amberley squeezed her eyes shut against the sudden, rising wet. "Thank you, Ella."

"It's my pleasure. You're a winner, Amberley. I'm just honored to be a part of it. Y'all take care, now."

She squeezed Amberley's shoulder, and her boots rustled the grass as she strode away.

Inside the stall, Amberley untacked Harley, located the comb and glided it through his luxurious mane, the repetitive motion settling her racing heart.

She'd compete again. With or without Jared.

Without him, or Harley, it all came down to her—as it should. No one to depend on except herself.

Would Jared change his mind, want her back, if he knew?

She encountered a snarl and teased it loose. Maybe.

Yet if he appeared, hat in hand, she wouldn't take him back. Jared might have his sight, but he didn't see the big picture. If he couldn't tell that they were perfect together, then so be it. Besides, he had his dreams to chase, and she wouldn't stand in the way of them. She just wished she'd been part of that dream.

No more shrinking from life again or letting a setback overwhelm her, no matter how badly she hurt. Winning in love, in life, wasn't some arbitrary achievement, but a series of steps taken toward a goal you set for yourself. Right now, her goal was to bring as much inspiration and happiness to others as she could.

Even if she couldn't have it for herself.

Not completely.

Not without Jared.

CHAPTER SIXTEEN

JARED SLUMPED IN his pickup outside the Sports Authority Field at Mile High stadium. The scoreboard's final tally flashed in his mind's eye: 24-26, Broncos. Given his dive over the Texans' linebackers at the one-yard line to win the game, he should feel elated. Instead, he felt defeated.

When his quarterback called the close game's final play, he'd worried his rehabbed ACL wasn't up to the challenge. The fact that they'd used him in such a crucial moment proved his coaches trusted him to get the job done, and he'd been determined to prove them right.

Now he was physically and emotionally wiped. He'd worked out harder than ever this week, his ACL not holding him back much if any. While he'd impressed his coaches, Jared just felt numb.

He drained his lemon-lime sports drink,

screwed the cap back on and tossed the empty behind his seat.

It seemed like he'd left his emotions in Carbondale with Amberley. He'd practiced all week on autopilot, feeling nothing but a sense of detachment.

And loss.

He missed her like crazy. His gaze swept the parking lot out of old habit, searching for the orange pom-pom hat she always wore when she'd attended his games. A long breath rushed from him. Looking for her was a fool's errand. She wanted nothing to do with him, not even as a friend, and her absence at today's game had kept him off balance, teetering, as if she'd torn away something vital when she'd said goodbye for good.

Jared flipped down his visor against the beaming afternoon sun. His skin still flushed hot beneath his muscle shirt and jeans and his body hummed with residual adrenaline.

The crowd's jubilant screams after the final touchdown still rang in his ears. After he'd scored, his teammates had surrounded him, thumping his helmet and back, saying "good game" or "way to go, Cade." But none of it brought him the pleasure it once had. He scooped up the game ball his coach handed to him on the way out and studied the pitted leather. Funny how much smaller it looked off the field. Inconsequential. Not nearly as important as...

He shoved down the sudden image of Amberley that'd appeared in his mind's eye.

His coach had told Jared he was a hero today and was glad to have him back on the team.

A hero. Jared twirled the football. He sure didn't feel like one.

He'd finally become the winner his father approved of, the older brother Jesse idolized, the hero he'd vowed he'd become.

Only...he wasn't satisfied...or happy.

Jared turned the key in the ignition, flicked on the air-conditioning, then pulled out his cell phone. He automatically scrolled to Amberley's number, his post-game ritual when she couldn't attend. His finger froze over the call button.

She didn't want to hear from him. Wouldn't want to celebrate. Without someone to share good times with, they didn't matter as much. Or at all.

He punched in another number and listened to the phone on the other end ring.

"Hello?" a young boy answered.

"Hey, Javi." Jared's lips curved, his first real smile in a week. "It's Jared."

"Uncle Jared!" A painful clattering erupted through the phone, and Jared pulled it from his ear. He barely made out Javi yelling, "Grandma! Come quick!" Then, clearer and louder, "I dropped the phone."

"That's okay."

"We watched you on TV! James called you a gridiron hero, and you flew, even though you don't have a cape." Javi's voice dipped, then brightened. "You're like a superhero."

Jared's eyes pricked. Javi reminded him of his father, Jesse. In fact, Jesse had used those same words.

"I'm no hero," he muttered, thinking of Amberley and how, if not for his return to pro ball, she'd be competing today at the ERA Premier touring team's final tryouts. He'd followed his destiny, only now that he'd achieved it, without Amberley, it felt hollow. Insubstantial.

"Yes, you are!" Javi exclaimed. "And football uniforms need capes."

"They'd let opponents grab us easier," Jared

asserted, enjoying this conversation despite his miserable mood.

"Take them off before you play."

Jared chuckled. "I'll suggest it to the coach. Is your grandma there?"

"Yes," Javi whispered. "And she's giving me those hurry-up eyes."

"Then I guess you'd better hurry up, buddy."

"Later, gator!" Javi shouted, and then there was a crashing sounded followed by his mother's voice.

"Why must he drop the phone like that, I—"

"Ma?"

"Oh, hi, honey." His mother's warm voice spilled over him like a balm. Healing. "What a great game. We all watched it."

Jared pictured the group crowded around the TV the way they had every Sunday, cheering on the Broncos...except James, who was a Cowboys fan for no good reason except maybe insanity. Football was an institution in his family, a tradition, one that kept them together through good times and bad. Now that he'd returned to the NFL, he could be their hero again and fill his father's void like he'd promised.

"And that final play!" his mother continued, gushing. "You must be thrilled."

A noncommittal sound, something between an uh-huh and an ugh, escaped him.

"You don't sound happy." Something scraped, and he imagined her pulling out a kitchen bar stool and settling behind their granite-topped island.

"I made the team. Had a good first game. Dad would be happy."

"He's not the one who matters right now."

He jerked the phone from his ear and stared at it. Had he heard her right?

"Jared?" Her distant voice floated up to him.

He pressed his cell back to his ear. "Here. I thought you said Pa didn't matter."

"Not when it comes to making your own life choices."

"Are you saying that because…because of Boyd?" He wouldn't fight his mother's late-in-life romance, but he didn't appreciate her shoving his father's feelings aside completely.

"No. I'm saying that because of you."

"He made me promise," Jared heard himself say, surprising himself. Over a decade had passed without him revealing this private conversation, but suddenly he wanted to share it. Needed to.

"Promise what?"

"Right before, before—" Jared cleared his clogged throat. "He said the family would need a hero after he passed. I promised him I'd be one."

"Oh. Honey." His mother's concerned voice reached right through the phone like a hug. "I'm sorry."

He rubbed his eyes. "For what?"

"That was a lot to ask of a young man."

"Seventeen, was that young? Pa said everyone had a role to play. Jack was the enforcer. He'd keep us all in line. James was the protector. He'd never let anything bad happen to us. Me, I was the glue, he said, that kept us together and gave everybody hope, especially given Jesse's struggles and Justin's troublemaking."

"Honey, he gave that speech to all of your brothers."

"What?"

"It's true. They told me."

So much for his father's request that they keep the conversation between the two of them. "What'd he tell Justin?"

"To watch over his twin."

"No wonder…" Jared drummed his fingers on the steering wheel, thinking of his troubled younger brother, who'd grown dark and withdrawn after his twin's death. "That was a lot to ask of Justin."

"Yes—and of you, too." He heard the splash of liquid poured into a glass, then the clink of ice cubes.

"He said we all had a responsibility to the family."

"True. But what about your responsibility to yourself? A poster at my support group says be the hero in your own life story. Not mine. Not your brothers'. *Yours*."

Jared stared out the windshield as his truck idled, mulling over her point. Players greeted girlfriends, wives and children. Their exchanged hugs sent a sharp spike of longing through him. No one waited for him. No one to hug. No Amberley.

"I got my spot back, first string."

"And that was for you?"

He frowned at his mother's skeptical tone. "No one else is here except me."

"Not Amberley either."

His fingers tightened around the phone. "That was her choice."

"Seems to me you only left her with one to make."

"We could still be close."

"You think so? If you saw her again, you'd be fine not holding her hand? Not kissing her? Seeing her with someone else? Maybe Maverick…heard he's taking a break from rodeo, so he'll be around more…"

He clenched his jaw, staring out the window, imagining Amberley with another man. "The hell I would…"

"Exactly. The heart's not a light switch. You can't turn off emotions that easily."

He nodded, and his eyes tracked a pair of ducks as they glided over a small pond, then landed, the water rippling behind them in a V. Every morning, he woke with Amberley's name on his lips, a dream of them together, happy, dissolving in his mind. If anything, his feelings had only grown while apart.

"Except for Jesse, I've worried the most about you."

Jared nearly dropped the phone. "Me? Why?"

"Everything came easily to you, and that's

not a good thing." Crunching sounded as his mother chewed, then—"Anything worth having is worth fighting for, is worth working hard to earn. You've never had to learn that skill, that lesson."

…until Amberley, he finished silently.

He'd always stuck to casual, short-term relationships because they were easy. He didn't have to worry they'd fail. A long-distance relationship meant hard work without a guarantee of success—the real reason he'd broken up with Amberley, he suddenly saw. Fear motivated him, not faith. He'd taken the familiar, easy route rather than the unknown road with Amberley, a futile gesture since his heart hadn't quit her, no matter the distance.

"You said you love Amberley?" his ma asked. "Are you *in* love with her?"

Memories scrolled though his brain, flash-bang: Amberley, fearless, astride Harley, blindly charging the barrels. Amberley determined, competing in the premier tour try-outs with a new horse on an unfamiliar course. Amberley, considerate, working with the kids on Spirit Ranch. Amberley reaching for him, finding him without her sight by following her heart.

He was blind, not her. She wasn't blind in the way it mattered.

Her challenges made her precious to him. They revealed her true grit and undaunted heart. Amberley didn't need him. She only wanted his love. He'd been so wrapped up in seeing what could go wrong between them, how he might fail her, that he'd stopped believing in what could go right. He loved Amberley, not just as a friend, but as a soul mate, a partner for life. She was his destiny. Not football.

"I'm in love with her."

"Well. What are you waiting for? Go tell her right this minute!"

"I'm still in Denver." Plus, he had to call his agent and announce his retirement. He wouldn't waste another minute chasing glory when he'd already found it, right in his arms, every time he held Amberley.

"So is she."

"What?" He pressed the phone closer to his ear.

"She competed in the final tryouts today."

His hands shook on the gear as he shifted out of Park. "How?"

"Ella's calling her through the course. You

might be able to make the tail end of it if you hurry."

"I will. Thanks, Ma. Talk to you later!" He clicked off his phone and gunned the truck.

He wanted to be the hero in Amberley's life story, and ask her to be the hero in his.

Starting now.

Was he too late?

"HANK ANDREWS HERE, live, with barrel racing's own Miracle Rider, Amberley James. Welcome, Amberley."

"Howdy." She shot Hank a wide smile, trying not to wince at the slightly condescending nickname. Getting to the final tryouts hadn't been a miracle, it'd been hard work, dogged determination and grit. Hearing that nickname all day had left her feeling singled out when she'd wanted to simply run the course like any other athlete. At least she'd reached her last interview, to end what had been a long, incredible day. She couldn't wait to call Jared and…

Her mouth drooped. She'd just secured a temporary spot on the ERA Premier touring team and she still pined for a guy who didn't love her for who she was. He saw her as a burden, a weight that'd drag him down; she deserved better.

And she'd proved it here today with a second-place finish that caught everyone by surprise, especially her.

"Amberley, you had an outstanding run today for any rider, especially one with your—uh—challenges. I know you've talked to a lot of people already today. Going in, you knew the times and that three of the girls had knocked barrels in the mud. How'd that affect you coming out?"

She angled her body toward Hank's voice, and the boggy ground sucked at her cowboy boots. It'd drizzled nearly nonstop until a half hour ago, leaving the world a shimmering, dangerous place. Petey's tail thumped reassuringly against her leg.

"I knew it was more crucial than ever to keep Calamity Jane standing. It's real hard to change your game plan or ride your horse any differently, so I just had faith in her—and myself—that if I did my job and placed her where I needed to that I could keep her standing."

The wind rustled a nearby tree and sent a shower of droplets spraying on them. Amberley shivered, despite the still-humid night. In the distance, car doors slammed and the last of the day's attendees called goodbyes to one another.

Who was waiting for her?

Her mother, sure, but that wasn't whom she really wanted.

"Another challenge today was I noticed this arena doesn't really have an alley to come out in. How did that affect your horse and just getting her used to charging out fast enough?"

"It's difficult when you don't have a long alley to get tapped off right, but speed's no problem for Calamity Jane. Every arena is different, and you have to be reactive to the moment and do what you need to do."

There. No excuses about her eyesight. Just a flat-out answer like any other competitor, and it felt good. For the past half hour, journalists commented about her "overcoming her disability," being "brave," how she "suffered from" vision loss, "defied the odds" and, her personal favorite, that she was "inspirational."

All true sentiments, no doubt, but somehow it sounded more like pity. They meant well and probably didn't know that people with challenges wanted to be treated like any other competitor. At least Hank seemed more focused on logistics. For the first time tonight, she felt like her old racing self, only better, with a deeper awareness and appreciation of this second chance.

"Calamity Jane's Ella Parks's horse. Can you tell us how you came to work together? You two are the dream team."

Amberley laughed. "Well. That's appreciated. Ella's a ten-time world champion, so it's been an honor working with her. When she heard about my horse's accident, she offered to help. I'm real lucky to partner with her and Calamity Jane."

"We were all sorry to hear about Harley's accident. He's a real champion. Can you give us an update on his condition?"

Amberley nodded. "Thank you. Harley's recovering well, and he's got a new job working with children in an equine therapy program at Spirit Ranch in Carbondale. He's their champion now."

"They're lucky to have him. And I understand you've been working there, as well?"

Somewhere in the distance a horse whinnied, followed by the sharp clatter of hooves on metal: an owner loading it into a trailer. Luckily, Ella, with Maverick's help, had taken

Calamity Jane home. Her husband's work demands kept him from attending, so Maverick, a Loveland through and through for always lending a hand, had stepped in to assist.

"It's the most fulfilling part of my life," she vowed, knowing it to be true with everything that she was, everything that she'd become. It'd been great to return to the ring, hearing the applause, the cheers…but somehow it didn't measure up as it once had; it didn't satisfy this new part of her that needed to make a difference in others' lives.

"I'm sure you'll be sorry to give it up when you begin touring next month."

"I'll miss the kids. And Harley. But I'm planning on returning to them once Ella rejoins to the team."

"Even if another permanent spot opens up?" Hank persisted. "Heard Windy Nelson may be retiring…"

"I'll cross that bridge when I come to it, but right now, my heart is with the kids."

And Jared, whispered the angel on one side.

He's one gorgeous cowboy, sighed the devil on the other.

She heard paper crinkling and imagined Hank flipping through his little notebook.

"Well, we're sure happy to have a rider like you competing again. You're a winner through and through."

She dipped her head momentarily, then lifted it. She hadn't run a flawless race today and she didn't earn the top score, things she would have berated herself for back when she'd only wanted to be number one. Now she saw that giving, not taking, defined winning. Hearing the children's excited cheers during the closing ceremony meant more than any trophy, any record, any score. "I appreciate that, Hank. Thank you."

"Any words of advice you'd give to athletes with disabilities who hope to win, too?"

She paused and weighed her words, careful to get this right.

"I think everyone faces obstacles, some are just more obvious than others, so my advice is the same for all athletes. Winning isn't a number, it's not a ribbon or trophy. It's a willingness to go longer, to try harder and give more than anyone else."

Hank fell silent, then he cleared his throat. "Well. Thanks for that. Now. I understand Jared Cade had been coaching you before Ella…"

She steeled herself to answer as neutrally as possible. "He played an exhibition game today against Houston."

"You two are real close." A sly note entered the blogger's voice. "Shame he couldn't be here with you."

"Who says I'm not?"

Amberley's head snapped around at the deep, familiar baritone.

"Speak of the devil!" crowed Hank. "Didn't expect to get a double scoop again like last time... Today marked quite a comeback for you, too. Congrats on scoring the winning touchdown."

"The team did an outstanding job. The players gave it their all, so it was a real group effort. My only regret was not seeing Amberley compete."

Amberley felt his eyes on her as he spoke, and her blood pumped in a strange rhythm. What was he doing here? Did he really have regrets?

"What can we expect from you this season, Jared?"

"Hank, last time we met, I offered you an exclusive, so here it is—I retired today."

Amberley's mouth dropped open. It sounded like he'd had a great game. Why…?

"What motivated your decision?" Hank's voice rose in excitement at this breaking news.

"I'm hoping to manage Amberley, full-time…" His large hands cradled hers, and his voice lowered. "If she'll have me and forgive me for being ten times a fool."

"Why should she do that?" Amberley gasped, uncertain, wanting him back, but only for the right reasons—not if he was doing it out of pity or even for loyalty to their old friendship.

"Because he loves her very much. Believes in her, too, and knows that she's the strongest, most independent woman he's ever met, much stronger than him since he can't live a day without her."

Everything inside her went still as she processed what he said.

"Lordy, Lord," she heard Hank exclaim. "My recorder clicked off. Would you mind repeating it?"

"But is he *in love* with her?" she urged, needing this validation, unwilling to accept anything less. Was he ready to commit and take the first steps into a future together?

Jared released her hands and slid his arms around her waist, eliciting a shivering, heady response. "Head over heels in love. You're the shoulder I lean on, the person I can turn to, the love of my life, my everything. I don't want anything else but my other half and my best friend."

"Why isn't this recorder working?" Hank grumped.

Overwhelmed, she nestled close and wrapped her arms around his neck. The delicious smell of his spicy aftershave wafted from his warm, smooth skin. "I didn't want to lose you as a best friend."

"You never did."

"But I needed more."

He reached his hand to her face, brushed his thumb slowly across her cheek, and Amberley's blood turned into shooting stars. "You have it. Everything that I am is yours because I'm nothing without you, sweetheart. You're the blue in my sky."

She grinned, recalling the cheesy Valentine's Day card he'd given her as a joke when they'd both been single (a frequent occasion for her—a rare one for him). She'd kept it in her nightstand and read it more times than she could count.

"You're the sprinkles on my sundae," she quoted from memory.

"You're the cheese on my chili dog." The smile in his gruff voice had her insides celebrating like it was Christmas morning. "And the beat of my heart."

"Now, that sounds serious."

He rolled his calloused thumb over her lips. "It is."

"For keeps?"

"Forever."

Her eyes drifted shut in complete and utter bliss. She'd never known a bond as strong as the one she shared with Jared: someone who truly cared about her, supported her, laughed with her and also happened to be in love with her. At first, the thought of falling for her best friend had paralyzed her with fear. But it'd been worth the risk. She had a best friend and a true love all in one, making her the luckiest girl in the world.

"Ah! There it is," Hank huffed. "Now. Would you mind repeating that for the record?"

"I don't mind," Amberley said, fast. It was her turn to speak her heart, and she wouldn't miss the opportunity. "I'm so in love with you, Jared Cade. I probably fell for you the moment I spotted you at our first junior rodeo competition. You've always been there for me—through the awesome times and the not-so-awesome times, through all my upside-downs and inside-outs, giving me your proud smiles when I achieved and your helping hand when I needed to find my feet, you were the gentle breeze beneath my wings that let me reach every one of my goals. You're my rock, my biggest fan, my best friend. I can't imagine my life without you in it."

"You'll never have to. Hank," Jared said without taking his eyes from hers. "I think you've got your exclusive."

"Oh. Ah. Yes. Yes. Thank you and—uh—congratulations," he said, his voice fading as he hurried off.

"Better?" Jared murmured once they were alone, and then his lips brushed hers in a tender kiss. Chills broke out over her skin and warmth flooded her insides at his sweet onslaught.

"Much better." She sighed when his mouth slid off hers to trail the length of her jaw and tease the sensitive flesh of her earlobe.

"I chose to be your best friend," Jared whispered as she kissed his face—just under his eye, not quite on his nose. "But falling in love with you was out of my control. I'll be here for you from now on, guiding you every step of the way."

"Um, yeah, but Ella is now my full-time trainer."

"You're saying you don't need me?"

She almost laughed, he looked so crestfallen. "I do because I love you, but not in order to function. You're my best friend and my fantasy all in one."

"I like the sound of that," he growled, then recaptured her lips, slanting them over hers with increased urgency, his broad hand on her back, molding her to his hard frame. He kissed her like she was gravity's center and he was falling into her, and she kissed him back like it was the end of the world. Her heart writhed as she understood what lay before them.

Everything.

The open road, the limitless sky, wherever their minds imagined and their hearts dared to dream.

* * * * *

Get 2 Free Books,

Plus 2 Free Gifts—

just for trying the Reader Service!

Love Inspired®

YES! Please send me 2 FREE Love Inspired® Romance novels and my 2 FREE mystery gifts (gifts are worth about $10 retail). After receiving them, if I don't wish to receive any more books, I can return the shipping statement marked "cancel." If I don't cancel, I will receive 6 brand-new novels every month and be billed just $5.24 for the regular-print edition or $5.74 each for the larger-print edition in the U.S., or $5.74 each for the regular-print edition or $6.24 each for the larger-print edition in Canada. That's a saving of at least 13% off the cover price. It's quite a bargain! Shipping and handling is just 50¢ per book in the U.S. and 75¢ per book in Canada.* I understand that accepting the 2 free books and gifts places me under no obligation to buy anything. I can always return a shipment and cancel at any time. The free books and gifts are mine to keep no matter what I decide.

Please check one:

☐ Love Inspired Romance Regular-Print   ☐ Love Inspired Romance Larger-Print
  (105/305 IDN GMWU)   (122/322 IDN GMWU)

Name _____ (PLEASE PRINT)

Address _____ Apt. # _____

City _____ State/Province _____ Zip/Postal Code _____

Signature (if under 18, a parent or guardian must sign)

Mail to the **Reader Service:**
IN U.S.A.: P.O. Box 1341, Buffalo, NY 14240-8531
IN CANADA: P.O. Box 603, Fort Erie, Ontario L2A 5X3

Want to try two free books from another line?
Call 1-800-873-8635 today or visit www.ReaderService.com.

*Terms and prices subject to change without notice. Prices do not include applicable taxes. Sales tax applicable in N.Y. Canadian residents will be charged applicable taxes. Offer not valid in Quebec. This offer is limited to one order per household. Books received may not be as shown. Not valid for current subscribers to Love Inspired Romance books. All orders subject to approval. Credit or debit balances in a customer's account(s) may be offset by any other outstanding balance owed by or to the customer. Please allow 4 to 6 weeks for delivery. Offer available while quantities last.

Your Privacy—The Reader Service is committed to protecting your privacy. Our Privacy Policy is available online at www.ReaderService.com or upon request from the Reader Service.

We make a portion of our mailing list available to reputable third parties that offer products we believe may interest you. If you prefer that we not exchange your name with third parties, or if you wish to clarify or modify your communication preferences, please visit us at www.ReaderService.com/consumerschoice or write to us at Reader Service Preference Service, P.O. Box 9062, Buffalo, NY 14240-9062. Include your complete name and address.

LI17R3

Get 2 Free Books,

Plus 2 Free Gifts—

just for trying the Reader Service!

YES! Please send me 2 FREE Love Inspired® Suspense novels and my 2 FREE mystery gifts (gifts are worth about $10 retail). After receiving them, if I don't wish to receive any more books, I can return the shipping statement marked "cancel." If I don't cancel, I will receive 4 brand-new novels every month and be billed just $5.24 each for the regular-print edition or $5.74 each for the larger-print edition in the U.S., or $5.74 each for the regular-print edition or $6.24 each for the larger-print edition in Canada. That's a savings of at least 13% off the cover price. It's quite a bargain! Shipping and handling is just 50¢ per book in the U.S. and 75¢ per book in Canada*. I understand that accepting the 2 free books and gifts places me under no obligation to buy anything. I can always return a shipment and cancel at any time. The free books and gifts are mine to keep no matter what I decide.

Please check one: ☐ Love Inspired Suspense Regular-Print ☐ Love Inspired Suspense Larger-Print
(153/353 IDN GMWT) (107/307 IDN GMWT)

Name _____ (PLEASE PRINT)

Address _____ Apt. #

City _____ State/Prov. _____ Zip/Postal Code

Signature (if under 18, a parent or guardian must sign)

Mail to the **Reader Service:**
IN U.S.A.: P.O. Box 1341, Buffalo, NY 14240-8531
IN CANADA: P.O. Box 603, Fort Erie, Ontario L2A 5X3

Want to try two free books from another line?
Call 1-800-873-8635 or visit www.ReaderService.com.

* Terms and prices subject to change without notice. Prices do not include applicable taxes. Sales tax applicable in N.Y. Canadian residents will be charged applicable taxes. Offer not valid in Quebec. This offer is limited to one order per household. Books received may not be as shown. Not valid for current subscribers to Love Inspired Suspense books. All orders subject to approval. Credit or debit balances in a customer's account(s) may be offset by any other outstanding balance owed by or to the customer. Please allow 4 to 6 weeks for delivery. Offer available while quantities last.

Your Privacy—The Reader Service is committed to protecting your privacy. Our Privacy Policy is available online at www.ReaderService.com or upon request from the Reader Service.

We make a portion of our mailing list available to reputable third parties that offer products we believe may interest you. If you prefer that we not exchange your name with third parties, or if you wish to clarify or modify your communication preferences, please visit us at www.ReaderService.com/consumerschoice or write to us at Reader Service Preference Service, P.O. Box 9062, Buffalo, NY 14240-9062. Include your complete name and address.

LIS17R3

HOMETOWN HEARTS ♥

YES! Please send me **The Hometown Hearts Collection** in Larger Print. This collection begins with 3 FREE books and 2 FREE gifts in the first shipment. Along with my 3 free books, I'll also get the next 4 books from the Hometown Hearts Collection, in LARGER PRINT, which I may either return and owe nothing, or keep for the low price of $4.99 U.S./ $5.89 CDN each plus $2.99 for shipping and handling per shipment*. If I decide to continue, about once a month for 8 months I will get 6 or 7 more books, but will only need to pay for 4. That means 2 or 3 books in every shipment will be FREE! If I decide to keep the entire collection, I'll have paid for only 32 books because 19 books are FREE! I understand that accepting the 3 free books and gifts places me under no obligation to buy anything. I can always return a shipment and cancel at any time. My free books and gifts are mine to keep no matter what I decide.

262 HCN 3432 462 HCN 3432

Name	(PLEASE PRINT)	
Address		Apt. #
City	State/Prov.	Zip/Postal Code

Signature (if under 18, a parent or guardian must sign)

Mail to the **Reader Service**:
IN U.S.A.: P.O. Box 1867, Buffalo, NY. 14240-1867
IN CANADA: P.O. Box 609, Fort Erie, Ontario L2A 5X3

* Terms and prices subject to change without notice. Prices do not include applicable taxes. Sales tax applicable in NY. Canadian residents will be charged applicable taxes. This offer is limited to one order per household. All orders subject to approval. Credit or debit balances in a customer's account(s) may be offset by any other outstanding balance owed by or to the customer. Please allow 4 to 6 weeks for delivery. Offer available while quantities last. Offer not available to Quebec residents.

Your Privacy—The Reader Service is committed to protecting your privacy. Our Privacy Policy is available online at www.ReaderService.com or upon request from the Reader Service.

We make a portion of our mailing list available to reputable third parties that offer products we believe may interest you. If you prefer that we not exchange your name with third parties, or if you wish to clarify or modify your communication preferences, please visit us at www.ReaderService.com/consumerschoice or write to us at Reader Service Preference Service, P.O. Box 9062, Buffalo, NY. 14240-9062. Include your complete name and address.

Get 2 Free Books,
Plus 2 Free Gifts -
just for trying the *Reader Service!*

YES! Please send me 2 FREE novels from the Essential Romance or Essential Suspense Collection and my 2 FREE gifts (gifts are worth about $10 retail). After receiving them, if I don't wish to receive any more books, I can return the shipping statement marked "cancel." If I don't cancel, I will receive 4 brand-new novels every month and be billed just $6.74 each in the U.S. or $7.24 each in Canada. That's a savings of at least 16% off the cover price. It's quite a bargain! Shipping and handling is just 50¢ per book in the U.S. and 75¢ per book in Canada*. I understand that accepting the 2 free books and gifts places me under no obligation to buy anything. I can always return a shipment and cancel at any time. The free books and gifts are mine to keep no matter what I decide.

Please check one: ☐ Essential Romance   ☐ Essential Suspense
                          194/394 MDN GMWR   191/391 MDN GMWR

Name _____ (PLEASE PRINT) _____

Address _____ Apt. # _____

City _____ State/Prov. _____ Zip/Postal Code _____

Signature (if under 18, a parent or guardian must sign)

Mail to the **Reader Service:**
IN U.S.A.: P.O. Box 1341, Buffalo, NY 14240-8531
IN CANADA: P.O. Box 603, Fort Erie, Ontario L2A 5X3

Want to try two free books from another line?
Call 1-800-873-8635 or visit www.ReaderService.com.

*Terms and prices subject to change without notice. Prices do not include applicable taxes. Sales tax applicable in NY. Canadian residents will be charged applicable taxes. Offer not valid in Quebec. This offer is limited to one order per household. Books received may not be as shown. Not valid for current subscribers to the Essential Romance or Essential Suspense Collection. All orders subject to approval. Credit or debit balances in a customer's account(s) may be offset by any other outstanding balance owed by or to the customer. Please allow 4 to 6 weeks for delivery. Offer available while quantities last.

Your Privacy—The Reader Service is committed to protecting your privacy. Our Privacy Policy is available online at www.ReaderService.com or upon request from the Reader Service.

We make a portion of our mailing list available to reputable third parties that offer products we believe may interest you. If you prefer that we not exchange your name with third parties, or if you wish to clarify or modify your communication preferences, please visit us at www.ReaderService.com/consumerschoice or write to us at Reader Service Preference Service, P.O. Box 9062, Buffalo, NY 14240-9062. Include your complete name and address.

STRS17R2

Get 2 Free Books,
Plus 2 Free Gifts—
just for trying the Reader Service!

YES! Please send me 2 FREE Harlequin® Romance Larger-Print novels and my 2 FREE gifts (gifts are worth about $10 retail). After receiving them, if I don't wish to receive any more books, I can return the shipping statement marked "cancel." If I don't cancel, I will receive 4 brand-new novels every month and be billed just $5.34 per book in the U.S. or $5.74 per book in Canada. That's a savings of at least 15% off the cover price! It's quite a bargain! Shipping and handling is just 50¢ per book in the U.S. and 75¢ per book in Canada*. I understand that accepting the 2 free books and gifts places me under no obligation to buy anything. I can always return a shipment and cancel at any time. The free books and gifts are mine to keep no matter what I decide.

119/319 HDN GMWL

Name   (PLEASE PRINT)

Address   Apt. #

City   State/Prov.   Zip/Postal Code

Signature (if under 18, a parent or guardian must sign)

Mail to the **Reader Service**:
IN U.S.A.: P.O. Box 1341, Buffalo, NY 14240-8531
IN CANADA: P.O. Box 603, Fort Erie, Ontario L2A 5X3
Want to try two free books from another line?
Call 1-800-873-8635 or visit www.ReaderService.com.

*Terms and prices subject to change without notice. Prices do not include applicable taxes. Sales tax applicable in N.Y. Canadian residents will be charged applicable taxes. Offer not valid in Quebec. This offer is limited to one order per household. Books received may not be as shown. Not valid for current subscribers to Harlequin Romance Larger-Print books. All orders subject to approval. Credit or debit balances in a customer's account(s) may be offset by any other outstanding balance owed by or to the customer. Please allow 4 to 6 weeks for delivery. Offer available while quantities last.

Your Privacy—The Reader Service is committed to protecting your privacy. Our Privacy Policy is available online at www.ReaderService.com or upon request from the Reader Service.

We make a portion of our mailing list available to reputable third parties that offer products we believe may interest you. If you prefer that we not exchange your name with third parties, or if you wish to clarify or modify your communication preferences, please visit us at www.ReaderService.com/consumerschoice or write to us at Reader Service Preference Service, P.O. Box 9062, Buffalo, NY 14240-9062. Include your complete name and address.

HRLP17R3

Get 2 Free Books,
Plus 2 Free Gifts—
just for trying the
Reader Service!

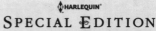

HARLEQUIN
SPECIAL EDITION

YES! Please send me 2 FREE Harlequin® Special Edition novels and my 2 FREE gifts (gifts are worth about $10 retail). After receiving them, if I don't wish to receive any more books, I can return the shipping statement marked "cancel." If I don't cancel, I will receive 6 brand-new novels every month and be billed just $4.99 per book in the U.S. or $5.74 per book in Canada. That's a savings of at least 12% off the cover price! It's quite a bargain! Shipping and handling is just 50¢ per book in the U.S. and 75¢ per book in Canada*. I understand that accepting the 2 free books and gifts places me under no obligation to buy anything. I can always return a shipment and cancel at any time. The free books and gifts are mine to keep no matter what I decide.

235/335 HDN GMWS

Name		(PLEASE PRINT)	

Address			Apt. #

City	State/Province	Zip/Postal Code

Signature (if under 18, a parent or guardian must sign)

Mail to the **Reader Service:**
IN U.S.A.: P.O. Box 1341, Buffalo, NY 14240-8531
IN CANADA: P.O. Box 603, Fort Erie, Ontario L2A 5X3

Want to try two free books from another line?
Call 1-800-873-8635 or visit www.ReaderService.com.

*Terms and prices subject to change without notice. Prices do not include applicable taxes. Sales tax applicable in N.Y. Canadian residents will be charged applicable taxes. Offer not valid in Quebec. This offer is limited to one order per household. Books received may not be as shown. Not valid for current subscribers to Harlequin® Special Edition books. All orders subject to approval. Credit or debit balances in a customer's account(s) may be offset by any other outstanding balance owed by or to the customer. Please allow 4 to 6 weeks for delivery. Offer available while quantities last.

Your Privacy—The Reader Service is committed to protecting your privacy. Our Privacy Policy is available online at www.ReaderService.com or upon request from the Reader Service.

We make a portion of our mailing list available to reputable third parties that offer products we believe may interest you. If you prefer that we not exchange your name with third parties, or if you wish to clarify or modify your communication preferences, please visit us at www.ReaderService.com/consumerchoice or write to us at Reader Service Preference Service, P.O. Box 9062, Buffalo, NY 14240-9062. Include your complete name and address.

HSE17R3

Get 2 Free Books,
Plus 2 Free Gifts—
just for trying the Reader Service!

HARLEQUIN *Desire*

YES! Please send me 2 FREE Harlequin® Desire novels and my 2 FREE gifts (gifts are worth about $10 retail). After receiving them, if I don't wish to receive any more books, I can return the shipping statement marked "cancel." If I don't cancel, I will receive 6 brand-new novels every month and be billed just $4.55 per book in the U.S. or $5.24 per book in Canada. That's a savings of at least 13% off the cover price! It's quite a bargain! Shipping and handling is just 50¢ per book in the U.S. and 75¢ per book in Canada*. I understand that accepting the 2 free books and gifts places me under no obligation to buy anything. I can always return a shipment and cancel at any time. The free books and gifts are mine to keep no matter what I decide.

225/326 HDN GMWG

Name _____ (PLEASE PRINT)

Address _____ Apt. #

City _____ State/Prov. _____ Zip/Postal Code

Signature (if under 18, a parent or guardian must sign)

Mail to the Reader Service:
IN U.S.A.: P.O. Box 1341, Buffalo, NY 14240-8531
IN CANADA: P.O. Box 603, Fort Erie, Ontario L2A 5X3

Want to try two free books from another line?
Call 1-800-873-8635 or visit www.ReaderService.com.

*Terms and prices subject to change without notice. Prices do not include applicable taxes. Sales tax applicable in N.Y. Canadian residents will be charged applicable taxes. Offer not valid in Quebec. This offer is limited to one order per household. Books received may not be as shown. Not valid for current subscribers to Harlequin Desire books. All orders subject to approval. Credit or debit balances in a customer's account(s) may be offset by any other outstanding balance owed by or to the customer. Please allow 4 to 6 weeks for delivery. Offer available while quantities last.

Your Privacy—The Reader Service is committed to protecting your privacy. Our Privacy Policy is available online at www.ReaderService.com or upon request from the Reader Service.

We make a portion of our mailing list available to reputable third parties that offer products we believe may interest you. If you prefer that we not exchange your name with third parties, or if you wish to clarify or modify your communication preferences, please visit us at www.ReaderService.com/consumerschoice or write to us at Reader Service Preference Service, P.O. Box 9062, Buffalo, NY 14240-9062. Include your complete name and address.

HD17R3

READERSERVICE.COM

Manage your account online!
- Review your order history
- Manage your payments
- Update your address

We've designed the
Reader Service website
just for you.

Enjoy all the features!
- Discover new series available to you, and read excerpts from any series.
- Respond to mailings and special monthly offers.
- Browse the Bonus Bucks catalog and online-only exculsives.
- Share your feedback.

Visit us at:
ReaderService.com

RS16R